MW00980217

Sky Knights

By Larry D Wagner

Copyright 2015

Sky Knights

Prologue

On a cool summer morning in 2013, a new Lincoln MKZ pulled into a parking spot in front of the office of a storage facility in Baton Rouge, Louisiana. Norm Davis, a thirty-something-year-old clerk was working at his computer when he heard the door chime sound. He looked up to see an older, well-dressed gentleman walk in, relying on the assistance of his cane.

"Grandpa" Norm exclaimed!

He rushed over to give him a hug then led his grandfather around the counter to a comfortable chair that was reserved especially for him. The elderly Ken Davis settled back into it with a big sigh. The man's poise and dignity suggested that he was a man worthy of respect.

With a noticeable southern drawl, he asked, "How's business, Norman?"

"Great, sir, we're 95% occupied!"

"Good… good." Ken paused then took in a deep breath before continuing. "Norm, I'm so grateful that you took an interest in running this place. Davis Storage has been a cash cow that's provided for this family for three generations. It put all you kids through college… *and* your parents. It amazes me that our family just wants to sell it."

"Well, it practically runs itself, Grandpa. I couldn't ask for a better way to make a living. It gives me all the time I need to work at my writing."

"How's that going, son?"

"I'm struggling at it, sir. It's *tough* to come up with a unique, interesting story. I think all the good stories have already been told."

"Well, Norm," Ken said, quietly chuckling to himself. "I could tell you an interesting story that I can *guarantee* you hasn't been told before, the story of how a German Luftwaffe pilot was responsible for our family getting into the mini-storage business."

"Really?!" Norm asked, shocked to hear that revelation. "I knew that you started the business when you were still in the service. Hey, I have an idea!" Norm said as he dug through a drawer. "Why don't I record this and you can tell me the *whole* story... from the very beginning!" Norm produced a tiny electronic voice recorder and slid it towards Ken. "I know you flew in the service, but you've really never talked much about it. As far as the family is concerned, we've only ever seen you and Grandma as the perfect grandparents. I'd love to know what your life was like when you were young."

Ken smiled. "So, you want the *whole* story? I've never told *anybody* the *whole* story, not even your grandmother. There are things in that story that were too painful to recall and other things I'd rather not have admitted to. There were some wonderful times though. Okay, Norman, I'll give you the whole story."

He settled back into his chair and began. "People of your generation seem to think that things were a lot different back when I was young… more primitive! Well, with technology, maybe so. We didn't have tiny voice recorders like this, and we didn't have computers or cell phones. But you know, life was as real back then as it is now. In fact, I'd say that it was *more* real… back in the '30s. The movies and pictures you see of those days are mostly black and white, but the world wasn't. Colors were just as vivid as they are today. The sky was just as blue and the smell of a fresh-cut lawn was just as wonderful. The youthful excitement over anything that was new was no different back then than it is now. You think *these* times are modern because of the things that you enjoy that weren't around in your parents' time? Well, you know something? *We* felt the *same way*.

"When *my* parents were young, homes had gas lighting. Horse-drawn wagons delivered ice and coal. Hell, most people still got around on horseback! No… I felt like *I* was living in a futuristic era when I was growing up. We had an all-electric house with a vacuum cleaner, electric kitchen appliances, and we had a radio in almost every room. We had two cars in the driveway! Airlines were flying people around the world! To us, life one generation earlier was the *Stone Age*."

Riveted, Norm replied, "You're right, Grandpa. Everything from back then seems old-fashioned to me... the music, the cars, the styles. It is really hard to imagine that to you, it was all new."

Ken replied, "Well, *try* to imagine it, Norm. Try to imagine what it was like to see it through my eyes when it all *was* new! Norm, you see my new car out there?"

"Yes sir. Your new Lincoln MKZ?"

Ken asserted, "My Lincoln *Zephyr*! The Z in MKZ stands for Zephyr."

Norm replied, "That's an amazing car! It does everything but drive itself!"

Ken laughed. "The body style might be new... but the truth of the matter is that my dad, your great-grandfather, bought a brand new Lincoln Zephyr back in 1939. It was a two-passenger coupe, streamlined with headlights molded right into the fenders, concealed running boards... with a V-12! It even had a locking steering wheel. It was ahead of its time."

He paused for a moment, reflecting. "1939... the year I graduated from Baton Rouge High was a year *full* of new and exciting things. *The Wizard of Oz* and *Gone with the Wind* were released—the first color movies! Glenn Miller was pumping out a brand new kind of music we just couldn't get enough of. The first jet aircraft flew in Germany, and that was also the year that television was first broadcast in New York."

Ken gazed up at a photograph on the wall of him and his late wife before he continued, "And it was in that 1939 Zephyr that I first kissed your grandmother. I was 18 and we were living there on the lake in the house my dad built… where I live today."

Chapter 1: Helen

There was a dance that night. It was the last school dance before the senior prom. I'll never forget how nervous I was. Oh God! My gut was in a knot. I stood at the bathroom mirror in my white sport coat, making sure every hair was slicked down into place. I splashed on some cologne and headed downstairs. I was expecting to drive the family car to the dance, but my dad blew my socks off when he handed me the keys to his new Zephyr. Wow! He'd let me drive it before, but only under his supervision.

The reason I was such a bundle of nerves was because I knew that your grandmother would be at the dance. I didn't want to go with anybody else, but I hadn't had the courage to ask her to go as my date. It's not like I had a problem asking girls out, but when it came to talking to your grandmother, I turned into a complete idiot. I couldn't utter a word. I'd been nuts about that girl since elementary school, but I could never talk to her. Over the years, there'd been a few times I thought I caught a glimpse of her returning one of my longing stares. Every man has a different idea of what a desirable woman is. In my eyes, your grandmother never had a close second. Anyway... if I couldn't muster the courage to talk to her on that night, not only would I miss the chance of having her as my prom date, but I might miss out on *ever* getting together with her.

When I headed to the car, my heart was pounding so hard that I could feel it throbbing in my temples. *What if she didn't come tonight? What if she comes with a date?* Thoughts kept running through my head. As I opened the door to the Zephyr, I was buffeted with that fantastic smell of a new car. I sure hoped that Helen would see me pull up in it.

I thought maybe I could get a good parking spot, right up close where everybody could see the car, but I wasn't that lucky. The parking lot was full, so I had to park way down the street.

When I walked into the dance, I saw that—of the kids that weren't already there as couples—the girls were gathered on one side of the hall and the guys on the other. I looked over and saw Helen there with her girlfriends. She was wearing a bright pink dress that made her stand out from the others. It looked like she noticed me when I walked in, too.

The first song they played that night was the newly released Glenn Miller song, "In the Mood"

Now I was faced with a double-edged sword. Not only did I have to muster the courage to go over and ask Helen to dance… but I didn't know *how* to dance! I was determined to try that night. Most of the kids streamed onto the floor and started dancing when the music started. Eventually there was a break in the dancers to where I could see across the floor. Helen was still standing there! I wondered why she wasn't dancing. Could she be waiting for *me*? When the song ended, I took a deep breath and headed across the floor.

I approached her and asked, "Hi, Helen. Suppose you might want to dance the next one with me?"

She said, "Oh, no, I'm… I'm sorry." My heart plummeted when she looked down and shook her head. Then she looked up and said, "I don't know how. I've never tried."

"Oh!" I said, elated. "That's great! I don't know how to dance either." Then I stood there feeling stupid when my mind went blank again. All I could think to say was, "Thank you." Then I turned to walk away.

Oh God! I thought to myself. *I can't let this happen!*

I took a couple of steps then managed to stop and turn back to her. "I don't suppose maybe, you'd just want to talk then?"

Her face broke into a big smile and her eyes brightened when she answered, "I'd like that!"

In that instant, I was on top of the world! My mind was still pretty much blank, but I was standing there with Helen. Eventually I regained my composure.

I said, "You look awfully pretty tonight. I noticed your dress when I walked in… and you smell wonderful!"

"Thank you. It's my mom's perfume."

"Well, you can tell her it was a hit tonight!"

She smiled and said, "You look pretty handsome yourself, Kenny," as she tugged the arm of my sport coat.

Wow! That was the first time I'd heard her call me by name… and she TOUCHED me!

With all the music and talking in the hall, we could barely hear each other, so I asked her if she wanted to go outside. I remember it was a warm night. Some of my buddies drove by in a convertible. Three of them were sitting up on top of the backseat, hooting and whistling, teasing me about being there with Helen.

That's a teasing I didn't mind.

I asked her, "So, we're almost out of school. What's next for you?"

"I'd like to be a nurse."

"You'd make a great nurse."

"Maybe... I'll have to work and save up for a while for school. My dad can't afford... well... he's not rich like your dad."

"Rich? My dad's not rich. I mean... we're doing *okay*."

She laughed. "You live in one of those big houses on City Park Lake, don't you? And I'd be willing to bet you're the only kid in school whose family owns an airplane."

"It's just a little Piper Cub. They don't cost much more than a new car. I'm surprised you heard about it."

"Well, when you took Stan flying this year, everybody in school heard about it."

"Really" I asked. "Would *you* like to go flying?"

Helen was visibly nervous over the thought. "I don't know. I'd have to ask my dad."

"Will you? We can make it a date!" I was starting to feel pretty bold.

"Okay. I'll ask him when I get home." She pulled a scrap of paper and pen from her purse and began to write her number. "Call me in the morning and I'll let you know what he said."

The next song began: "Moonlight Serenade." It was smooth and slow. We were still outside.

I asked her, "Do you want to try dancing to this out here? Nobody's watching if we mess up!"

She smiled and nodded. I took her hand, pulled her close, and she placed her other hand on my shoulder. We started to sway to the music in the moonlight.

I couldn't help but wonder if that moment meant nearly as much to her as it did to me.

"Am I keeping you from your friends..."

"No," she answered. "I'm where I want to be right now." Then she rested her head on my shoulder as we danced.

I said, "Me too."

I smelled a scent in her hair that was uniquely hers. When I drew in a breath of it, it seemed to feed a hunger in my soul.

After dancing a while, she quietly asked, "I suppose you're going off to some college back east after we graduate?"

"No, as a matter of fact, I'm going to college here at LSU. It was good enough for my dad."

"What is it that he does? He's an architect, isn't he?"

"No. He's an engineer. An architect is kind of like an artist. They'll design a building to look good, but then the engineers take over to make it safe and functional. And this is a great time to be an engineer. The government is spending millions on new highways, bridges, and buildings to help us recover from this depression. My dad was one of the engineers that worked on the new state capitol building."

"So are you going to be an engineer too?"

"That's the plan. When I get my degree, Davis Engineering will become Davis and Son Engineering."

She said, "Nice!"

"Your friends are probably wondering what happened to you. We'd better get back in there."

It didn't take Helen long to tell her girlfriends that I had asked her to go flying.

One of them asked her, "Do you think your dad will let you go? I mean, if you just ask him out of the blue if you can go flying with a boy from school that he doesn't know?!"

Helen looked concerned over the thought.

So I offered, "Maybe it would be better if I came over in the morning and we could ask him together? I can show him my pilot's license and have him call my dad if he has any questions."

"Okay. That might be a good idea. Do you know where I live?"

"I will if I drive you home tonight." I didn't want to admit that I'd known where she lived since grade school.

Helen blushed, a little surprised by my asking. "Okay."

We both felt more comfortable with the idea of dancing since we'd practiced outside, so we managed to make it through a few more of the slower songs before the night was done.

What a night! So many times I'd daydreamed about having Helen in my arms, but those dreams didn't nearly measure up to the way that night actually played out. Life doesn't often give you that.

I got to show off the Lincoln after all. Only, I wasn't quite so proud of it after Helen's comment about my dad being rich. I didn't want to seem like I was flaunting it. As we drove along, I noticed that she sat her hand on the seat between us. I took it in mine.

My heart began to race again as we pulled up in front of her house. I shut off the car and looked over to see if she was in a hurry to go in. God, was she beautiful! Her lipstick was as pink as her dress. Her perfume was so enchanting… and the look in her eyes let me know that a kiss from me would be welcome.

Oh, and was *that* a kiss! Until then, I figured kissing was just something guys did because girls liked it. No… my perspective on that topic was forever changed that night. It was like years of yearning were satisfied in that kiss. But then, of course, that only gave rise to a whole new kind of desire!

Dad was up when I got home, so I told him about the night and asked if I could take the plane out the next day. He was happy for me.

I was up early the next morning.

My mom asked over breakfast, "Your dad says you met somebody special last night."

"I've known her since second grade. Last night was just the first night we talked... and danced." I added, "And she *is* special."

I kissed Mom, dashed out to hop in the family sedan, and headed towards Helen's house. She appeared at her front door before I came to a stop. As I neared her, she extended her hand then led me to the living room to her dad who was sitting, reading the paper. He closed it and looked up as we approached.

She said, "I already told Daddy about the flying."

"She did," her dad said as he stood to shake my hand. "Ed Phillips."

"Kenny Davis," I replied.

"Well, Kenny. I don't mind saying that it makes me more than a little nervous... the thought of my Helen going up with such a young pilot."

I pulled my license from my wallet and handed it to him to examine as he continued, "I'll tell you what I *would* be comfortable with. What do you say to the three of us going down to the airport? You can take me up for a quick spin, and if

I'm confident that you know what you're doing, you kids can go and have fun. Sound like a deal?"

"Yes sir. That sounds like a great idea."

Helen's dad followed us down to the end of Government Street to the Baton Rouge airport where we kept the plane.

"Thanks for doing this," she said.

"I really *do* think it's a great idea. I can't think of a better way to assure your dad that you're in good hands."

"To be honest with you, I think he was just looking for an excuse to go up with you. He's never been flying either."

I liked that! What a way to start out my relationship with Helen's father… by offering him something that he was really excited about.

Helen said, "Kenny… I *am* scared."

I took her hand and gave it a squeeze. "Believe me, Helen. I'd never let anything bad happen to you. You couldn't be safer."

We pulled up next to the plane at the airfield. It was a shiny, bright yellow 1937 Piper Cub with a single high wing that carried two passengers, one in front of the other. I asked Mr. Phillips to climb in and buckle up while I untied and fired up the plane.

We bounced along to the end of the grass field then turned into the wind to take off. I opened the throttle and the plane gained speed. Within a moment, we lifted free of the field, airborne!

We circled around and I looked down to see Helen at the car waving. We slowly gained altitude.

"Mr. Phillips, why don't we fly over your house? It's only a couple of miles over there."

He responded with a thumbs-up. Once we reached it, I circled their house a couple of times to be sure that Mrs. Phillips could hear us and come out to wave.

Landing is a lot more difficult for me than taking off. With Helen and her dad both watching, I was really nervous about it. It wasn't my best, but they didn't seem to notice.

I taxied back to where the car was and shut the motor down. "Well, sir. Did I do okay?"

He laughed as he climbed out and patted my shoulder. "You did fine, Kenny. Very impressive! So where are you kids going?"

"Well, I thought maybe we'd go down to New Orleans for lunch. It's about an hour's trip each way. What do you think, Helen?"

"Sure!"

I could see that Mr. Phillips was still apprehensive. "Honey, will you please call me when you get there to let your mom and I know you're okay?"

As I buckled your grandmother in, I was grateful over how lucky I was that day, combining two things that were so important to me: flying and being able to share it with your grandmother. Mr. Phillips took pictures as we taxied out for takeoff. Once again, I eased the throttle out, and off we went.

I circled the field so she could wave to her dad then flew around the town and over the high school before heading south.

It seemed to thrill Helen to pass through clouds, so I made a point to pass through quite a few along the way. What a first date! In the clouds! I looked back to see the wonder in her face.

That little plane was so noisy and drafty that we couldn't really talk much until we landed in New Orleans. After calling our parents, we had lunch at a diner at the airfield.

The first thing she asked me over lunch was, "How come you never asked me out before? You went out with other girls. I figured you weren't interested."

Pride kept me from telling her the truth… that I was terrified of her because I wanted her more than anyone else. So instead, I told her a half-truth.

"Oh, I was interested alright. I was just waiting for the right time. And last night was it."

She said, "I was starting to give up hope."

"So you were interested too?"

"Well, maybe a little."

We spent hours talking about the times over the years when we almost got together… or wished we had. My secret was out, but then, so was hers. We returned to Baton Rouge at dusk, just in time to see the city's lights against the twilight sky.

I wasn't scheduled start college until that fall, so I spent that summer getting better acquainted with Helen. Our parents soon became friends, and I think they realized before we did that eventually we would all be one family. Our families went to New York together that summer to the 1939 World's Fair. We came away from that long train ride and visit to the fair with some priceless memories.

Every place I went and everything I saw felt magical as long as I was sharing it with Helen. Every morning that I woke, I couldn't wait to see her. Every night, it broke my heart when we parted. That was new to me and I liked it... a lot.

I had four long years ahead of me to earn my bachelor's degree in engineering. The fact that I was working part-time at my dad's engineering firm gave me quite an edge over my classmates.

Knowing that Helen was looking for a job so she could start saving for college, my dad asked me if I thought it would be a good idea for the firm to hire her for office help. I thought it was a great idea.

So we did, and that was a good thing, because between school and work I wouldn't have seen her much otherwise.

As the holidays approached that year, our families were spending a lot of time together. It was about then that I decided to ask Helen to marry me.

I talked to my dad about it and I kind of expected his response.

"Kenny, I really do think a man should be at least 25 before getting married. He should be financially stable so he can provide for his bride and family to come."

"I know, Dad. We've had this talk before. You got married at 20 and it was really tough for you to get through college. But what if you had waited... and lost the girl you were meant to spend the rest of your life with? We wouldn't be having this conversation right now, would we?"

He laughed. "Point taken. And you're sure that Helen is that girl for you? You've only been dating for five months."

"Dad, do you have to ask? All of us... both of our families find ourselves talking about what we'll all be doing 10 years from now, together."

He said, "Well, at least consider a lengthy engagement. I'll talk to your mom about it tonight."

Thank God that my mom was on my side. In fact, she got really excited over the idea and started making plans right away. There was an apartment above our garage that we used for storage. Mom suggested that we clear it out to make a place for us to live until I was done with school. She also wanted me to offer Helen my grandmother's ring.

Now, if only Helen wanted the same thing. Christmas was fast approaching, and I came up with a plan. Our families were going to have Christmas dinner together. I figured I'd make my proposal a Christmas surprise. Whether she said yes or no, it would surely make for a memorable Christmas! But before then, I asked for—and got—her dad's approval. I just hoped that he and Mrs. Phillips wouldn't let the secret slip before Christmas.

On Christmas Day, we had dinner then went into the living room to exchange gifts. Bing Crosby's new hit, "White Christmas," was playing on the radio when Helen picked up my box. I'd put the ring in a larger box so she wouldn't know what it was right off. She really wasn't expecting it. When she saw the ring, I could see in her face that she didn't understand that it was an engagement ring. By the time I dropped to my knee, it registered.

I took her hand and asked her, "Helen. There could never be anybody else I'd want to share my future with. Will you marry me?"

She didn't make me wait for an answer. We set the wedding date for May of the next year. We figured it should be set for a year from our first kiss.

In early months of 1940, there was a lot of talk about war overseas on the radio and newsreels. To me, those wars seemed worlds away.

Business was good at the firm and Helen's natural organizational skills made her quite an asset at the office. She seemed to love the work so much that I was starting to think she might just be content to stay with the firm over working to become a nurse.

As May rolled around, our parents took care of most of the planning for the wedding. We held the wedding at the house in the front yard overlooking the lake. Helen made such a beautiful bride. My parents were thrilled about my choice for a wife. How could they not be?

An orchestra played on our large front porch. Its music spilled down to the ceremony, and then later, in through the open windows of the house for dancing. Between our families and friends from school, we couldn't have asked for a better wedding.

I flew Helen down to Miami for our honeymoon.

When we returned, it was back to the grind of school and work... only from then on, when Helen and I went home after work, it was together.

Since business was doing so well, Dad bought a new airplane, a Cessna Airmaster.

Now that was a *real* airplane! It scared the crap out of me though. I had to learn to fly all over again. The Piper Cub was a nice little plane, but it was light with a tiny engine. It had a top speed of about 90 miles per hour. The Airmaster was a four-passenger plane, more than twice the size and weight of the Cub. It had a huge radial engine and cruised at 150 miles per hour, which was as fast as most commercial airliners at the time. It was a practical investment for the company since it expanded our service area for clients. We could be in Houston in two hours; Washington DC in eight. When we had to shuttle clients or staff back and forth, I was usually the company pilot.

In 1941, the Federal Government decided to build Harding Field, an Army Air Force base just north of Baton Rouge to train fighter and bomber pilots. We weren't the primary engineering firm on the project, but we had to hire extra staff to take care of the work they did send our way. The increased business was reflected in my salary. Granted, with school, I only worked part-time, but doubling as the company pilot certainly bolstered my paycheck.

We were able to move out of the garage apartment and into our own home. It wasn't nearly as grand as my parents' house, but it was ours.

CHAPTER 2: War

As the holidays arrived once again, the days had grown shorter, cooler, and grayer.

I was anticipating another joyous holiday season and decided to start my Christmas shopping early. Just as I'd pulled into a parking place in front of Sears, a news report flashed over the car's radio. I'll never forget the moment when I heard the announcement about Pearl Harbor. At first I thought that maybe it was a false report, like when "War of the Worlds" was broadcast the year before and so many people thought the program's fictional newscasts were real. After switching stations, I realized that it *was* real.

I hurried back to the office and found that everyone had stopped working and had gathered in Dad's office, silently listening to the radio broadcasts. I sat next to Helen and listened. Then a new announcement came in from the president's office. The Japanese had attacked a second target, the Army and Navy posts in the Philippines. All we knew was that the United States was under attack from Japan. Two attacks: Pearl Harbor and now the Philippines. We were waiting to hear where the next one would be. San Diego?!

Dad sent the staff home early and closed the office. Helen and I followed him home, where we continued to listen to the news.

The next day, the United States formally declared war on Japan. Three days later, we declared war on Germany.

The community spirit reminded me of how it felt in my childhood when a hurricane was approaching. Whatever people were involved with at the time suddenly became unimportant. People banded together to brace themselves for the storm. It was almost a good feeling, of unity and excitement.

I hadn't known the horror of war, but my father had. Anxious for adventure as a teenager, he'd joined the Army during the First World War. What he experienced wasn't the romantic adventure he'd imagined.

Dad told us, "We suffered unimaginable misery. It didn't matter if we were sick, hungry, cold, wet, or exhausted beyond our limits. We still had to fight, watching our friends die beside us. At times, I felt they were the lucky ones. When that war ended, I thought that civilized man had learned his lesson, that in the future we'd find other ways to settle our differences." He let go a sorrowful sigh. "And son, I prayed that my children would never have to see that kind of hell." He looked up at me. "As long as you're in school, you're safe. They'll need officers, and they will want you to graduate. You'll be safe for a few years, so let's pray that this war is over by then."

We still shared a pretty wonderful Christmas, but the shadow of war and the uncertainty it brought couldn't be ignored.

In the months that followed, I saw friends that I went to school with called upon to serve. Dad was right. Those who weren't in college were called first. Through the daily report in the newspaper, we began to hear of those who weren't coming home.

The places where these battles were raging were places I'd only read about in National Geographic, faraway places that didn't seem real.

Business declined. The engineering firms that were in demand at home were those that designed and built war machines, not so much the ones that designed roads, buildings or bridges.

Another day whose every detail would leave an eternal impression in my memory came on the afternoon of March 12th, 1942. When I was done with my classes, I headed for the office. It was a miserable winter's day and the warm, bright office was a welcome refuge. I found comfort in the sounds and smells of the office that I'd known since my childhood. Half of the employees had a cigarette burning in an ashtray and the air was heavy with the bitter smell of carbon paper. The sound of clattering typewriters was ever-present. My dad's office was enclosed in large windows which kept distractions out but also allowed him to keep an eye on all of us. As I only had a couple of hours to contribute that day, I quickly went to work on my project at my drafting table.

A telegram arrived for Dad. I glanced over and noticed him open it. I looked over five minutes later to see that he was still staring at the telegram. That was odd. I walked over and knocked on his door. He looked up and motioned me in.

He had a bewildered expression. "I've been drafted!"

"What?" I asked in disbelief.

He repeated himself. "It says here that I've been drafted. I have two weeks to get my affairs in order and report."

I was sure that it was a mistake. "This must have been meant for me."

"No. They want me back in the Army, only this time as an officer. There's my commission," he said, pointing at the telegram. "Second Lieutenant."

"They can't do this! You have a company to run. People depend on you. I thought there was an age limit."

"Well, I'm 42. Apparently that's not too old. And I don't think there's a lot we can do about it."

We sat quietly for a couple of minutes before Dad continued, "Son, I think you know what this means. I've got two weeks to groom you to run this place."

"Dad, I can't do that! How can I? I'd have to quit school."

"No! Absolutely not! If you quit school, your butt's going to be drafted so fast it'll make your head spin... as an enlisted man!"

I couldn't help but feel that the draft board figured they'd leave me in school and to take Dad instead.

In the following weeks, Dad taught me things about running the business that weren't taught in my engineering classes. He did his best to teach me how to manage people, but two weeks wasn't nearly enough time. Two years wouldn't have been enough. Until the end, I didn't believe that it was real. It wasn't until the day he actually left that it sank in. He was to report to Fort Benning in Georgia for OCS. Helen and Mom and I flew up with him in our plane.

The next time I saw Dad, he was looking pretty dapper in his new uniform. He was in good spirits and seemed to be enjoying the experience. I guess that's why everybody loved my dad. He always saw the best in everyone and in every situation.

He got to come home for a visit before he shipped out to his duty station. He was assigned to join the 151st engineers in Dutch Harbor, in the Aleutian Islands.

When he left, I missed him so badly. We all did. And life was hard. I was struggling to keep my grades up in school while running the firm. Clients were leery about whether we could maintain our quality of work without Dad, so we had to try extra hard to impress them. I was so grateful that Helen was there to support me. The staff was helpful too. A couple of the guys had been with the firm longer than I could remember. As a kid, I'd sit in Mark's lap while he coached me on how to draw at his drafting table. Now I sat at Dad's desk. I was in charge, and they were gracious in accepting it.

A letter from Dad arrived at the office. I read it to the crew.

"Well, I'm here and settled in. As I expected, I'm the old-timer of the lot. I'm surrounded by young engineers that aren't much older than you, Kenny. Now I understand why they needed someone like me with a little experience in both engineering and management to whip them into shape. I'm not at liberty to say what our assignments are, but I will say that our work is all that keeps us sane. This little island is pretty desolate. I've attached a picture. You can see that, aside from our barracks and fuel docks, there just isn't a lot here. I'd say the greatest hazard of war here is the threat of dying of boredom. I will say that I have plenty of time for reading, so please write, all of you!"

I was anxious to show the letter to my mom, so when we closed the office, Helen and I drove over to the house.

It was kind of strange: there was an Army car parked in the driveway.

"Could it be Dad, home for a visit? Did he actually beat his letter home?"

We rushed in to see. My mom was sitting in Dad's chair with two soldiers standing in front of her. When they stepped aside, I saw a look on my mother's face that horrified me. She cried out to me, "Kenny!"

Oh God, I knew what this meant! I couldn't breathe. I heard our maid, Mary, in the kitchen crying without restraint. Helen ran to my mom. I turned and walked out to the front porch. One of the men followed me out. I managed to catch my breath. He started to talk, but I held up my hand to stop him.

"I know what you're here to say; just give me a minute."

"Sure," he answered. "But your mom really needs you right now."

I fought to regain my composure then went back in to join them. As I approached Mom, I asked her, "Is he dead?"

She nodded and reached for my neck, sobbing uncontrollably. I'd never heard my mom cry before. It was the most devastating sound I'd ever heard.

I turned to the soldiers and demanded, "How?! What happened?! He hasn't been gone a month!"

One answered, "The Japanese fleet was planning on retaking Midway, a small island about 1,500 miles from Honolulu. They didn't want us to know it… so as a distraction, they attacked our bases in the Aleutians. They hit the barracks and the fuel depot at Dutch Harbor yesterday at about 0400 hours. Your dad was asleep when they hit. I don't think he even woke up. We lost eight of our engineers."

I walked the men out to their car. One of them said angrily, "You know, I hear so much about the dignity and honor of the Japanese warriors. The Samurai!" he scoffed. "I don't see much honor and dignity in the way they're fighting. What I see are sneaky little cowards. They launched a sneak attack on Pearl Harbor on a Sunday morning when we were least prepared for it. And Dutch Harbor? People were asleep in their beds."

I agreed with him. The thought of it made my blood boil.

Helen was wonderful, knowing just what say and do to be a comfort to my mom. I didn't have a clue. We decided to stay the night. After dinner, we sat around the fireplace with the lights off, listening to music on the radio—the way we used to with Dad.

I shared some of my thoughts. "They didn't give Dad a chance to defend himself. I don't know how y'all feel about it, but I don't much like the thought of my going to war like Dad… just waiting for them to sneak up on me when I'm not expecting them."

Helen asked, "So what can you do differently?"

"I'm thinking about maybe serving as a pilot instead of as an engineer."

My mom and Helen both gave me their full attention as I continued, "This way, I'd have a fighting chance with them. I figure they fight like sneaky cowards because they aren't much good at fighting like men! And I would LOVE to give them a lesson in what it's like to fight like men! Maybe I'll even get the spineless little bastard that killed Dad in his sleep!"

I really didn't expect my mom to like the idea much, but she surprised me by saying bitterly, "You do that, Kenny. You get those bastards!"

A while later, my mom asked, "What will we do about the firm when you go?"

"To be honest, Mom, I've felt kind of silly running the firm. I mean... most of those guys have worked for Dad since before I can remember. It just doesn't feel right for me to be their boss. What do you think of the idea of us selling the firm to the employees? Rather than take a lump sum payment, they can pay out a monthly salary to you, Mom, as long as you live. And they'd have to guarantee Helen a job there as long as she wants it, too."

She considered it for a minute before answering. "I'll think about it. It sounds like it might be a wise decision." Then she hugged me.

"One more thought, Mom. There won't be anybody here to fly the plane while I'm gone. We should think about selling it. I'd rather see the money in the bank than see the plane sit there unused."

"Oh, Kenny, that plane was your father's greatest joy!"

"No, Mom. *You* were his greatest joy. I'm sure he would agree with me on this."

When Helen and I turned in for the night, I said to her, "I'm leaving soon, and I don't like the idea of you living alone. I also don't much like the idea of Mom living alone."

She asked, "You'd like me to move in here with your mom?"

"What do you think? It's a big house."

"I'd be okay with that, but would we have to sell our house?

"No… we can just rent it out," I answered. "There are a ton of GIs at Harding Field that have families, needing housing."

The guys at the firm took the news about Dad hard. They agreed that the idea of buying the firm on the terms that we proposed, was most practical.

It was still a year before I was done with school, which gave us all the time we needed to make the transition.

I'm glad that your grandmother kept her position at the firm. Customers and staff alike took comfort in knowing that there was still at least one Davis left at Davis Engineering.

I drove up to Harding Field to find out what I'd need to do to become a pilot for the Army Air Force. It didn't take long to find the right person to talk to. I explained to him that I already had almost five hundred hours of flight time and that I had a year left in college to get my bachelor's degree.

He explained, "You don't need your bachelor's degree to be an officer *or* a pilot. Until just recently, you only needed your two-year degree. But now, we have a program where we are promoting *enlisted men* into the pilot training program. If you want to fly for us, you're more than qualified to do so now."

I was shocked and a little disappointed to hear that. "And these enlisted men are being promoted to officers?"

"They are. It's not open to just anybody though. They have to be an extraordinary candidate," he replied.

I shook my head. "I'm sorry, but I only have one year to go to get my degree in engineering. I promised my dad that I would."

The man said, "We'd love to have you as a pilot. The army needs engineers, but right now we need pilots a whole lot more."

It was decided. I would be a pilot, but I would complete my degree in engineering first.

When you're busy, time flies quickly. Before I knew it, I was graduating from LSU with my degree. It was time for me to leave Baton Rouge, my wife, my mom and the firm.

At Davis Engineering, the engineers had only wanted to be engineers and were happy to leave the public relations and the management of the firm to Helen and me. With my leaving, it all fell on Helen, on top of keeping the books.

Before I could be transferred to Harding Field in Baton Rouge, I had to first report to OCS in Georgia and then, in August of 1943, to Texas to start basic flight school. I was feeling cocky when I got there with the flight experience I had, but that only seemed to make them want to humble me.

I loved the flying, but it was there that I experienced my first serious bout of homesickness. I missed Baton Rouge, and I especially missed Helen.

Flying the military trainers was easier than flying the Cessna. They were more like the Piper Cub we had, where the pilot and copilot sat one behind the other, only these planes were much faster than the Cub.

When I was sent back to Harding Field, they were training pilots in bombers, P-47s, and Mustangs. Actually, they called the Mustangs A-36s rather than P-51s. It was the same plane, only it was an attack version with more guns and dive brakes for its role as a dive bomber. I would have been happy with either the Mustang or the P-47.

They put me in the Mustangs. The first time I actually walked up to one, I was amazed at how small it was. It was smaller than our family's Cessna. It was a small plane built around a huge V-12 engine. I could barely fit into the cockpit with my parachute. It was a beautiful machine. It cruised more than 100 miles per hour faster than our Cessna and, with its turbo-charger, the Mustang could fly more than twice as high! It was quite a thrill to be flying one over my hometown.

I was lucky to be stationed in Baton Rouge. The guys I was flying with were from all over the country. When the workday was over, they had dinner at the chow hall, hung out in the recreation room playing cards all night, then showered in a community shower before hitting their racks. I, on the other hand, drove home to a home-cooked dinner and, after a day of cruising at 30,000 feet in sub-zero temperatures, got to soak in a hot bath, then fall asleep in my own warm bed in the arms of my wife. It didn't seem fair, so sometimes I'd invite some of the guys I flew with home for dinner.

The fighter planes they trained us in at Harding Field weren't used in the Pacific War. My motivation for becoming a pilot in the first place was so I could go raise hell with the Japanese pilots that killed Dad! No, instead, I would be shipping out to England to fly P-51s that escorted bombers into Germany. I was happy to learn that I'd be flying the fighter version of the Mustang rather than the attack version I'd trained in. The P-51 Mustangs had a more powerful engine designed by Rolls Royce.

It was early in 1944 that the time came to leave for England. I was 21. It had been over two years since Dad died. Mom was doing much better. She'd gotten involved with a lot of social and fundraising groups. It was comforting to know that Helen wouldn't be her sole companion after I left.

Before leaving, Helen and I drove around town, visiting places that had special meaning to us. The truth of the matter was I felt that it might well be the last time I saw those places. I'm sure that, when my dad left Baton Rouge, he hadn't considered that he would never see it again.

Things didn't look a whole lot different around town at that time than they did before the war. It wasn't very obvious in the peaceful town of Baton Rouge that the world was involved in such a horrific conflict, a conflict that I would soon be leaving to join.

CHAPTER 3: England

The first leg of my trip to England consisted of a train ride to New York. It was the same route I'd taken to the World's Fair in 1939 with Helen and our parents. But this time, I was making the trip alone. Leaving Helen and my mom at the train station in Baton Rouge was one of the most difficult things I'd ever done. Again, I heard the devastating sound of my mother crying, only this time it was even worse. Helen joined her. At least I left knowing that I was loved.

The thought that most saddened me about going to war was the prospect of dying alone like Dad, with my loved ones thousands of miles away; but I couldn't dwell on that.

I have to admit that, although I felt fear and anxiety over going to war, I was also excited over the prospect of flying in battle. By the time I reached Tennessee, snow began to fall. It fell heavily during most of the remainder of the trip. It was beautiful to look out at from within the warm and cozy train. I only wished that my Helen were there to share it with.

The second leg of the journey to England was aboard the *Queen Mary*, which had been converted to a troop ship during wartime. They say that the *Queen Mary* was never torpedoed in all of its years of transporting troops to and from Europe, because it was too fast for the U-Boats to catch. Nevertheless, the thought of being torpedoed was a constant concern.

The trip over the ocean was crowded and noisy. Fortunately the officers had more privacy than the enlisted men. I did quite a bit of reading.

When I arrived in England… maybe it was just my imagination, but it smelled like war. Although everything was covered in a shroud of snow, it couldn't mask that parts of many major towns were laid waste—evidence of the German bombings. The newsreels I'd seen of the devastation back home were in black and white and didn't seem as real.

People talked funny and drove on the wrong side of the road in England, but they were friendly enough—especially considering what they were going through.

I arrived at Royal Air Force station Leiston, where the 363rd fighter squadron was stationed. I was led to my bunk where I stowed my gear before beginning my in-processing. The weather had been rotten for a few days, so all missions had been scrubbed. The guys were enjoying the downtime. I listened to stories of their missions, of their successes and also stories of their colleagues who hadn't returned.

My flight leader took me over to the hanger to introduce me to my crew chief, Steve. Damn, he was tall. He could work on a plane's engine without using a ladder.

Steve took me over and introduced me to my plane, one of the new P-51Ds that just arrived. Its polished aluminum skin and bubble canopy glistened under the hanger's lights.

"It's beautiful," I said.

Steve replied, "Sir, I'd appreciate it if you'd try to keep her that way. Have you thought about what you're going to name her?"

"No, I haven't yet. I suppose it would be nice to name her after my wife, Helen."

"Well, you can't just name her Helen. It's got to be something catchy, like... *Hell Raisin' Helen* or *Hurricane Helen!*"

"I don't know. She's a sweetheart, not much of a hell-raiser or a hurricane. She's more like an angel. Maybe... *Angel Helen?*"

"Hmmm," Steve replied, sounding unimpressed. "I suppose that would work."

"I know." It dawned on me. "How about *Heavenly Helen?*"

He thought for a second. "Yeah. I like that better. *Heavenly Helen!* Kinda snappy! You got a picture of her? One of our line mechanics does the nose art on the planes. He's pretty damned good at it. He'll make her look real sexy too. We gotta keep those Jerrys thinking our gals are prettier than theirs!"

I explained, "The night that I first got together with Helen was at a dance. She was wearing a pink dress. I'm not just talking about pink... it was bright pink. She stood out like she was the only gal there. Think he could manage to paint her in a pink dress?"

He said, "I'm sure he can manage that. A bright pink dress, and... how about we give her some wings and a halo? *Heavenly Helen!*"

Yes, I liked that! I liked Steve too. For a guy of his size, he was a gentle soul, but I guess he could afford to be.

During that bad stretch of weather, I was able to take my new plane up for a few short local runs to get familiar with it.

When the weather finally broke, we reported to the early morning flight briefing, way before dawn. The briefing hut smelled heavily of coffee, cigarettes, and leather jackets. It was warm though, as opposed to the biting cold outside. I wasn't looking forward to how cold it would be when we reached our cruising altitude.

Our group was to escort a group of bombers headed for Germany. Since fighters didn't have the range of bombers, they had three groups of us trading off on the escort. We had the first shift, upon which we were instructed to defend the bombers until we met up with the second escort group... then on the way home, we were to look for "targets of opportunity" to strafe. Targets of opportunity were trucks, trains, airfields, or even enemy barracks. I was being ordered to do the same thing as the pilot who'd strafed my dad's barracks. This was different though. When my dad died, we were defending ourselves against an aggressive enemy. This time, we were attacking the aggressors.

When the briefing was over, jeeps took us out to our planes. I found my crew chief, Steve, waiting at my plane. Though I wasn't surprised, I was a little disappointed that they hadn't yet had a chance to paint Helen on the plane's nose.

I tried to hide the fact that I was trembling as Steve helped load me into the cockpit. I don't know if it was from the cold or from the anticipation of what lay ahead. Maybe it was a little of both. I only wished that it were daylight. Having to join up into a formation in the dark was something I'd trained for but didn't much like. I fired up the engine and let it warm up. Steve hopped up on the wing of the plane to listen for any abnormalities in the engine as we taxied out towards the strip. Once he was satisfied that all was right, he hopped off. He slapped the wing and gave me thumbs-up. Then he walked over to join the other crew chiefs in the darkness.

I made sure that a picture of Helen was in plain sight. If anything did happen to me, I wanted her face to be the last thing I saw.

My flight leader and I taxied out to the end of the runway, and when it was our turn, I eased the throttle up and felt that powerful V-12 push me back into my seat. After forming up, we headed out over the English Channel towards the coast of France where we met up with the flight of B-17s that we were sent to escort. Dawn was breaking just as we met them. At our altitude, we were shining in the morning sun while the Earth below still remained in darkness. What an impressive sight—

bombers as far as I could see! Being part of that made my chest swell with pride. It was sad that it was a sight I could never share with anyone who wasn't there.

We zigzagged back and forth, looking for enemy planes. I watched and waited, more than ready to challenge the enemy, but it wasn't going to happen on that trip. Hours later, our relief showed up to escort the bombers to their target.

It wasn't over yet though. We still had our orders to strafe targets of opportunity on our way home. Looking down over the countryside below, with its farms and cozy rows of houses, was a lot like looking down over the countryside in Louisiana.

The targets weren't so clearly defined. A set of railroad tracks below happened to run in the same general direction as our flight coordinates towards home. I saw a plume of smoke from a locomotive on the horizon.

My flight leader radioed me. "Here's your target of opportunity. Let's see what you can do."

My pulse was racing and my hands were shaking. I took a deep breath and remembered my lessons from my flight training. Being trained in the Mustang A-36, I had more training in ground attack than the pilots that were trained in the P-51 Mustangs. As I neared it, I arced into a dive and lined the train up clearly in my sights. But I could see that it was a passenger train: no freight cars, no military equipment, just passenger cars. The thought crossed my mind: *What if it was a train full of civilian passengers, like the one I took to New York?* I passed on the opportunity to strafe the train itself and focused my first burst of gunfire on the locomotive. There was nothing wrong with my aim, as it instantly exploded in a burst of steam. As I pulled up, I could see that my flight leader had fallen in directly behind me... but he didn't spare the passenger cars, spraying the length of them with a deadly blast of 50-caliber rounds.

"One more pass," I heard over my headset. Reluctant as I was, I knew that I had to follow the order. As I came back around and lined up on the train, I could see enemy soldiers pouring out of the cars, shooting up at us. This time I didn't hesitate to fire.

On the remainder of my flight back to the field, I had time to ponder what had happened. When I lined up on the passenger train on my first pass, I was picturing that it was full of civilians. Instead, it was filled with German soldiers who were wholly focused on killing me with their small arms fire. If my hesitation had spared any of them, those who survived would go on to the battle lines to fight, to kill our soldiers who have families waiting for them at home back in the States.

I was surprised that I didn't feel more remorse over the casualties from the train. Was it that they were so far away that they didn't seem like real people or was it because they were German. I felt that Germans weren't like us. It was as if they were another species. I thought of the German people as mean and scary. And it wasn't like they were stupid and mean. What made them scary was that they were smart and mean. The appearance of their uniforms, tanks, aircraft, and submarines all looked so serious and formidable. What really dumbfounded me, though, was how such an intelligent, disciplined people like that could fall under the control of a high-strung little guy like Hitler, with his Charlie Chaplin mustache.

The pilots in my group were something else. When the guys weren't flying, they drank and laughed a lot. They were an awfully cocky bunch. There was quite a bit of prestige and glamour in being a fighter pilot. The girls in town were awfully friendly to us, and these guys made the most of it. I got a lot of teasing about being old-fashioned, mostly because I wouldn't go into town to the nightclubs with them. I thought about going along and was tempted, but then I'd talk myself out of it. I was married! Okay. So maybe I *was* old-fashioned, but I was okay with that. I got the bright idea to buy a motorcycle and spent a lot of my downtime exploring the English countryside. I'd write to Helen and send her pictures of my adventures.

They finally got around to painting Helen's image onto my plane. Steve was right. The likeness was amazing... except that he did take the liberty of enhancing her figure, just a little. He also managed to find just the right shade of bright pink for her dress. For luck, I'd kiss my glove and press it to her lips before each mission.

When I was escorting bombers, I'd sit cramped in my tiny cockpit for hours, flying so high above the clouds that the sky above as nearly as dark as night. The crisp white contrails from the other planes would flow past me, and the only sound was the constant droning of the engine. I relied on my thoughts and daydreams to pass the time.

Then someone would shout over the radio, "Bandits!" In the next instant, both enemy and friendly fighters were zipping in all directions, through and around the bombers. The brilliant tracers from gunfire would cross in all directions around me. Often it was hard to tell if the gunfire was coming from the bombers, friendly fighters, or the enemy.

In my first few encounters, I was so busy trying to evade bandits that it was damned near impossible to concentrate on lining one up in my own sights. The duration of our battles was limited to the amount of ammunition we had, on both sides— friend and foe. It was spent in a short time and the battles were over as quickly as they had begun. One thing that frustrated me was that, if I had ammo left after the battle, I couldn't pursue the fleeing enemy planes. Orders were to stay with the formation.

General Doolittle changed that rule in early 1944, which gave us the freedom to roam away from the formation to search for enemy planes. That might not sound like a big deal, but it changed the outcome of the entire European War. We no longer had to wait for the enemy to come to us. This gave us the advantage of surprising them, for a change.

We often knew which airfield the enemy fighters would fly out of to attack our bomber formations. With the new rules, we could intercept them as they headed towards our formations—or, better yet… when they were most vulnerable: while they were taking off. It was also nice to engage them away from our bomber formations, where we didn't have to worry about casualties from friendly fire.

In just over a week after this change, the Luftwaffe lost 17% of its pilots. Within a month, half of the Luftwaffe was destroyed.

It was a stroke of luck for me to arrive just as this change in strategy was initiated. If I had arrived a year earlier, I might not have survived my introduction to air battle. In fact, I'm pretty sure of that.

Within a week of this new strategy's implementation, I claimed my first kill. It wasn't at all like I expected. The G-forces involved in a dogfight push you to the edge of blacking out, and the smell of the cordite from the machine guns made it hard to breathe. At the same time, I had to pay constant attention to keeping the plane operating within its limitations. Otherwise I could stall or go into a spin. Then, when my guns finally did find their mark, I felt the heat on my face from the flames trailing off of my opponent's plane. And I could see the pilots of those planes, bail out or die. There is no way they could have prepared me for that in training.

The more I flew, the more I felt one with my plane. I could tell when the pilots I was flying against were inexperienced by how easy it was to anticipate their moves. In those days, it wasn't uncommon for our group to score twenty-five victories on a mission to three of our losses.

It wasn't always that way though. The Luftwaffe lost most of their best pilots over the years, and most of those that were left made easy prey.

This all happened just before the Allied Invasion of France, D-Day. By then the Germans had almost no air cover, which made our landing at Normandy a lot easier. Everyone was excited about the Allies actually fighting and advancing in German-occupied France.

By June, we liberated Paris. We began to capture and utilize enemy airfields in France for our bases of operations. In months that followed, I downed five more planes, which earned me the status of "Ace"—along with a promotion to captain. My hometown newspaper in Baton Rouge made a big deal of my accomplishments. The person at home that I most wanted to share it with would have been my dad. It broke my heart that I couldn't.

In December of 1944, as the Allies advanced further into France, we captured and occupied Haguenau, an important German airfield. The Germans were determined to retake it though and made an aggressive move to do so. The Allies had to evacuate the field until it could be re-secured. One morning, my group was called upon to offer the ground troops air support. Usually P-47s would have been sent on this mission, but we just happened to be available that morning. I welcomed the change.

It was still pretty damned cold, but on that mission, we wouldn't be flying bomber escort in the upper atmosphere with its sub-zero temperatures.

I knew the airfield that we were trying to retake. We'd flown against HE-111s based there a number of times before.

As we neared our target, we were intercepted by German fighters. This time, rather than HE-111s, it was a flight of at least twenty FW-190s. We had the advantage of a higher altitude, so we dove on them head-on. I maneuvered like crazy to avoid their oncoming gunfire and was able to squeeze off a burst that nailed one of them right in the engine. We closed on each other with a combined speed of over seven hundred miles per hour—so close that I could feel a burst of turbulence as they passed.

Since our Mustangs were lighter and more maneuverable, we were able to swing around into firing position before they could. I took down a second 190 within two minutes of the first. It was like jousting! Only on this pass, I noticed that one of the 190s peeled off to gain a better position on us as we passed.

He was a tricky one. I peeled off from my group as well to pursue him. When he saw me, he began evasive maneuvers. My God, could this guy fly! I'd never seen anything like it. This was obviously no green cadet. He seemed to anticipate and counter my every move. This scared the hell out of me. I felt like I had a tiger by the tail. If I lost my position to him, I knew

I'd be in serious trouble! Every time I came close to hitting my guns, he'd slip right out of my sights. He was rolling and banking at such extremes that I was close to blacking out from the G-forces as I followed.

On one of the banks, I did black out for a couple of seconds. When I regained my vision, he was gone. Damn it! That slick bastard was behind me and he didn't waste any time in unleashing his cannons. He was outfitted with both 20- and 30-mm cannons. He may not have been able to fire off nearly the number of rounds that I could, but if one of his rounds hit me, I'd likely be done for. It was my turn to show him *my* evasive maneuvers. I could only hope that I could regain my position, or outmaneuver him into spending his ammunition. He didn't appear to be wasting ammo though. He was waiting until he felt like he had a clear shot before firing. Damn!

His cannon rounds streaked past me. Then, with a deafening bang, I was hit! What a sound! He hit me 30mm with a cannon round right in my radiator beneath my feet. Steam exploded from the radiator, filling the cockpit and instantly fogged up my canopy and windscreen. I knew better than to breathe it in as it would have toasted my lungs in a second. I quickly slid my canopy open. My ears were ringing from the explosion and my left leg was numb. I moved the joystick around to see if I still had control of the plane. That worked, but nothing happened when I tried to move the rudder pedals. I couldn't tell if it was due to the injury to my leg or if something was damaged in the controls. I just knew that I had limited control of my plane. I could see my temperature gauge climbing quickly and I knew that I only had a minute or so before the engine would fail.

All this happened in a split second, and my challenger was still behind me in a position to finish me off. I thought: *It's my time.* And I thanked God for a wonderful life then looked up at my rear view mirrors, expecting to see the flash of his cannons. He wasn't there! Instead, he eased up next to me on my right... wingtip to wingtip. He couldn't have been sitting 30 feet from me. The pilot nodded and gave me a salute, then peeled off. I couldn't believe it. He had spared me. I was dumbfounded, but grateful.

The engine's temperature continued to climb. I thought I could nurse a few more minutes of flying time out of the plane if I eased back on the throttle. Where the hell was I though? Somewhere in France! I hadn't exactly been paying attention to my heading and location during the dogfight, and the sky was totally clear of other aircraft—friend and foe. The only exception was that of my enemy's plane departing on the horizon.

I knew that I was behind enemy lines, but not how far. Without rudder control, I managed to turn back to the south by using the ailerons. The engine began to shudder, made a horrible squeaking sound then abruptly seized up. Then there was silence, aside from the sound of the wind blowing past my open canopy. I didn't have a whole lot of altitude and P-51s didn't have a very impressive glide ratio. I lowered my flaps for a little extra range, then nosed the plane down to keep my airspeed above stalling.

It's funny how time slows down in a situation like that. I looked down to see how bad my leg was. I could see that my suit was torn and there was a lot of blood. I could also see the ground through a hole torn in the floor. It was a struggle, but I managed to climb out of the cockpit and dive overboard.

Once I was free of the plane, I yanked my ripcord and was relieved to see and feel my parachute canopy inflate above me. I was also relieved to see that the cannon round that had exploded under my seat hadn't damaged my parachute. Since I was no longer in the plane pushing the stick forward to maintain airspeed, the plane stalled, then fell like a rock. Great! I was going to come down practically on top of it with everybody in the countryside watching. So much for a quiet getaway!

On my way down, I wondered how difficult life would be as a prisoner of war. Would they take me as a prisoner, or shoot me on the spot?

Boom! The plane hit the ground, sending a mushroom of flame upwards from beneath me. The heat from the explosion filled my parachute and lifted me, actually helping to carry me away from the wreck. My baby, *Heavenly Helen,* was no more. Maybe I'd be lucky enough that there were no German troops in the area. Maybe they were all off fighting to take the airfield.

I'd heard great things about the French Resistance helping pilots to find their way out of France. I could only hope.

I checked to see if I had lost anything when I bailed out. My .45 was still in its holster and, more importantly, I still had my first aid kit. I looked down and could see blood dripping from my boot, falling to the ground below. The shock that had numbed the pain was starting to wear off. I wasn't much looking forward to hitting the ground with my injured leg.

I landed, instinctively using both legs to absorb the impact before rolling. It hurt. Oh God, it hurt, so bad! I'm no sissy, but I screamed when I hit the ground. The last thing I remember was unclipping my chute, and then I must have passed out.

When I came to, I was in a lot less pain. In fact, I was feeling pretty damned good. A nurse was looking down at me, smiling. A nurse? I looked around and saw that I was lying on the ground in a forest. My leg was bandaged. There was a soldier sitting next to her, and he was watching me, too. The nurse was wearing a white uniform and the soldier was definitely an American GI who looked like he was Army Air Force. Odd!

Before I could ask, the nurse said comfortingly, "Just relax. I gave you some morphine for the pain and I stopped the bleeding."

I remember saying, "So... I get shot down behind enemy lines and wake to an American nurse tending to my wounds and a sergeant from the Army Air Force. I suppose you're here to fix my plane?"

The sergeant chuckled and replied with a Southern drawl. "Yeah... I'm afraid that your plane isn't fixable. We were at the Haguenau Airfield when it was evacuated, and got left behind. We didn't want to wait around for the Krauts to retake it, so we ran. We figured we'd try to keep from getting captured 'til our boys retake this area... so we've just been hiding out!"

"I'm sure glad you found me. Anyway, I've got a map and a compass so we can head back towards our line, but I don't know how mobile I am. How bad is my leg?"

The nurse answered, "Nothing's broken, but you have a pretty good gash there. It's wrapped for now, but you'll need surgery. Looks like shrapnel. Was it flak?"

"No, a cannon round from a 190 exploded right under me. I guess I'm lucky that it wasn't worse."

The sergeant asked, "Do you know how far we are behind enemy lines?"

"I'm not too sure. I was in a pretty intense dogfight when I got shot down. I believe the line was about ten minutes behind me."

He reacted optimistically, "Ten minutes?!"

I said, "Well, you got to figure I was flying over three hundred miles an hour. That would make it... about fifty miles back if I was flying in a straight line. I really don't know what my heading was though. We could have been flying in circles."

The nurse said, "Well, for right now, we need to get you into town to find somewhere to bed down for the night."

"Town?!" I asked. "Do we have friendly help in town?"

"Yes and no," she answered. "The French civilians would be shot for helping us, so they don't—not directly, anyway. We've been on the run for two days now. When they see us, they just look the other way. When we find a shed or a garage to bed down for the night, breakfast mysteriously shows up at the door in the morning."

I laughed. "How could they *not* notice you two? With you in uniform and you in that white nurse's dress, they can spot you a mile off!"

I introduced myself to them. The nurse's name was Sandy. She was from Cleveland, and the GI was Lonny, who was from Atlanta—another Southern boy. Turns out that he was a mechanic on one of the cargo planes that abandoned them at the airfield. Sandy was a red-haired, freckled, blue-eyed woman who might have been mistaken for a boy if she wasn't wearing a dress. She did have a gentle touch, a soothing voice, and a sincere goodness about her. Lonny, well, he was lanky and looked like a mechanic.

"So they left y'all behind? That was pretty crappy of them."

Lonny answered, "They didn't have much of a choice. I was helping the medics load the last of the wounded onto the last plane out, and then the lieutenant asked me to go back with her to get more medical supplies. I guess the Germans were determined to hit the plane before it left, so they started shelling the field really hard. The plane couldn't wait for us and I don't blame them a bit for taking off."

I replied, "The battle for that field isn't over. I was on my way there to support our ground troops when we ran into these 190s. I trust we'll have it back soon."

I didn't really need to explain that the battle was still on. The distant thumping of artillery made that fact pretty obvious.

I said, "It sounds like they're still at it. We don't really need a compass. All we have to do is follow the sound of the shelling to find our battle line."

We knew that we shouldn't stay close to the crash site. Lonny fashioned me a pair of crutches out of some branches and Sandy rigged up a splint to help keep the pressure off of my wound. She only had one vial of morphine in her bag, so I prayed that we'd find help before it ran out. Sandy gave me another dose before we began the slow and painful journey towards friendly lines.

We were traveling in daylight and trying not to be too obvious, sticking to sparsely populated back roads. We'd hide in the brush when a car passed. I doubt that we traveled a whole mile before dusk. We turned off the road, down a long gravel driveway that stretched through an open meadow with split-rail fences on either side. At the end of the drive was a house, but it wasn't a typical German home. It had a modern design with a flat, pitched roof and lots of glass. It was kind of a Frank Lloyd Wright-looking house, which unfortunately had a carport rather than a detached garage. We needed shelter and remembered passing a shed halfway down the driveway. It wasn't locked, but it was full of farming equipment. There was barely enough room for us to bed down. Pain sure saps the energy out of a person. I hardly remember lying down before I was out.

We were awakened the next morning by the sound of a vehicle passing down the gravel road outside. Lonny peeked out as it passed. "It looks like the couple from the house is going to work."

I asked, "So, nobody's at the house now?"

"Doesn't look like it. I'll go scout it out. Maybe we can find something to eat."

"Maybe we can find some clothes that will help us blend in," Sandy added.

It was good that the house was at the end of a long drive with no visible neighbors. We watched as Lonny drew his weapon and went to check it out. We lost sight of him as he went around the back of the house. I heard breaking glass as he gained access to it. He appeared soon after at the front door and motioned for us to join him.

The home was warm and inviting. The Christmas tree, with all of its gifts crowded around it, made me feel like we could have been at a home in the States. That thought saddened me when I pictured the tree at our house, with only Mom and Helen to sit around it by the fireplace.

Sandy gathered what she needed to cook breakfast while Lonny and I looked for clothes that would fit. Poor Lonny was so tall that everything was too short for him, but anything was better than his uniform.

After finishing breakfast, I said, "It would sure be nice if we could come back after the war and properly thank our hosts."

Sandy replied, "Let's do that. It's a date!" She went to the trouble of washing and putting away the dishes, then turned to Lonny and said, "I have to wash and dress this wound, Sergeant. It might be a good idea for you to stand watch."

"Yes ma'am," he replied and went out to the front porch.

I followed her into the bedroom and sat down on the bed. After tending to my leg, she gave me the last of the morphine, then put her hand on my chest and pushed me back onto the bed. "You lie down and rest for a while. I want to take a quick shower. Lord knows if I'll get another chance."

I settled back onto the bed to relax. The bathroom was directly at the foot of the bed. Sandy didn't close the door behind her! She stood facing the mirror with her back to me, and she unbuttoned her dress and let it fall to the floor. Holy crap!

Should I turn away?! I think that she meant for me to see her. In that one instant, all of my moral convictions vanished. The fact that we both wore wedding rings no longer mattered. I couldn't believe how horribly excited I became from one second to the next. Then she undid her brassier and let it fall. That nurse's dress had done a great job of concealing the woman's magnificent form. She was looking at my reflection in the mirror to see if I was watching. She smiled, let her panties fall to the floor then stepped into the shower.

Damn! What I was feeling wasn't love. I was consumed by a powerful, heavy-duty lust. Trembling, I couldn't remember ever having been moved that way before. My leg may have been in bad shape, but everything else was working just fine! Oh, the sweet, intoxicating anticipation of waiting for her to finish that shower. As I heard the water running, I could picture it washing down her beautiful body.

There was a loud squeak from the knobs as she shut the water off. She stepped from the shower, faced me and picked up a towel and slowly dried herself, all the while watching me through the corner of her eye.

I sat up on the end of the bed so there would be no doubt that she had my full attention. She walked over and stood before me. I'd never seen the body of a red-haired girl before. Freckles complimented her fair skin, and she was indeed a true redhead. Sandy took my face in her hands and I gently ran my hands up her hips. That last dose of morphine must have kicked in about then, because that's the last thing I remember.

I don't even remember leaving the house. Next thing I could recall was that we were walking down the road again, surrounded by a forest. Then we saw a vehicle approaching in the distance. Again, we dove for cover, but not before noticing that it was a military vehicle... and more than one. My head cleared pretty fast as we made our way deeper into the woods. We could hear the vehicles coming closer. How we were hoping that they hadn't seen us. That wasn't the case. We heard brakes whistle as the vehicles came to a stop, and we could hear muffled voices in the distance. There was no doubt that they were looking for us.

As we hurried through the brush, I had to stop. I was feeling pretty weak, and I leaned against a large log in a little clearing. "I don't mean to sound like a hero... but there's no way we can outrun them. Not with me holding you back."

Sandy snapped, "We're not leaving you!"

Lonny pulled out his .45. I laughed and said, "Put that thing away, Sergeant. You're going to get us all killed. I think I'd rather be a prisoner than a corpse. Really, y'all should go!" Then I turned my attention to Sandy, "I'd hate to think of what they might do to a pretty redhead like you, Sandy."

Lonny looked at Sandy for a response. Her resolve hadn't changed, so I said to Lonny, "You go anyway, Sergeant. There's no sense in all three of us getting captured."

His shoulders dropped and he sighed as he returned his gun to its holster. The three of us sat against the log and waited for our captors.

Talk about a burst of joy! As the soldiers emerged from the brush, we saw that they were Americans! We were so excited that we all screamed and rushed towards them.

One of soldiers blasted a stream of machine gun fire across the ground in front of us, yelling, "Halt!" It sent sprigs of grass flying up and pelted us with dirt. We halted and raised our hands.

"We're Americans," I said.

He barked, "Identify yourself!"

I slowly reached into my shirt and produced my dog tags while answering, "I'm Captain Ken Davis, U.S. Army Air Force."

They immediately relaxed and lowered their weapons. "Well I'll be damned!" the sergeant replied. "We've been looking for you. Who're your friends?"

The soldier in charge, Sergeant Paulson, approached us. I answered as we handed him our dog tags, "They're from Haguenau. They were left behind in the evacuation."

Once Sergeant Paulson saw the dog tags, his group followed his lead as he snapped to attention and saluted me. "Yes sir." He looked down at my leg, "I see that you are injured."

"Yeah, my leg's in pretty bad shape. As luck would have it though, these two found me and the lieutenant just happens to be a nurse. She saved my life!"

Sergeant Paulson saluted Sandy, "Ma'am!" Then he turned to another GI and ordered, "Get a medic over here, quick... with a litter."

One of the GIs handed a grateful Lonny a cigarette. The GI commented after looking at his pants, "Those clothes don't fit you very good, do they, sport?"

Lonny sarcastically quipped, "I'm afraid my tailor's on holiday."

I asked, "So are we behind enemy lines?"

"We are, sir," the sergeant answered. "But most of the enemy forces are focused on the airfield right now."

Lonny asked, "How far are we from the line?"

The sergeant answered, pointing, "It's about five miles over that way."

"Really?!" I was amazed to find that we were so close. I asked, "And do you know where my plane went down?"

He turned the opposite direction and answered, "About two miles up there. We got word from the French Underground that you bailed out, so we started at the crash site and backtracked towards the battle line... and we found you!"

"Great work, Sergeant!"

"Word is, sir, that you downed two 190s before they got you."

"That's some consolation." I turned to Sandy and Lonny. "We had quite an adventure in our two-mile journey, didn't we?"

The medics arrived with a litter and loaded me onto it. Sandy walked alongside, explaining to them the care that she'd given me so far. Her hand was on my chest. Without thinking, I took it in mine and squeezed. In an instant, she slid her hand away and continued her conversation with them. It kind of hurt my feelings, but I understood. We were both married and we certainly didn't need a scandal. I was still fuzzy from the morphine, and I figured that her judgment was likely better than mine at the time. When they loaded me into the field ambulance, Sandy moved to join us.

One of the medics stopped her. "Thank you, ma'am. We've got it from here." Then he pulled the door closed. Damn. I could have pulled rank on them and insisted that they allow her to accompany us, but then, after the little "hand" thing, I figured that maybe I should just wait 'til she came to see me at the hospital.

But she didn't come. In fact, that was the last time I saw her. I kept thinking that she'd at least come by to say "hi" or "goodbye" when they stitched me up at the infirmary. Nothing!

As I lay there recovering I pondered whether, in my drug-induced stupor, I could have said or done something to offend her. I couldn't remember, since I was delusional most of the time. That's when it dawned on me that maybe the *whole encounter* was a hallucination from the morphine. Well yes, that would make sense of things. Because in reality, it's not likely that I would have cheated on my wife... and if the encounter with Sandy was real, she would have come to see me.

Of the music I heard playing while I was at that hospital, I especially remember the voice of a French singer, Edith Piaf. Her hauntingly unique vibrato echoed through the halls during my short stay there. Whenever I think of France, I remember her voice and recall the bittersweet memory of Sandy.

I was awakened the next morning by people talking about my condition outside my door. I recognized one of the voices as my commanding officer from the airfield where I was based in England, Colonel Douglas. His voice was unmistakable—loud and confident.

He entered the room with the doctor and another colonel I didn't know. He came over to me and patted my shoulder and said, "Here's the man of the hour! Congratulations, Captain Davis. You battled it out with the legendary Luftwaffe Ace, Major Hans Kirpes, and lived to tell about it. I heard you gave him quite a run for his money."

"You're kidding me!" I shot up in bed. "Hans Kirpes?! Are you sure?"

He handed me a grainy black and white photograph of an aircraft. "Here are the markings on his plane. Is this the one that shot you down?"

The vertical bands painted on the rear of the fuselage and the crest over them, were very unique. "Yes. That's the plane." I answered. "Wow. I could tell that he was an extraordinary pilot. You should have seen him fly!"

The commander said, "Major Kirpes has 206 kills to his credit, which makes him one of the top five Aces of all time. That you survived a dogfight with him says a lot about your skill as a pilot."

"I, uh... I can't claim that it was my skill, sir" I replied.

"Then what was it?" he asked.

"He let me go. It *was* truly an epic dogfight, and it was obvious that he was a far better pilot than me. Anyway, after he disabled my plane, he had the position to finish me off, but he didn't. Instead, he flew up next to me, saluted then went home."

The colonel with my C.O. spoke up. "I'm Colonel Clark with the Army's Public Relations Department. Captain, your story makes Kirpes sound downright chivalrous, but that's not the story we're going to publicize. Captain Davis, we need your help. We need *you* to be the hero in this story. And I've got some good news for you. We're pulling some strings and bypassing a mile of red tape so we can send you home in time for Christmas. In return, we'd like you to do some public relations for us while you are Stateside, recovering."

"Sure! Hey, that *is* great news!" I answered.

"Like I said," the Colonel continued, "the headlines will say that you are the hero, an Ace who's downed eight enemy planes and has survived against one of Germany's most notorious Aces who only downed you with a lucky shot. There'll be speaking engagements, war bond sales events, and maybe even a parade or two."

"Really?" I asked. "I don't really understand why I'd be celebrated for eight kills when I was flying against a pilot who has over two hundred."

"You don't have to. You just have to do what we tell you to, and we're telling you to play up the role of being a national hero. This PR business is a little more complicated than you might think. I'll have to coach you on what you can and can't say, so you're going to be seeing a lot of me on this trip home."

The doctor spoke up. "We're releasing you a lot sooner than I'd like, but we're sending a nurse along with you to take care of you. Just sign here and you can go. Sounds like you have a plane to catch!"

I have to admit that, at least for a moment, I entertained the notion that perhaps Sandy would be the nurse they sent to accompany me. It wasn't to be.

They flew me home in a C-47. It was a long flight by way of Iceland, but it beat the heck out of traveling across the Atlantic by ship. Colonel Clark spent a good deal of the trip educating me in the business of public affairs and national security. Eventually, the colonel dozed off. I tried to do the same, only my mind was reeling from everything that had happened in the previous 48 hours.

CHAPTER 4: Home

Everything happened so quickly that I hadn't had a chance to send a telegram to Helen to let her know I was coming home. What I didn't know was that Colonel Clark had already had the airfield contact her to update her.

As we descended into the Baton Rouge area, I strained to see familiar landmarks through the breaks in the clouds below us.

The colonel had quite a reception organized for me upon landing at Harding Field. When we taxied up to the tarmac there, we were greeted by a brass band, reporters, the airfield's officials, and even the mayor of Baton Rouge. He had the whole event planned in advance—down to who I greeted and what I was supposed to say. I struggled to get down the steps from the plane and was handed a set of crutches. The colonel decided that, for appearances, I should be standing with crutches rather than seated in a wheelchair when I faced the press.

I'm grateful that they allowed me hug my wife and Mom first.

"Oh, honey, they told me you're hurt!" Helen said.

"It's not serious. Nothing I won't heal from, anyway."

"Why didn't I know you were shot down?! We just heard this morning!"

"Well it just happened the day before yesterday! It's really *not* that serious. Hey, it got me home for Christmas! I couldn't have planned it better."

The reporters were snapping pictures and struggling for position. Then the officials lined up to be photographed with me. The reporters were all asking questions at the same time.

Colonel Clark raised his hands to silence them, then spoke. "We will have a press conference at nine tomorrow morning at the Heidelberg Hotel. Captain Davis will make a brief statement now. Then we're going to let him go home to spend some time with his family."

My statement was well-rehearsed. I said, "All I'm going to say for right now is that, if I was going to be shot down in a dogfight, at least it wasn't by some lucky green Luftwaffe pilot. It was by one of the most notorious German Aces to ever threaten the skies over Europe. And he hasn't seen the last of me!"

Upon completing my statement, we were hustled into a car and driven to Mom's car. Colonel Clark patted my shoulder and said, "I'll pick you up at 0700."

It was nice to leave all that commotion behind and head towards home. Mom drove, giving Helen and me the backseat. The sight of Helen and the feel of her touch brought me such peace. I'd come back home to reality. It felt like my time away had simply been a dream. I relished the drive home through

Baton Rouge. The state capitol building towered into the sky ahead. I always thought of Dad when I saw it.

As we navigated the winding road around the lake, the welcome sight of my home came into view. The front of the big white house was graced with columns that supported two levels of sprawling porches that faced out towards the lake. It was surrounded by oak trees draped with Spanish moss.

A decade earlier, City Park Lake had been a swampland, dense with cypress trees. Dad fell in love with the lake when his firm was involved in clearing it, and he decided to build our home on it.

The house was decorated for Christmas with a full, tastefully decorated tree at its usual place in the living room.

"We weren't expecting you, Kenny," my mom said. "We would have had the place fixed up nicer."

"You can't imagine how beautiful it looks to me right now, Mom. And I didn't expect to be home either, so I've got some Christmas shopping to do!"

Helen squeezed me from behind and said quietly, "Being together for Christmas is a better gift than we could have hoped for..."

It was nice, feeling Helen in my arms again, but then I felt unworthy of her when I remembered Sandy. I quickly dismissed the thought, choosing to embrace the idea that the forbidden encounter was only imaginary.

A doctor and nurse from Harding Field came over that night to assist us in making it possible for me to convalesce at home rather than at the hospital. They brought me a wheelchair and gave me a medication to help with the pain that wouldn't muddle my mind like the morphine did.

In the morning, I woke to the smell of one of Mary's wonderful home-cooked breakfasts. The morning paper was waiting at the breakfast table. A picture of me shaking hands with the mayor was on the front page.

Colonel Clark was at the door at 0700 sharp. Mom and Helen were going to spend the morning shopping while I was doing my interviews.

"Beautiful home, Captain," the colonel commented.

"Yeah, I'm afraid I took it for granted before the war, but I certainly don't now."

The morning news on the car's radio was also brimming with the news of my homecoming for Christmas.

We drove through downtown on our way to the Heidelberg Hotel. It was as beautiful as it ever was, all trimmed out for Christmas. I almost felt that I should thank Hans Kirpes for shooting me down. If he hadn't, I'd have been in my cold drafty Quonset hut in England for Christmas.

The press conference was a bigger deal than I expected. It wasn't just the local press. The national radio networks were there, with newsreel cameras and reporters from newspapers all over the country. Colonel Clark must have notified them of the conference before we even left France. I nervously offered the reporters the rehearsed answers I was authorized to give. Then I made a comment that I hadn't run by Colonel Clark beforehand.

"I would also like to say that, when I bailed out, I was bleeding pretty badly from my leg wound. When I hit the ground, I lost consciousness. Somehow, out in the middle of nowhere behind enemy lines, nurse Sandy Burkhart and Sergeant Lonny Gann appeared. They dragged me to safety and saved me from bleeding to death. Wherever they are, I want to extend my heartfelt thanks for being my heroes."

Apprehensively, I looked at the colonel's face for a response. I could see that I was in trouble. He waited until we were in the car to confront me.

"Captain Davis. I've been doing my job longer than you've been alive. Wars are won and lost on *information*. Maybe I didn't make myself clear enough. You are not to disclose unauthorized information to the press. To do so is direct insubordination and will not only go onto your record, but you could also face a court-martial for it. Is that clear?"

"Yes sir," I answered. "I knew the second it came out of my mouth that I messed up. I'm sorry, and it will never happen again."

"You didn't just recount an event. You gave soldier's names out. *I* can't authorize you to do that without the Pentagon's approval. Now I've got to go back and straighten this out with the press. It won't go on your record this time, but

I guarantee you, if there is a next time, you *will* be held accountable!"

"Thank you, sir," I responded. "Damn. I'm starting to think this Public Affairs business is a lot more complicated than flying!"

The colonel pointed out, "A hell of a lot more damage can be done with information than with an airplane." He let go a sigh, then continued on a lighter note, "I'm going home to spend Christmas with *my* family. You relax and do the same, and we'll hit the road after the first of the year."

"Can Helen come with us?" I asked hopefully.

"There you go again, not taking this assignment seriously. This is *not* a vacation. It's a very important assignment! The information we need to discuss on these tours is not for civilian ears. I'll try to get you home for the weekends."

"Okay, but I do have one request regarding Helen that's personal. What do you think the chances are, after my leg's healed, of my taking her up in one of the Mustang tandem trainers? I would love for her to experience what I do for a living!"

Clark nodded his head thoughtfully. "It might actually be a good bit of public relations exposure. I'll check on that for you."

Mom and Helen weren't home when he dropped me off. I started a fire, turned on some Christmas music, settled back into my dad's favorite chair, propped up my leg, and gazed out of the large front window over the lake beyond. The smell of the Christmas tree and the crackling fire took me back to the happy memories of Christmases of my childhood. Emotionally drained from the day's activities, I dozed off.

I must've really been out. I didn't hear the ladies come in. Helen woke me with a kiss.

I said, "We can relax now. I'm off 'til after New Year's. What do you say we have a big New Year's bash here and invite all of our family and friends from school?"

Helen's face lit up at the thought of it. "Everybody would love to see you!"

I suggested, "Let's invite the crew from Davis Engineering, too!"

Her expression changed when I mentioned the firm.

"What?" I asked.

"Nothing."

"Come on... you're keeping something from me. What is it?"

Mom answered. "We weren't going to talk to you about this just yet, but the firm isn't doing too well. One very important thing your dad took care of when he ran the firm was to check everybody's work to be sure that nothing was overlooked. We've had some oversights, caught by the inspectors, that cost a couple of our biggest accounts a small fortune... and we lost them."

"Oh."

Helen commented, "We can't afford to lose another client. I manage the books. We're operating at very close to break-even."

Mom said, "Helen and I both have our salaries for the moment, but we can't depend on that lasting."

I said, "My income should be helping."

"That's going in the bank. And your dad's life insurance is in the bank if we should need it. Things are fine, Kenny. It's just that there's a little bit of tension between us and the firm right now. We'll invite them. I'm sure they'll be happy to see you."

I wasn't going to let that put a damper on my holidays.

We loaded the wheelchair into the car and headed out to go shopping. I was pretty famous that day. As we drove along, one of my interviews from that morning was playing on the radio.

Baton Rouge had a morning and afternoon newspaper. When that afternoon's paper came out, I found myself, again, on the front page with a headline reading, "Baton Rouge's Fighter Ace, Captain Ken Davis, home for Christmas!" The real topper was that there was a picture of me standing by the nose of my P-51, proudly showing off *Heavenly Helen*. I was happy that Helen was included in the publicity.

Christmas music spilled out from the stores we passed and the downtown sidewalks that were crowded with holiday shoppers. It seemed like we couldn't go five feet without someone recognizing me and wanting to congratulate me. I suppose, if I hadn't been in a wheelchair, I would have been less conspicuous. When we got to Kress's department store, the manager himself came out to help us. He asked one of his assistants to run and get a camera so he could be photographed with me.

"You just tell me. What can we do for you?" he offered.

"My leg is killing me," I answered. "Is there someplace quiet I can rest for a few minutes? I love all this attention, but I don't see how I'm going to get any shopping done."

The manager whispered something to his assistant, who hurried away, and then he led me to his office where he sat me in front of his desk. The assistant came back beaming and told him, "Yes sir. Absolutely!"

He turned to us and said, "I had an idea. Why don't you go home and rest up. We close at nine. Come back then and we'll stay open for you. You'll have the store to yourself."

Amazing! I was starting to like the hero business. I said, "Y'all are wonderful! You got a deal!"

I turned to Helen. "You know what I'd like to do now? I've been dying to go to the Piccadilly Restaurant down the street."

Mom said, "But honey. They've got lines down the street, and with your leg…"

Kress's manager held up his hand. "I have a solution for that too. I'll just make a quick call to their manager."

It just kept getting better!

That restaurant had been my dad's favorite. The last time I was there, the family went together just before he left. When we arrived, the restaurant manager came out to greet us and held up a copy of the newspaper, announcing to the crowd as we moved past them, "Make way for Captain Davis, our injured fighter Ace!"

I got a lot of smiles and pats on the back as the manager led us in.

He told us, "Your money's no good here, Captain! Your dinner's on the house!"

After we were seated, I looked over to see a couple of familiar faces approaching our table. It was John and his wife Rose, friends from high school.

He said, "Hey, buddy. It's great to see you. Am I intruding?"

He'd changed. His voice was lower, and there seemed to be sadness in his eyes that hadn't been there before.

"Of course not!" I said, as I motioned for them to join us. "It's great to see you two! We haven't seen you since the wedding."

"That was forever ago. I did a hitch in the Marines since then, South Pacific," he answered. "But geez, look at you... all over the news! You're famous!"

"Yeah, well the attention is great, but I'm not really comfortable with it. There are a *lot* of wounded heroes who came home to Baton Rouge who aren't getting any publicity. It's mostly arranged by the Army's public affairs department to raise money for war bonds. They've got most of my healing time booked up with events all over the country. I've only got 'til New Year's to enjoy some time off. So, you fought in the South Pacific. That must have been hell."

"It was. There's a lot of misery and death out there, on both sides. The heat, humidity, and bugs really got to us when we weren't fighting. All the time we were each carrying a full backpack with soaking wet feet. I'll tell you what—at times, we envied the casualties." Then he smiled and squeezed Rose and said, "But it sure makes me appreciate being home again!"

"That's exactly what my dad said about the First World War. Guys like you deserve the credit for fighting this war."

John lowered his head, "Sorry to hear about your dad, Kenny. Everybody loved that guy." Then he looked up with an idea, "Hey! What are you guys doing for New Year's?"

"We were going to have a big party at our house like we had in the old days. You two want to come?"

John and Rose looked at each other, then answered, "I'm sorry, Kenny. We've already got a party planned at our place, mostly a bunch of our friends from school. I was going to invite you two."

"Bring them to our house! Unless you're set on having the party at your place, let us foot the bill!" I told him. "You remember the parties we used to have at our place. There's plenty of room."

It was agreed: New Year's at our house.

As they walked away, I sat there feeling guilty. I mentioned to Helen and Mom, "It's likely that John has a lot more enemy kills to his credit than I ever would, and under some pretty horrible circumstances too. I'm the one getting all of the glory and he didn't even get a free dinner."

Helen replied, "If he'd gone on to college like you, he could have been an officer."

I argued, "The guys trudging through those tropical forests were led by officers, who fought right there beside them. Besides, not everybody can afford college. Before I enlisted, I found out that some people didn't have to go to college to be an officer *or* a pilot. One of our pilots, Chuck Yeager, was a car mechanic from a little town in West Virginia who wound up working on airplanes in the Army. He joined the Enlisted Pilots Program and now, not only is he an officer, but he's one of our top Aces."

"Well, when this war's over and he's looking for a job, he's going to wish he had a college degree!" Mom asserted.

"Well, the best thing about my staying in school to get my degree was that I was able to spend more time at home with you guys. Hey! Let's quit talking about war. What's important is that I'm home now and we've got some Christmas shopping to do!"

We went home after dinner. Mom said she wanted to stay home and bake cookies and that Helen could take me back to Kress's. I think she understood that Helen and I could use a little time alone together. We left a little early so we could drive around town to enjoy the Christmas decorations.

Helen's parents came over for Christmas. Having them there took a little bit of the emptiness away from Dad's absence.

In getting ready for the New Year's party, I had a huge enlargement made of a photograph of me standing by Helen's image at the nose of my P-51. I had it framed to hang in the foyer for all of our guests to see. I even had color airbrushed onto the picture to show off *Heavenly Helen's* bright pink dress.

At the party, my friend John wasn't the only one of my guests who'd returned from combat overseas, and I wasn't the only one who came home wounded. A number of my classmates couldn't be there because they were either overseas or had lost their lives fighting.

Colonel Clark arrived at the house on January 2nd, ready to work. He joined us at the dinner table and Mom poured him some coffee. He turned to me and said, "I've talked to the brass about your little idea with Helen."

She looked at me curiously, "What idea?"

I answered, "I didn't mention it to her because I really didn't think there'd be much chance that they'd agree."

Clark continued, "So you haven't told her?"

I turned to Helen and asked, "How would you like to go up in a Mustang, the plane I fly? They have two-passenger trainers at Harding Field. You'd be one of the few civilians to go up in one."

We didn't have to ask her twice. She replied excitedly, "I can't wait to tell Dad. He'll be green with envy!"

Colonel Clark said, "We'll set it up for tomorrow morning at ten hundred hours. We'll have full press coverage." He smiled and looked at Helen, "Tomorrow, you'll be as famous as that husband of yours." Then he turned to me and said, "We'll have two more Mustangs flying along with you. It'll make for a better show."

As we stood to leave, I noticed that Helen was looking rather pale. "You're not nervous about flying with me, are you?"

"No," she answered. "It's not the flying that I'm uncomfortable with. It's the publicity. Will I be in newsreels, on the radio?"

"I'm sorry, sweetheart. I really didn't think they'd go for the idea, so I didn't mention it before. Besides, I thought that if they *did* go for the idea, it would be after my leg healed a little more."

"I'm not saying it won't be a thrill. It's just that the thought of all of those cameras and reporters being directed at me really scares me. I was proud I as could be when they were all trained on you! And, yes, I *would* have appreciated your asking me before volunteering me."

"We don't have to do it if you're not comfortable with it. It *is* a once in a lifetime opportunity though."

She gave me a hug. "Oh, we'll make it through it."

The colonel and I got everything coordinated for the next day, and I even managed to get passes for Helen's parents to be there. I knew how much it would mean to her to have them there.

After an early breakfast the next morning, we headed for the airfield. It was a chilly morning, but the sun was out bright. Once we arrived, an AAF liaison took our parents to join the press while I went off to get into my flight suit. They took Helen to be fitted into one as well. She looked so damned cute and sexy in her flight suit, complete with a leather cap and goggles perched on top. Her pretty face and bright red lipstick gave the outfit a whole new look. The real teaser was that she was wearing that perfume that I was so crazy about. I have to admit, the whole thing kind of excited me!

I didn't question it, but I was surprised that the event had been planned without the flight surgeon checking to see if I was fit to fly. My wound was just over a week old and still hurt like hell. I decided to conceal the pain as best I could and would try not to use my left rudder pedal any more than I had to, so I told the other pilots that we'd be making mostly… right turns.

Once again, the press experience was preplanned. They photographed us together, then together in front of the plane, and we even got some photos of us with our parents.

One of the reporters commented, "It must take a lot of courage to be a fighter pilot."

I laughed as I answered, "Yes, it does. But not nearly as much courage as it took to ask Helen for our first dance!"

If Helen was nervous, I certainly couldn't tell. By the way she was smiling and waving at the reporters as she was lowered into the cockpit, you'd have thought that she was the queen of the Mardi Gras ball! I climbed in ahead of her and waited until the ground crew confirmed that the press was clear before starting my engine. Then I taxied over to join two other Mustangs that were waiting for us. Both of the other planes were also tandem trainers, one carrying a reporter as a passenger and the other a cameraman.

The three of us formed up at the end of the runway, one behind me to my left and one behind me to my right. We took off in formation as one. I have to admit that, even to me, it looked pretty damned impressive! After leaving the field, we headed south over downtown Baton Rouge and took a heading down along the Mississippi River. Helen could hear the chatter between the control tower and me over her headset, and then with the other pilots as I called out the maneuvers we were to make.

I announced on the radio, "Okay. We're going to show those folks what a strafing run looks like with a low pass over the field."

I told Helen, "When we're flying over three hundred miles per hour at this altitude, it seems like we're moving pretty fast... but when we drop down to treetop level, you can really get a sense of our speed."

With that, I rolled the plane over and dove down to an altitude just above the treetops, with the other two planes in formation behind me. We shot past Harding Field in a flash then I yanked back on the stick. The ground fell away behind us at an amazing rate.

I'm sure the reporters were a little queasy from the ride, but they experienced what it felt like to pilot one of those awesome machines. Next, I swung around to cross over the downtown airport (the airfield where Helen and I had taken our first flight together), down Government Street, over Baton Rouge High, and then on to the river before heading north to Harding Field. For the benefit of the news cameras, we made another high-speed low-level pass before coming in for a landing. I opened it up to full throttle on that run and the three of us, still in tight formation, passed the spectators at just over 400 miles per hour.

We then swung around wide, lowered our flaps and gear, and settled gently down to the runway. I had to apply the brakes to come to a stop, which meant that I had to assert quite a bit of pressure on the top of the rudder pedals. That was awfully painful on my leg. As we taxied back up to the area where the press was waiting, I could see Colonel Clark and the rest of the field's brass, beaming. It was like a Hollywood premiere as we climbed out of the plane with flashes popping in the frenzied mass of reporters.

The flight really took its toll on my leg, between my braking and pulling those G's when I buzzed the field. I could feel blood squishing between my toes in my boot, and it was hurting. I motioned for Mom to bring me my crutches as I climbed down from the plane. Fortunately, all of the attention was on Helen, and no one seemed to notice that I was in distress. I wasn't complaining though. I wouldn't have traded that experience for anything!

Before leaving the field, I stopped at the infirmary. Turns out, I didn't mess the wound up too badly, but I did get my butt chewed for flying without being cleared first. I figured that the reason that step was bypassed was because the brass likely knew I wouldn't have passed. Nothing more was said about it.

When the afternoon paper came out, the front page was plastered with a picture of Helen stepping into the plane's cockpit, next to a photo of the nose art from my actual plane.

The headline read, "Heavenly Helen Davis of Davis Engineering steps into her husband's Mustang's cockpit for a wild ride above their hometown of Baton Rouge."

When Helen got home from work the next day, she could hardly contain her excitement. "The phones rang all day at the office. It seems like since the newspaper tied us to Davis Engineering, everybody wants to deal with us now."

I was glad to hear that. "If they get some new accounts out of this, I hope they don't blow it with them like the others!"

"We'll see," Helen said. "Hopefully they'll be paying more attention to their work in the future. I think losing the accounts they did might have wizened them up."

"I sure hope so. Maybe we can quit worrying about whether they can keep their doors open now."

That was to be my last evening home that week. The colonel took me on a road trip the next morning that spanned the Gulf Coast. We stayed pretty close to home on the first trip out, considering the condition of my leg.

We flew on commercial airlines, stayed at nice hotels, and ate well as we roamed the country making our fundraising engagements. Colonel Clark made good on his promise to try to get me home for weekends—I think mostly because he wanted to spend weekends with his family as well. I really gained a lot of respect for the man during our travels.

As January passed, I found that my leg was healing nicely. It was still painful to walk on, but I was able to trade my crutches for a cane.

I'd been following news of the war closely and saw that the Russians, British, French, and the Americans were converging on Germany on all sides. It looked like it was just a matter of time before the war with Germany was over.

By the middle of February in 1945, I'd fulfilled my usefulness to the Army's Public Affairs department, and the doctor at Harding Field certified me as ready to return for duty in Europe.

CHAPTER 5: Back to Work

My departure from Harding Field wasn't quite as exciting as my arrival. Mom and Helen saw me off. If I died and never made it home again, I would have died content. On that trip, I'd come home a hero, spent Christmas and New Year's with the people who mattered most to me, and brought the struggling engineering firm the publicity that would no doubt solve its problems. But as much as I hated leaving home, I *was* itching to get back into combat.

I certainly felt like February in England—cold, gray, and wintry. Like when I had first arrived at the 363rd, there were often days when no one could fly missions.

My first appointment was with the infirmary to prove that I was fit to fly. I still needed my cane, but my injury was looking good.

I found my bunk and locker as I had left them two months before and also found that my motorcycle had been safely stored out of the elements. While we were grounded, the guys spent much of their days gathered around in a Quonset hut, trying to keep warm and shooting the breeze. They had read about me while I was gone. Though some resented that I got so much attention when I'd only scored eight kills, they were still excited over my celebrity status. I traded tales of my State side travels for their stories of current events with the war. They talked about George Preddy, our top P-51 Ace, who got shot down by friendly fire on Christmas Day. The Germans had greatly intensified their bombardment of England with V1 and V2 missiles. The pilots were also encountering a lot more of the ME-262 jet fighters on their missions, which I'd yet to experience in combat.

Being grounded made it easy to forget that I was in a country at war. As I walked back to my hut, the thick blanket of snow compacted beneath my boots in a muffled crunch. The large, fluffy snowflakes that were falling seemed to absorb all other sound. Even the barking of a nearby dog seemed muffled. The smell of coal from the potbellied stoves in the huts hung heavily in the air.

Before returning to my hut, I walked out to the flight line to see that a new P-51 was waiting for me. Though it was draped in a snow-covered tarp, I could still see the image of *Heavenly Helen II* peeking out from under it… bright pink dress and all.

We finally got word that we'd be on for the next day. Since my leg was still rather tender, it was more of a challenge to get dressed, so I got into my layers of underwear and socks the night before. Considering how little the stove did to warm the hut on winter nights, I slept surprisingly warm that night.

I was already awake when they came to roust us for the mission, and I quickly climbed into my flight suit. After breakfast, we assembled in a large Quonset hut for our briefing. With a "Ten Hut!" the mission commander laid out the mission and showed us the leg of the bomber formation's route that we are assigned to serve as escort.

He said, "There's a good chance you'll be flying against ME-262s today. I don't need to say that they are presenting us with a whole new challenge up there. Flying a full 100 miles per hour faster than us, they're able to hit us and go before we have time to react. Their greatest vulnerability is that it takes quite a while for them to reach that speed. Their acceleration is sluggish. So, if we can catch them either on the ground or while they're attempting to accelerate to their most efficient speed, we have the best chance of downing them."

I looked around the room and counted the new faces, then noted those whose faces I didn't see.

The forecaster was right. Bulldozers had cleared the snow from the runways while we were sleeping and the cold morning sky was filled with broken clouds. With the weather as it was, I hadn't had a chance to try out the new plane. Turns out, it wasn't new like my last plane, but it looked like it hadn't been abused too badly. I formed up with my wingman and we were off. The sound and feel of the takeoff brought me a renewed sense of exhilaration. I was again filled with the mixture of emotions I felt when I was flying into battle. I was also nervous over the prospect of engaging the ME-262 jet fighters for the first time.

The closer we drew to the anticipated point of intercepting the 262s, the more nervous I got. My senses had to be at their absolute peak and I had to be prepared for a fight like I'd never fought before. If the 262s were where we expected them to be, they would still be gaining speed and altitude. I was playing scenarios in my mind of how I'd engage them. I found myself breathing heavily. I needed to relax and focus!

"BANDITS, one o'clock, low!" blared over the headset. Damn it, so much for relaxing. The bandits were 262s.

They were far enough below us that I could roll and loop down behind them without losing airspeed. Of course, if they didn't take evasive action, that would work out perfectly. I could only hope that at least one of them wasn't anticipating my move.

As I maneuvered, I fell right in behind one. What luck, or maybe it was more than luck. A factor I hadn't considered was that the pilots of these remarkable aircraft were likely green. I blasted a volley from my 50-caliber guns at the 262 and saw my tracers make contact with him. Before I could line up on him for another blast, I saw cannon fire flash past me. It wasn't aimed at me though. My wingman was its intended target. I saw his plane blow apart when he was hit. I violently maneuvered to gain a position behind his attacker as he shot past me, and I gave him a blast as well. He suffered the same fate as my wingman.

In the instant that I was watching that 262 go down, I hadn't seen that another one had dropped behind me. I realized it when he sprayed me with a volley of 20mm cannon fire. Tracers zipped passed me in the same instant that I felt the hard knock of a round hitting the backside of the armor plating behind my seat. It nearly winded me. In the same instant, I heard the sound of aluminum ripping and of another round glancing off of my canopy. I rolled and dove out of his way to avoid him, but if I'd been smart, I would have stayed put and he would have flown right past me, giving me a clear shot at him.

When I leveled out, I realized that my plane was still operable and I wasn't hurt. Fuel was spraying out of my right wing. Luckily it hadn't ignited. The gauges looked okay… oil and temperature, etc… I figured that I had enough fuel in my other wing tank to get me home, so I headed back towards the Leiston Field. I tried to radio the tower to let them know I was coming in damaged, but the round that hit the armor behind my seat had also taken out the radio which was located behind the seat. The flaps wouldn't lower, which meant I'd have to land at a high rate of speed. Someone in my flight must have notified the tower that I was in trouble, because the emergency vehicles were waiting alongside the landing strip as I approached. It took me the entire runway to bring the plane to a stop, but I made it down in one piece. Then I taxied off of the runway and shut the engine off out of concern over the fuel leak.

My crew chief, Steve, came out with the emergency vehicles. I let him know that my wingman hadn't made it back so he could notify his crew chief. He walked around my plane, shaking his head in disbelief over how chewed up it was.

He said, "First time out since you've been back and you bring your plane back like this? Looks like a flying cheese grater!"

"Those 262s have a pretty mean bite, but I downed one of them and left another looking like this. Can you patch her up?" I asked.

"I've seen worse," he answered. "It'll be a while though. We'll have to find you a loaner."

As we gathered for debriefing, one of the other pilots patted my shoulder. "Nice going, Davis!"

"It was just luck. The one I downed was the one that got my wingman. I nailed him as he shot past me. If I'd been his first choice for a target, I would have been the one who didn't make it home."

I found out later that the first 262 I hit did go down, so I had two 262 kills to my credit that day.

Before Kirpes had shot me down, I felt invulnerable. That experience made me realize that I wasn't, and getting my plane shot up so badly on that last mission shook my confidence even further.

My leg continued to get better. Although it was pretty much healed, it was still painful to walk on, so I still relied on my cane to get around.

As February gave way to March of 1945, we felt more confident that the end of the war was near. On our bomber escort missions, I could see that most of Berlin was devastated.

It was hard to imagine what the Germans had left to fight for. I couldn't help but feel compassion for the people who lived in the bombed-out cities, both in England and in Germany.

I felt blessed that those of us from the States had our peaceful hometowns to return to, untouched by the ravages of war.

The aircraft that we were flying against were disorganized and, consequently, made easier prey for us. They would send up a hodge-podge mixture of planes to fly against us... whatever was left airworthy. Many of their planes were grounded from a lack of replacement parts. Other fighters were grounded simply because they had no fuel. I felt that the Luftwaffe pilots knew the war would be over soon and were only flying against us in a desperate attempt to prevent further destruction of their cities. I'm sure that they were as anxious as we were to live to see the end of the war.

We heard that the remaining 262s were sent to a unit called JV44, headed by one of the Luftwaffe's top Aces, Adolf Galland. He assembled the best pilots from the Luftwaffe in this unit, who had attained a kill ratio of 4-to-1. Needless to say, we were all apprehensive about running into them on our missions.

When I returned from a mission in early April, my crew chief said the C.O. wanted to see me in his office. I was pretty sure I knew what it was about. Since I had returned to combat, I only scored the two kills on my first day back—the day I came back with my plane shot up. I hadn't scored any kills since. I suspected that he was going to lecture me about being too cautious and about not being aggressive enough.

When I walked into his office, Colonel Douglas motioned for me to sit. "I've volunteered you for a unique assignment, Captain Davis."

"Yes sir?"

"You're a damned fine pilot, but you also have a degree in engineering."

"Yes sir."

"We've taken several Luftwaffe facilities and have captured some of their most advanced aircraft."

I liked the way the conversation was going. A grin broke across my face. "Yes sir."

"Some of the top engineers in the aviation industry are on their way over to assess our findings before these aircraft are boxed up and shipped Stateside. These guys are civilians. We'd like an engineer there as an observer representing the USAAF. I figured that you'd be one of our best options, since aside from being an engineer, you have actual combat experience flying against some of these machines. The mission is called *Operation Overcast.*"

I couldn't conceal my excitement. "I'm honored to have been chosen for this assignment, sir. When do I go?"

"I should have your orders in a couple of days," the colonel answered.

"Could I bring my crew chief to assist me?" I asked.

"Good thinking," he answered. "I'll have his transfer drawn up immediately. Let him know that he'll be shipping out with you as well."

I was downright giddy! It would be such a thrill to actually see a ME-262 in the flesh. I'd also be seeing the other planes I'd been flying against... the Focke-Wulf 190 and the ME-109. Wow. I was damned glad that I'd held out for my engineering degree.

I tossed and turned that night, my mind filled with thoughts and images of what the assignment would bring. I had a funny feeling in my gut that I wasn't familiar with. I felt like, in analyzing the enemy's planes, that somehow I'd be staring evil in the face. I'd barely dozed off when we were rousted for the next morning's mission.

After the briefing, I was anxious to break the news to Steve. I walked up to him with a serious look and said, "Steve. The C.O. himself wanted me to break the news to you. You're being reassigned in a couple of days."

"Reassigned?! I'm not going to be your crew chief? Why?! Did I screw up?"

"No, I'm being reassigned too. And you're going with me."

"Where?"

"Well. Considering that I'm a pilot with an engineering degree, they figured I'd be a good candidate to help assess the aircraft we've seized from the Nazis. I told them that I needed you to assist me."

His eyes were glazed and his jaw dropped as I explained. It only took a second for it to occur to him what a fantastic break it was. It took me a while to convince him that I wasn't kidding.

"That's right," I said. "Next week, we'll be evaluating ME-262s, FW-190s, and the like... taking them apart to see what makes them tick."

Steve was definitely the envy of all the other crew chiefs on the flight line.

I wasn't just being generous by including him on the assignment. The truth of the matter was, I may have had an engineering degree and might have known all the theories involved, but Steve, with his hands-on experience, knew more about actual operation of the mechanical systems in an aircraft than I did.

As I took off on the next mission, I was thinking about my lack of recent kills. Maybe I *was* flying scared and wasn't being aggressive enough. If that was the case, that's something I needed to fix. If I allowed a Luftwaffe pilot to escape me due to my lack of aggression, he might well be the one who returned to kill me or one of our other pilots the next day.

I had plenty to think about on the long trip to intercept our bombers who were on a mission to Frankfurt. If the new assignment lasted very long and the war in Europe came to an end soon, this might be one of my last combat missions.

When we met up with the bomber group, they hadn't yet faced any opposition on their run. For a while, it looked like we wouldn't either, but then I spotted contrails of enemy fighters above us. We all watched, fighter pilots and bomber gunners alike, as they seemed to spread out to preplanned locations before they descended on us for the attack. It was kind of like watching a football team take their positions before a play.

Thank God for their vapor trails. We could see exactly where they were coming from and we were prepared. We'd been instructed on this mission to stick tight to the bombers rather than prowl the surrounding fields on our way. That gave me the impression that somehow, our intelligence had foreseen this coordinated attack.

In the next moment, all hell broke loose. I hated fighting in the midst of bomber formations. Their plan of attack may have been well thought-out, but it was apparent that the pilots themselves were, for the most part, inexperienced. We were flying against a mix of 109s and 190s. I scored a kill. The bomber's gunners were taking down quite a few as well.

One of our bombers broke apart and spun out of control. Then, I took a blast of gunfire straight-on. A few rounds came right through my propeller and glanced off of my armored windscreen. I could tell that the propeller had been hit by the sound of a round hitting a blade and the sudden vibration that resulted. The gauges indicated that the engine was still okay. It all happened so fast that I couldn't say for sure, but it looked an awful lot like that blast of gunfire came from one of our B-17 gunners.

As the attack was winding down, a 109 dropped right down into my sights. Poor devil did everything to evade me, but within a few seconds, he became my eleventh confirmed air combat kill. It was the third time I'd downed two planes on a single mission.

That last encounter had taken me away from my group. I got my bearings and headed back towards the airfield, alone. The vibration from my propeller was annoying, but it didn't affect my plane's performance. I was soon lost again in my thoughts about my new assignment.

Then all of the sudden, without the least bit of warning, a lone ME-262 appeared behind me with a whoosh! It came up from beneath me and was so close on my tail that I could hear the whistling of its jet engines. It scared the crap out of me. I could see the pilot in my rear view mirrors, pointing at me as if he were calling me out on a personal challenge. Could it have been Kirpes?! It must have been. Flying a 262 now? And why didn't he just shoot me down? Why the challenge? Maybe he knew about the story of our last encounter in the *Stars and Stripes* newspaper. In their account of the dogfight, they said I had eluded Kirpes with my superior flying skills and that he only downed me with a lucky shot.

If that was the case, I guess I could understand why he'd have taken it personally.

Then as quickly as he appeared, he peeled off to give me a chance to position myself for the battle. As he did so, I could see the same markings that I'd seen on the 190 he was flying when he shot me down. Yes, I had no doubt that it was Major Hans Kirpes.

In the seconds that passed, it seemed like I had an eternity to consider the situation. I was alone in the sky with a superior pilot, who was flying a superior aircraft, who was determined to *prove* his superiority. I knew that my chances of surviving were slim, but I was certainly not going without a fight. My ammunition was half-gone as well. I had to think fast. What were my advantages over a 262? He had the speed and firepower. I had maneuverability.

I remembered that, in my previous encounter with a 262, I could never match their speed. My best chance of having a shot at one was when it passed me after making a run at me, or if I was lucky when it was approaching head-on. It looked like that was going to be my first option, since he had passed me and was turning to come back at me. I had to guess at which way he was anticipating that I would turn to avoid his fire. I decided to do a quick barrel roll, fire a volley towards him, then nose straight down. It happened quicker than I could say it. Several of his rounds hit my plane, but because of my maneuver, I couldn't see if any of mine had found their target.

By the time I pulled out of my dive and lined him in my sights, he was already well out of range. In our next encounter, I wanted him to blow past me; so rather than face him head-on, I turned away from the battle to try to convince him that I was making a run for it. Whether or not he bought it, he did come after me. As soon as he approached firing range, I pulled another barrel roll, only this time, in the opposite direction from what he would have expected. His tracers zipped by me to my right and in the next instant, he shot past me low. I couldn't believe he fell for it! I was able to snap back into firing position and blasted a volley at him before he was out of range. My 50-caliber rounds tore through his right wing. His engine puffed out a trail of black smoke. I could also see that he was losing speed. Wonderful!

Just as I felt that I could close the distance between us, he went into a dive. I followed. He used the speed he gained from the dive to execute some really impressive maneuvers. I wasn't about to let him get behind me this time. Though he managed to stay out of my gun sights, I was able to maintain my position behind him. This was a fight to the death. I couldn't assume that he was less of a threat just because he had a damaged engine.

He dove even lower until we were barely skimming the treetops. Why did that scenario seem familiar? I remembered the Luftwaffe pilot that led George Preddy into friendly anti-aircraft fire on Christmas. I was pretty sure that's what he was up to, since we were heading right towards enemy lines. I had to end it. Even though I was low on ammunition and wasn't sure of the shot, I blasted a volley at him, and missed. I fired another volley. In that fraction of a second, I looked past Kirpes' plane and saw something that made my blood run cold.

"Oh God," I screamed in horror. "Dimmit, NO!"

Not only did I miss his plane, but I could see my rows of 50-caliber bullets shoot past him to plow up a schoolyard... full of children. Passing them at nearly 400 miles per hour, there was no way I could see how many casualties there were.

In the instant that I was distracted, Kirpes managed to swing away from me. I broke off my pursuit and let him escape. It was actually a relief that he decided to run. I was so distraught over the schoolyard that there wasn't much fight left in me. With Kirpes gone, I gained some altitude and swung around to look at the schoolyard again. They must have thought I was coming back for another strafing run because they scattered to take cover. Even from my altitude, I could see blood. It looked as if a teacher was trying to pull a wounded child to cover as well.

As I turned towards my airfield, an unfamiliar voice sounded on my radio. "You should watch where you are shooting, Captain Davis... a lucky shot *indeed!*"

With its distinct German accent, it was without doubt the voice of Hans Kirpes. I wanted to respond and point out that it was he who led our battle down to that town... but I knew that I'd be in serious trouble for conversing with the enemy.

It was a long, lonely trip back to the airfield. It seemed that 90% of the land we flew over in Germany was sparsely populated farmland. What were the chances that a low-altitude air battle would bring me not only to a town, but to a schoolyard of children in that town? Fate was especially cruel that day.

When I touched down, I inspected the damage to my plane. I was right about the propeller. There was a big dent in one blade where a round had glanced off of it before hitting my windscreen. The plane had suffered from quite a few other hits that were inflicted by Kirpes, but none had been severe enough to keep my *Heavenly Helen II* from getting me safely home.

Upon landing at my airfield, I headed to the hut for the mission debriefing. As I walked in, the guys were congratulating me on my two kills of the day. When a pilot has ten aerial combat kills to his credit, he earns the title of "Double Ace." I asked them to calm down so I could tell them about my encounter with Kirpes on my trip back and of how I mowed down a schoolyard full of kids as a result. The room was solemn, but the consensus was that it couldn't have been anticipated or avoided. I tried to put it out of my mind. It was war. Innocent people die. It's just that children aren't usually involved—at least, not that I could see.

As we were excused from the debriefing, one of the guys grabbed me by the shoulder, "Get dressed buddy! We're taking you into town to celebrate... Mr. Double Ace!"

Maybe that wasn't such a bad idea. I figured that a few beers might have been what I needed right then. I was wrong about that, being as inexperienced at drinking as I was. The first half of the night was a lot of fun, but I spent the second half of it hugging a lamppost out at the curb in front of the tavern, waiting for my buddies to take me home.

When 5:00 came around the next morning, I wasn't feeling much like getting up. Obviously the guys that I was out with the night before were more experienced at the drinking than I was. They bounced right out of bed, ready to go. My leg hurt like hell. I must have strained it when I was drunk. And, damn it, I couldn't find my cane! My head was still spinning when I stood. Breakfast helped.

When I walked into the morning briefing, I was told, "Davis. You're not flying today. C.O. wants to see you at 0800."

Oh gee, what a relief! If I had flown that day, I would have died for sure.

Steve found me, saying he'd been instructed to be at the C.O.'s at 0800 as well. This could only mean that our orders were in. I downed a couple cups of coffee while we waited.

At 0800, we were promptly ushered in to Colonel Douglas' office. There was a photographer and a reporter from the *Stars and Stripes* newspaper waiting for us. We saluted, and the colonel said, "Good morning, Major Davis."

I corrected him, "Sorry sir... it's *Captain* Davis."

The colonel smiled knowingly as he replied, "Nope. It's Major Davis! Along with your new assignment, you are being promoted." And he handed me my insignia.

Steve chuckled with excitement and said, "Well, I'll be. Congratulations, sir," while giving me a salute.

Colonel Douglas added, "The timing couldn't have been better for your promotion, the day after you made Double Ace!"

After the photographer got a shot of the colonel presenting me with the promotion, I turned to the reporter and said, "You know, the last story *Stars and Stripes* wrote about me just about got me killed yesterday."

"How's that?" he asked.

"When I finished my run yesterday, Major Kirpes came after me in a ME-262. He tracked me down and personally challenged me to a fight! You know why?! At the end of our battle, he quoted your story over the radio: 'A lucky shot, indeed!' "

The room burst into laughter.

"Wow! He read the story we wrote about you?" The reporter was amazed. "So, even Luftwaffe Aces read *Stars and Stripes*."

"Yeah, but since y'all made it sound like I was bragging that I out flew him, he's gunning for me now in a personal vendetta!"

The reporter replied, "You're standing here in front of me. You must have out flown him yesterday."

"I had to fly like I'd never flown before to survive that fight, and the only reason I did survive was because I gambled on a maneuver that took him by surprise."

"So... you out flew him! This is going to make a fantastic story. An American P-51 Ace against a Luftwaffe Ace in a ME-262 emerges victorious!" The reporter could barely contain his enthusiasm.

"Well, if you put that in print, Kirpes is really going to blow a gasket!"

Nobody mentioned the schoolyard incident. You could bet that the German newspapers would be writing about it.

CHAPTER 6: Special Assignment

My first destination for Operation Overcast was Münster-Handorf field, which had been taken a week before on April 5th. We were told that the Germans had destroyed most of the aircraft that they left behind at that airfield. I had a really strange feeling as we boarded the C-47 to head north. I'd flown hundreds of missions over Germany, but this would be the first time that I actually set foot in the country. The prospect was a little scary.

When you're at war, you're taught to hate your enemy— to view them as something other than human. I wondered if I would come into contact with any of the townspeople from around the airfield. We were still at war with their nation. I tried to imagine how I would feel towards my conquerors if I were in their shoes.

I really had a case of butterflies in my gut as Steve and I looked out of the plane's windows at the towns and farmlands passing below us. I'd flown this route before, escorting bombers to the same airfield that we were heading for.

The landing at Handorf was a rough one. Our engineers were just beginning the process of filling bomb craters and repaving the runways that had been destroyed by our bombing missions.

A group of our P-47 Thunderbolts had already taken up residence at the field. There truly wasn't much to see there. The sight of utter destruction there was hard to digest. What wasn't destroyed by our repeated bombings had been finished off by the Germans themselves as they retreated. The aircraft that lay in ruins looked as if they had been brand new. Some had been destroyed after they sat unused for lack of fuel.

When we got off of the plane, we were taken directly to the Operation Overcast group leader, Colonel Sanderson. Next, I met engineers from the largest aircraft manufacturers in the States. These guys knew who I was from the stories in the papers and newsreels, and they treated me with a surprising amount of respect.

I learned quite a bit from these guys. I hadn't known that the FW-190s that I was flying against were originally powered by a variant of an American Pratt & Whitney engine that BMW had acquired the rights to manufacture before the war... or that its airframe was influenced by the experimental racing airplane that Howard Hughes designed and flew before the war. Once they mentioned it, I saw the amazing resemblance. It made me feel good to know that some of the superior German war technology was actually stolen from the United States.

I was humbled that the engineers responsible for designing our planes, men that I'd idolized, knew who I was.

Once we were in private, Steve commented, "Major. I may not be an officer and I might not have your education, but one thing I can tell you... if you tell these guys that you're not worthy of their respect, they'll believe you. So enjoy it. Play it up and make the most of it."

There was wisdom in those words. Steve often impressed me with his casual insight.

Even though they were rendered unusable, it was still a thrill for me to sit in the cockpit of the planes that I'd been flying against. Steve and I didn't have much to contribute to the evaluation of that airfield's aircraft. The civilian engineers there had already examined the same kind of aircraft that had been captured that were in flying condition.

We got word on April 15th that our 3rd Army captured a research facility, located a hundred or so miles east of us, that was developing Germany's most promising and secret experimental jet aircraft: the HO-229, flying wing.

As the Allied forces advanced deep into Germany from the West, the Russians were advancing from the East, each claiming the treasures of arts and science that they were lucky enough to capture. Both sides were anxious to capture the German engineers who were responsible for the technology that they claimed. Claiming and evaluating the HO-229 was a top priority. We barely had time to throw our things together before we were on our way.

The Gothaer Waggonfabrik facility was near a town called Gotha. The facility was by no means new. WWI aircraft were built there, and between the wars, it was used to build BMW automobiles. One small area was devoted to the Horten

Ho flying wing. Several prototypes were lined up inside of a building in various stages of construction. It was truly magnificent. The plane itself was constructed of very thin layers of wood that were laminated together over molds to make three-dimensional forms. Was this because it was cheaper or faster than constructing them from aluminum? Not likely. The American engineers there decided that plywood should be used so that the plane wouldn't be detected by British radar. In fact, the whole design of the plane was intended to produce a minimal radar reflection.

Only one of the aircraft looked like it was near completion. I wondered if there had been others that were completed that were flown to airfields which the Nazis still controlled. It wasn't likely in production yet. None of our pilots had reported seeing them in battle.

I was assigned to the chore of searching through the facilities' records to find the HO-229's engineering and design specifications. The offices had been trashed. It was apparent that the staff had removed, and had likely destroyed, the information I was looking for. We still went through every file cabinet in the building in an effort to find something of value. There were plenty of photographs of the prototypes hanging on the walls—photos of three versions of the aircraft. One was of a glider version, another of a propeller-driven version, and one of a jet-powered version—all actually photographed in flight.

I sat at one of the drafting tables and looked across the room that had likely been filled with German engineers less than a week before. The drafting room wasn't a whole lot different than Davis Engineering. A calendar on one of the desks was dated April 12th, 1945—just three days earlier.

After interviewing witnesses, we learned that there had only been one jet-powered model to fly—which crashed after its third test flight—and that the other prototypes were still under construction. So, this meant that we had captured all there was to the HO-229, except for its engineering documents. During the following week, our guys packed up the one that was nearest to completion and shipped it back to Norton Aircraft in the States. It broke my heart to see them destroy what was left behind out of fear that the Russians would get it.

Just south of Gotha, our troops also liberated a one of the concentration camps we'd heard about: Ohrdruf. In it, they found thousands of bodies heaped in piles, still smoldering from where the Nazis had tried to burn them. General Eisenhower was mortified by the gruesome sight and insisted that every American soldier who wasn't actively fighting be made to tour the camp so we could see what kind of people we were fighting. Steve and I went up with a group from the facility in Gotha.

I was curious, like everyone else, to see with my own eyes that these horrible rumors were indeed fact. But what I saw there was far worse than the rumors—far worse than I imagined it would be. Whenever I think about that tour through the camp, my sinuses seem to fill with a hint of that horrible smell. I felt such a sorrow when I considered that each of those bodies belonged to a man who once lived in a home surrounded by a loving family. These men were taken from their homes, stripped of the possessions they'd worked a lifetime for, separated from their families, made to work as slaves, then slaughtered with indifference and left to rot. Why? Simply because they were Jewish? I had gone to school with Jewish kids. I wouldn't have known that they were Jewish if they hadn't told me. Aside from the places we went to church, they didn't appear to be any different than the rest of us.

In order to carry out my job as a pilot, I'd had to kill and maim people—sometimes by the dozens—on strafing runs. I'd always had stop myself from thinking about those lives. It was war: us or them. That wasn't the case in that camp. The Nazis abused and murdered and abused these people, simply because they could. Because it made them feel superior? Whatever the reason, I wouldn't be losing any more sleep over the casualties that these coldhearted killers had suffered at my hand.

On April 29th of 1945, as we were wrapping up the HO-229, we got word that our forces had taken the Messerschmitt factory in Augsburg. What a prize! Operation Overcast was there within hours of its capture. We walked into the plant, expecting it to be abandoned and cleared of its important records and engineering. Instead, we were greeted by a delegation of Messerschmitt's engineers.

One stepped forward and introduced himself, speaking fluent English. "I'm Karl Baur, Messerschmitt's chief engineer and test pilot, and this is my crew."

What luck! I was humbled to be in the presence of such giants in the aviation world. I was standing between the men who had designed the world's most advanced aircraft, both from the States and Germany.

From his appearance, Baur wasn't someone you'd expect to be very important: not very tall, with thinning blond hair and wire-rimmed glasses. His manner was a different story: confident and somewhat condescending.

Colonel Sanderson introduced our party, and when he got to me: "And this is Major Ken Davis. He's not only an engineer, but also one of our P-51 Aces."

We cordially shook hands and nodded.

The colonel continued, "I'm sure you appreciate that we're interested in your aircraft, especially your jet aircraft. Unfortunately, most of the 262s we've recovered have been purposely damaged. Can we count on you and your crew to restore some of them to flying order?"

"Yes," Baur answered, knowing that it was a request he couldn't refuse.

Colonel Sanderson continued, "And once we have operable 262s, as an instructor, can we count on you to teach our pilots to fly them?"

He answered, "Certainly," then turned to me. "Major Davis?"

I turned to our group of engineers to see them nod approvingly.

Inwardly, I was jumping for joy! Outwardly, I politely nodded and answered, "I'd be honored."

I realized that it might be a while before they had a plane ready to fly, or before Baur would have time to begin my instruction, but there was plenty to keep me busy until then.

That night, we stayed in a nice hotel in Augsburg. The courtesy shown us by the townspeople was surprising. They didn't seem to be terribly disappointed at being liberated from Nazi control. Maybe all German people weren't as evil as I'd thought. After dinner, I retired to my room where I opened the curtains and turned down the lights. It was a quiet end to an incredible day. The only sound in the room was from the hiss of the gas heater and the ticking of the clock. I watched as it rained on the empty city street below. I switched the lamp on and pulled stationary from the desk drawer to write Helen.

After enjoying a hearty German breakfast the next morning, we returned to the Messerschmitt facility. Baur led us on a tour of the plant, telling us of the conventional and exotic aircraft that he had designed and tested. He didn't have a choice about whether to cooperate with us. He certainly reveled in boasting of their superior innovations. Baur made it clear that if

Germany was losing the war, it wasn't due to a lack of technical superiority.

At the end of the day, I called Colonel Douglas back at my base. I couldn't wait to tell him about my invitation to fly the ME-262. He said that he was both thrilled and envious over my mission. His tone of voice lowered as he said, "I do have some bad news for you, Major. We sent a new pilot out on a mission in your plane yesterday."

I knew what was coming. He continued, "I'm afraid he was shot down on his first mission. We lost a fine young man, *and* your plane. But, with your being given the opportunity to be trained to fly the 262 there, you probably wouldn't have needed your plane again anyway."

That seemed to close the door behind me as to the path my military career would take.

I was awakened the following morning before dawn by people yelling in the street in front of the hotel. I thrust the window open to see people shouting and waving their arms excitedly. Something was wrong, but I couldn't understand what they were saying. Maybe the Nazis were retaking the town?! Suddenly, there was a pounding on my door. I grabbed my .45 and asked, "Who's there?!"

"It's me, Steve!" It was my crew chief. I stowed my gun, grabbed a bathrobe, and opened the door. He thrust a newspaper in my face. Before I had a chance to focus on it, he shouted, "Hitler's dead! He shot himself."

"What?" I sat on the bed, staring at the German newspaper. Hitler's photo dominated the front page. That explained what all of the shouting was about. I only wished that I could understand if the people outside were shouting for joy or sorrow. I could never tell. To me, Germans sounded angry even when they were happy.

I figured that, when I got to the Messerschmitt facility, I'd get an idea of how Germans felt about the news. But nobody seemed willing to offer an opinion on it. I respected their privacy, appreciating that these people lived in a world where a person could be shot for voicing an unpopular thought, and the war wasn't over yet.

With the news of Hitler's death, the Allies became more concerned about the Russians seizing our German assets. It was decided to ship Baur, his crew, and all of the ME-262 parts back to the States to continue their work... as well as my instruction.

Word came in that Western Allied forces had overtaken Salzburg, home to JV44, the special fighter unit made up of the Luftwaffe's elite pilots who primarily flew the ME-262s. Unfortunately, we also heard that the Luftwaffe had destroyed the engines on the 262s at the field by inserting grenades into the engine's intakes.

A team from Messerschmitt and my crew chief and I set off for Salzburg to disassemble and ship out what was salvageable. When we landed, we went straight to the flight line to have a look at the planes. The airframes themselves appeared to be in good shape. Only the engines had suffered damage, and the Messerschmitt factory had more engines. The fact that the planes hadn't caught fire told me that they had been drained of fuel.

I saw something on one of the planes that stopped me in my tracks. It had the markings and crest of Hans Kirpes' plane. Damn! That was the plane that I had engaged. How strange to see it on the ground. I walked around to see the wing I'd shot up. I expected to see a series of aluminum patches over the bullet holes I left on it. There were none. I was positive that I'd hit the starboard engine. Could they have replaced the skin for the whole wing, or was this indeed his plane?

I asked the soldiers escorting us, "Where are the pilots of these planes?"

"They're here, being held in the officer's quarters."

"Take me there," I demanded.

We climbed into a jeep and headed towards the captive pilots. I should have figured that Kirpes would be among the JV44 fighter group, but I never imagined that I might meet him face to face.

When I walked into the officer's club, it was tough to tell that these guys were our prisoners. They were smoking and kidding around with their captors as if they were our guests. When the Luftwaffe's officers surrendered to us, they were wearing their finest dress uniforms. Even as prisoners of war, they looked sharp and proud. It always bothered me that we wore puppy dog-colored khakis while they wore such smart, official-looking uniforms of gray and black. As I walked in, I saluted the group and received a casual reciprocation.

I spoke up. "Is Major Hans Kirpes here?"

A dark-haired, good-looking officer with a Clark Gable mustache walked up, eyeing me curiously. He was about five years older than me. The fact that he was our prisoner didn't seem to humble him in the least.

With a confident smile, he saluted, "At your service, major. And you are?" His command of the English language was impressive.

"Major Ken Davis," I answered as I extended my hand. "We finally meet."

His cocky expression gave way to one of genuine shock. "I'm surprised to meet you, Major… considering, I killed you."

"No… you didn't. Although, I do have you to thank for this!" I answered, holding up my cane.

"I was certain of it! I shot you down. I saw your plane explode."

"You did shoot me down and my plane exploded alright, but I bailed out first."

"No… well, yes. I assumed that you bailed out the first time I shot you down… but not the last time. Your plane exploded, instantly!"

It took me a second before it dawned on me. "Oh! God! You are the one who shot my plane down last week!"

"I take it you weren't in it?!"

I laughed, "Now we're getting somewhere!"

"I am relieved! I felt really bad for killing you. Well, this explains a lot. I wondered why you didn't put up much of a fight."

"The pilot flying my plane was a new recruit. That was his first... and last combat mission."

"Oh," Kirpes replied. "Bless his young soul, but he wasn't much of a pilot."

He stepped back and made it clear that he was upset with me. "If you will remember, I LET you survive our first encounter. Later, I read an article in *Stars and Stripes* that quoted you as saying that you had out flown me and that my taking you down was a lucky shot on my part!"

"Damn it. I *knew* you read that story! Look, I'm sure you know what propaganda is all about. I told the press the story just the way it happened, but that wasn't good enough for Army morale, so they got a little creative in revising the story."

"I was thinking you were an arrogant ass who needed to be humbled. What about that second story?"

"It was the same thing, only a different reporter. It was his job to make *me* out to be the hero."

Kirpes smiled and said, "Well. In that case, I hope you'll accept my apology for killing you."

I shook his hand, "Apology accepted."

Then Kirpes said, "I noticed in that story that you only boasted about having damaged my plane on our second encounter. You must not have known that I didn't make it back to base. I had to bail out and the plane was lost."

I was floored by that news. "No, I didn't know! That brings my total kills to an even dozen."

Kirpes chuckled. "Well, I'm glad that makes you proud. It's about 200 fewer than I have, but it's not bad for an American."

"I was curious as to how you managed to find me that last time."

"Well," Kirpes said, "When I heard my pilots mention they were engaged with the 'Pink Lady,' I rushed to intervene."

"The 'Pink Lady?' " I asked.

"Yes. That bright pink dress on your nose made you very easy to recognize!"

"Oh. I hadn't considered that."

"The lady in the pink dress is an attractive woman. Is she your girlfriend?"

"She's my wife, Helen." I pulled a photo from my wallet to show him.

"Impressive! She's actually more attractive than your plane's image."

"Thank you." Then I asked him about something that was bothering me. "Why did y'all destroy your planes here?"

"Actually, we were trying to arrange the surrender of our unit to the Americans. We planned on flying our planes to you and were actually involved in dialog with Eisenhower himself. Only, your troops shot down our messenger. The final terms of surrender were never delivered. So when that effort failed, we destroyed our planes to keep them from the Russians' hands. To be honest with you, we are hoping that your forces will run the Russians out of Germany after we surrender, which will be easier to do if they aren't flying our 262s against you. If we'd known that you Yanks were going to capture our base before the Russians, we wouldn't have destroyed them. Why is that a concern of yours?"

"I'm also an engineer. I was asked to evaluate the planes we are capturing. That's why I wasn't flying my plane last week. Anyway! I'm glad I had the chance to explain those newspaper stories. I have a great deal of respect for you and for your outstanding abilities as a pilot. I know that I'm very fortunate to have survived our encounters. I also appreciate that, on our last encounter, that rather than just shoot me down, you challenged me to give me a fighting chance. Thank you."

Major Kirpes replied, "Don't underestimate yourself, Major Davis. You are indeed a challenging adversary. I looked forward to our encounters and was truly saddened when I thought I'd killed you." Kirpes gave me an intense look. "Major. I'd like to ask a favor of you."

"Yes?"

"We wanted to surrender to the Americans for a reason. There are horrible stories about what the Russians are doing to our prisoners and I've heard talk that the Americans are going to turn us over to them. Is there any way that you can help to keep that from happening?"

"I don't know. I'll see what I can do. I might be able to help you, but I don't know about the others. Karl Baur is going to teach me to fly the 262. He can teach me to fly it, but he doesn't have your combat experience in it. Your combat experience combined with your fluent English might just be your ticket to go back to the States when we go."

"Karl Baur. He's a good man. Share with him what I've asked of you. I think he will be willing to help as well."

"I'll talk with him and let you know. I agree that a request from him would carry more weight with the brass."

Kirpes then grabbed me by the shoulder and turned to his colleagues, announcing something in German over which they burst into laughter. The only part of it I understood was my name.

As we turned to leave the room, he explained. "I told them that this is Major Ken Davis, my late nemesis, who has returned from the dead to torment me!"

I laughed and said, "Let's hope that our days of tormenting each other are in the past."

As I started to leave, Hans asked if he could walk out with me. I motioned for him to walk out ahead of me, since he wasn't being guarded so much as supervised.

He glanced back to be sure that we could speak privately and said, "My commander, Adolf Galland, is recovering in the hospital now, but he left me the authorization to share a bargaining chip with your people. The six surviving 262s that we were going to turn over to Eisenhower, weren't destroyed. We flew them to small airfield, tucked away in the mountains in Innsbruck, Austria. The field is so small that the aircraft would never be able to take off from it, so they'll have to be dismantled in order to be moved."

"That *is* some very valuable information. Operation Overcast will be thrilled to hear it. Unfortunately, as you know, Innsbruck is still occupied."

Kirpes said, "True. But now that you know the 262s are there, your people can make a priority of capturing Innsbruck before the Russians do. Please be sure that this information gets to Eisenhower. I want it to be a factor when he's considering our fate."

After evaluating the planes at Salzburg and arranging the shipment of what was usable, the remaining planes were ordered to be destroyed.

Before leaving to return to the Messerschmitt plant in Augsburg, I called ahead to arrange a meeting with Karl Baur and Colonel Sanderson. I arrived late, so we met for dinner.

I started by saying, "When I was at Salzburg, I met Major Hans Kirpes, who is interned there."

Karl Baur responded, "One of our best pilots. His feedback has been very helpful in refining both the 262 and the 109 in combat performance."

I said, "First, Mr. Baur, Major Kirpes wanted me to let you know that he would be agreeable to sharing his combat experience with the American 262 pilots you are training. He feels that his combat experience, combined with the fact that he's fluent in English, would make him a valuable asset."

Baur answered, "Indeed, it would. I'll see what I can do to acquire him."

Colonel Sanderson piped in, "No, I'm afraid that won't be possible. We've decided to turn the pilots of JV44 over to the Russians in a matter of days."

Baur was very distressed at hearing this. "They'll either be shot or spend the rest of their lives in prison… for doing no less than any American or Russian pilot had for their countries. Isn't there a way to prevent this? It would be such a waste. These men are our best, our brightest."

Then I turned to Sanderson. "Colonel, I'm sure you were involved with JV44's surrender negotiations with Eisenhower."

Sanderson answered, "Yes. That's when they were talking about flying their remaining 262s to our base to surrender."

I asked, "Were you aware that the plan didn't materialize because their messenger was shot down before Eisenhower could receive their response?"

"Yes, I heard that story. I also heard that they were hoping that the Allies would declare war on Russia to drive them out of Germany. We figured that JV44 decided to keep their planes in hopes that we would employ them to assist us in our battle. It was only when they were afraid the Russians were going to capture the planes that they destroyed them."

"Okay," I said. "I wasn't told about this."

The Colonel replied, "That's because it didn't pertain to your mission... which was to analyze and recover aircraft."

I responded, "It seems that my job description has broadened, since they've asked me to deliver a message to you that might affect their fate. All of the ME-262s weren't destroyed. Out of their twenty-five 262s, only six were flyable. They confided in me that they'd flown those six planes to a small field in Innsbruck. It's such a small field that they couldn't be flown out again. They'll have to be disassembled and trucked out. The planes they destroyed at Salzburg weren't operable anyway. They were destroyed to keep the Russians from being able to repair and use them. Anyway, they confided this in me, hoping that it would influence Eisenhower in his decision on whether to turn them over to the Russians."

That news sure changed the colonel's attitude. "So we have six flyable planes. Or, we will once we've secured the

Innsbruck area. I can assure you that this news will certainly affect Eisenhower's consideration of JV44's fate."

CHAPTER 7: Hans

On May 8th, 1945, the day arrived that we'd all been praying for.   Germany formally surrendered.   Overnight, Germany went from enemy to ally and Russia went from ally to enemy.

I didn't have time to celebrate.   The moment the surrender was announced, Colonel Sanderson arranged a convoy of trucks to head to Innsbruck to recover the 262s before the Russians found them. We flew on ahead with the Messerschmitt technicians. When we arrived at Innsbruck, I saw that our troops had already established a secure perimeter around the airfield. It was beautiful there, but easy to understand why the 262s' arrival there was a one-way trip. The small airfield was surrounded by rows of tall mountains. Propeller-driven planes could make a slow, powerful ascent from the field, unlike jet aircraft.

A number of the townspeople watched from the distance as the Messerschmitt crews quickly began to dismantle and crate the 262s. These planes were my ticket home. They were being shipped back to Wright Field near Dayton, Ohio, where they would be reassembled and where I would be taught to fly them. I was given the credit for finding these six planes, but it was only because I was in the right place at the right time. Like Steve had said earlier: if I say I'm not worthy of the credit I'm given, people will believe me, so I kept my mouth shut and acted worthy!

We were there for a couple of days until Colonel Sanderson was satisfied that the project was under control. Then he told me it was time to leave.

I asked, "We're flying back to Augsburg?"

"No, Major," he answered. "Our next stop is Peenemünde. I'm sure you've heard of it?"

Had I ever! It had the mystique of a Nazi Atlantis, the home of their greatest innovations. Peenemünde was one of the most important targets on our bombing runs and one of the most heavily defended. I hoped that it hadn't been so heavily damaged that there would be nothing left to see.

We weren't the first to arrive on the site. Other engineers were already examining the rocket and pulse jet engines they found there. Colonel Sanderson and I wandered around the site, looking for something the others might have missed. What an eerie feeling it was to be wandering through such advanced technology, abandoned by its creators.

We came across a strange little aircraft that was small enough to fit in the bed of a pickup. It was sitting on a stack of scrap wood, piled up alongside an unpainted wooden building. It had been discarded like trash. Its wings and tail were short and stubby, like its fuselage. The nose of the thing was flat, but packed full of what appeared to be missiles. It was an evil looking little thing.

The colonel asked as he studied it, "What the hell is it? It doesn't have any landing gear or any signs of pilot controls inside. Those look like rocket boosters on its sides, but without landing gear, how would it take off or land? It doesn't make sense."

"Well, sir, it looks to me like something that would be launched from a larger plane to shoot missiles at our bombers. The fact that it doesn't have landing gear would tell me that when its mission is complete, the pilot parachutes out of it, letting it fall to the ground. And as far as the controls go, judging by the wooden jigs and templates that it was dumped on top of, I'd say that this was only a mock-up rather than a prototype."

Colonel Sanderson was impressed with my observations. "I believe you're right, Major. That makes sense. Let's go see what else we can find."

Later that day, I chuckled when I heard Colonel Sanderson telling his colleagues of his earlier find. Then he took the credit for deducing its purpose. That was fine by me. I was just grateful as hell to be a witness to that page in history.

We came across some incredible machinery there. There was no doubt that, if the Germans had had just a little more time to develop those weapons, there's no way we could have defeated them.

In peacetime, if an inventor produces a better mousetrap, the old mousetrap producers and distributors will do everything in their power to bury it. The old cliché—"If it ain't broke, don't fix it"—prevailed. In wartime, not only is man's creativity unrestricted, but it's wholly encouraged. Nowhere was that more apparent than at Peenemünde. Though the place had an air of evil about it, it saddened me to see that the raging innovation that once lived there had been bought to a halt.

When Colonel Sanderson and I returned to the Messerschmitt plant in Augsburg, we were met by Karl Baur and Hans Kirpes. For a second, I didn't recognize Major Kirpes, since he was wearing a suit in place of his uniform.

I extended my hand to him. "I see they released you. Good deal!"

Baur said, "And they decided not to turn JV44 over to the Russians, but most of our other pilots were. And those JV44 pilots in Allied custody now will remain there until they're tried for crimes as Nazi sympathizers," scoffing, as if he thought it was ridiculous. "Major Kirpes was given a hasty trial, then released to us, like so many other Nazis that Operation Overcast finds to be of value. I suspect that our appeal was responsible for that."

I asked, "Did they release Adolf Galland?"

"No, they shipped him to England for interrogation."

I could tell that Baur was grateful for the fact that our application of justice to Nazi sympathizers was a matter of convenience. Willie Messerschmitt was being held on charges for using slave labor to build his planes, whereas Wernher von Braun—who was guilty of the same crime—was not being held accountable for it because of the Allied interest in his rocket technology.

Kirpes said, "As it turned out, I've been given a comfortable position as a consultant for your government. Isn't fate amazing?"

Colonel Sanderson told me, "Major Kirpes will be traveling to Wright Field with you and Mr. Baur. We appreciate your hard work these past few weeks, Major. And, we are especially pleased with the recovery of these planes! You're shipping out in about a week, so take a little time to relax before you go."

Major Kirpes said, "Why don't we start with me buying you a beer to celebrate the war's end?"

I answered, "Well, Major Kirpes. That's the least you could do after killing me!"

"I'm a civilian now, Major Davis. You can call me Hans."

"Hans it is. And... since you're a civilian now, you can call me... Major Davis."

He laughed and said, "Kenny it is!"

We went out to the parking lot to Hans' personal car. It was a beautiful black Mercedes 540K convertible. It was one impressive automobile! That beat the heck out of taking a jeep back to the hotel.

I finally felt that I could relax and celebrate the war's end. What a strange twist of fate, though, to be sharing the celebration with Hans Kirpes. His air of confidence seemed to border on arrogance. As we navigated the narrow streets, they were lined with people who were either going home or leaving what was left of their homes. Hans impatiently shouted and blew his horn at them to make way. It was unsettling that he didn't have more compassion for his own people.

It was a breezy summer afternoon. The sun sat low in the sky, casting a golden glow over the city of Augsburg. Since the war was over, I could appreciate its beauty.

The unbalanced ratio of women to men in the tavern we stopped at was no doubt typical since the war's end. The young men who hadn't died in the war were likely still being held in prison camps. Maybe I should have changed out of my uniform first. I felt that the patrons there were apprehensive about my being there.

After relaxing over a couple of beers, I asked Hans about something that had been bothering me, a lot. "You know in our last dogfight, when I hit your engine and you dove to get away from me?"

"Yes," Hans said, "the schoolyard."

"I was... mortified. I could see my rounds shooting past you into that schoolyard full of children. I have nightmares about that."

He sighed woefully before responding, "I think about it too. Collateral damage, my friend. It happened so quickly, so unexpectedly, there was nothing either of us could have done to avoid it."

I replied, "I guess we'd all go crazy if we thought about the casualties we were responsible for in a war, but when it comes to children, it's hard to get over. After it happened, you kept going, but I circled back for a look. I wish I hadn't."

He asked, "Were there many casualties?"

"I could only see a couple, but there had to be more."

"Ultimately, it was my fault," Hans said. "It was my duty, as a pilot in the service of my country, to have finished you off in our first encounter. If I had, that schoolyard incident wouldn't have happened. Tell me, Kenny, how many planes did you down since then?"

"Three," I answered.

"Three of my fellow pilots likely didn't make it home to their loved ones because of my choice to let you go."

"Why *did* you let me go?" I asked.

Hans took a drink from his beer and searched for the words to answer me. He took a deep breath and stared at the table. "I have to be honest with you. I could see immediately that you... were an extraordinary pilot. It took every bit of my ability to escape and gain position on you. Once I had the position, I couldn't get a shot. You were one slippery bastard. Knowing that if I didn't down you that you'd most likely down me, I did something that I almost never do... something I'm not proud of. I fired aimlessly in your direction, hoping that you'd fly into my ordinance. You did. And that was indeed… a lucky shot. To finish you off would have been as dishonorable as claiming a victory over a billiards game in which the winning ball wasn't dropped where you intended. I had to let you go so we could fight another day. My mission to catch you wasn't because I thought you'd lied about my downing you with a lucky shot. My mission was to confront you in a fair fight. We had that in Frankfurt. And, my worthy adversary," he said, raising his glass, "you won!"

I raised my glass and thanked him for his honesty.

"Will this be your first trip to the States?" I asked.

"That, it will. Can I count on you to show me around?"

I answered, "This will be my first trip to Ohio. It'll be new to the both of us. I hear they've got quite a collection of German and Japanese aircraft there at Wright Field."

Hans said, "We have a week left before we leave. How about, in the morning, I pick you up and show you Germany—at least, what's left of it?"

I graciously accepted his offer. There's a fuzzy line between fear and respect. When I was flying against Hans and his fellow Aces, I had good cause to fear them, but I also respected them. I was grateful for the opportunity to work on removing the fear aspect from my attitude towards Hans.

Hans was knocking at my door early the next morning, ready to discuss our travel plans over breakfast. He really seemed motivated about being my tour guide. I dressed in clothing that wouldn't cause me to stand out so much from the locals.

He said, "I grew up just outside of Munich, which is only about 60 kilometers from here. I thought we'd start there."

The weather cooperated with us enough to allow us to put the top down on the car. Although the countryside was beautiful, it was kind of hard to enjoy. We passed so many people on the roads who were going back home—some with vehicles loaded with their belongings, some in horse-drawn carts, and others simply walking. I felt arrogant, driving past them in a flashy new Mercedes. One of Edith Piaf's songs came on the radio.

"What do you think of this little French whore?" he asked.

"Edith Piaf? I like her!"

"I think she sounds like a damned goat!" Then he made a "baaaa" sound, imitating her vibrato.

I was offended that he was belittling my choice in music and asked defensively, "Why would you call her a whore?!"

"That's what she was. So was her mother. She grew up in bordellos, but was too short and flat-chested to make much of a living as a whore, so she started singing in bordellos for tips."

I said defensively, "France doesn't seem to agree with you. She's thought of pretty highly."

"Ehhh… the French are idiots!"

I was amazed at how confident he seemed in his conviction.

"Idiots?" I asked.

"Yes! Ask them for music, they sing like goats; ask them for art, they give you Picasso. Do you think they would have overthrown us if the Yanks and Brits hadn't interfered? I think not! It was our moral *duty* to rule France. It would have been irresponsible of us to leave a country of idiots to govern themselves."

I sat quietly, brooding; feeling like I'd made a big mistake in helping this guy escape the Russian prisons. I was starting to think that he was a monster who should have been left locked up with his Nazi buddies. Then it dawned on me that he seemed to take delight in antagonizing me. He was challenging me for a worthy rebuttal. So I thought for a minute and replied.

"You know, a dog's sense of smell is said to be a thousand times more sophisticated than man's… yet when he sees a pile of shit, he runs right to it and sticks his nose in it. To us, with our unsophisticated sense of smell, shit stinks, yet if you held the dog back from sniffing it… it would ruin his day!"

Hans laughed, impressed with my response. "You are suggesting that the French have a sense of artistic appreciation that's a thousand times more sophisticated than mine?!"

I chuckled, "Maybe not a *thousand* times!"

The highway system was impressive in Germany. Many of the major towns were connected by divided highways with overpasses that allowed traffic to cross over. The traffic signs featured modern modern-looking symbols that were recognizable throughout Europe, regardless of language. At home, two-lane highways that passed through every town and intersection were the best we had and if you didn't speak English, our traffic signs wouldn't be much use to you.

As we drew near to Munich, Hans pulled off of the highway into a gravel parking lot that had nothing but two long, light blue buildings with rows of white roll-up doors on them.

When we got out of the car, he motioned to the buildings and said, "This is my security. I bought this piece of land some time ago. It sat for quite a while, but then it occurred to me that if I placed storage buildings on it, I wouldn't have to bring in water, sewer, or power to create an income from the property. I got the idea when so many people in Munich lost their homes. Most of them moved in with relatives out of town and had to find a place to store their stuff. These units filled up overnight and have since provided me with a nice little income. I have a local attorney oversee them."

I replied, "Nice, but I wouldn't imagine that it would work as well in America, since we don't have war refugees."

He answered, "You might be surprised. The refugees have a tough time paying rent. Lately, I've found that my best renters are simply people who need more storage space."

"Maybe I'll give it a try when I get back home."

Hans grabbed my shoulder and said, "Let's go have lunch at the little airport where I learned to fly. It's not far. I still have a plane there."

I wasn't entirely comfortable with him touching me, but I could tell that it was sincere.

It was different to be entering Munich by car rather than by air. We pulled into a small airfield that bore quite a resemblance to the Baton Rouge airport, only with more bomb craters. There were only a few planes tied down in front of the small terminal building, which housed a little café. The windows were boarded over since their glass had been long since blown out. When I told Hans what I wanted to order, my English seemed to attract the attention of everyone there. Again, I sensed that it wasn't an unfavorable reaction. I'd say it was of curiosity more than anything.

After breakfast, we walked out to see Hans' plane, which was hidden under a tall stand of trees at the edge of the field along with dozens of other planes. Though it was weathered and dirty from neglect, it was an amazing aircraft to behold... a Messerschmitt 108, the civilian predecessor to the ME 109 fighter. I recognized it instantly from my ground-school training which taught me to identify enemy aircraft. Even if it was older, it was far superior to our family's Cessna. With its low wing and streamlined fuselage, the four passenger plane had an air-speed of nearly 200 miles per hour. It had retractable landing gear and a luxurious interior that rivaled Hans' Mercedes. It must have cost him a small fortune!

He explained, "Once you and the Brits started bombing Germany, you'd strafe any flyable aircraft you came across, so we hid our private planes under the trees here."

As we walked through the airplanes, I was overcome with a sorrow and emptiness inside. I knew that most of these planes' owners wouldn't be returning for them. The people who owned those planes had likely worked hard to afford them out of their love for flying. It was a small comfort to know that those who died flying in combat had died doing what they loved. I wondered if any of the planes belonged to any of the pilots I had shot down.

The fuel in the tanks and carburetor of Hans' plane had been there for over a year. We drained the old fuel, which was rancid-smelling—like old varnish. Some underhanded bargaining was required to acquire a fresh load of fuel for it. With a little tinkering, we got it to fire up. Once we had it sounding strong and dependable, we took it up for a spin around Munich. Our flying together in the same plane seemed surreal, but also pretty fantastic.

"What got you interested in flying?" I asked him.

"Dirigibles! Those huge, magnificent airships like the Graf Zeppelin and the Hindenburg. In my boyhood, I'd watch them glide through the skies above Munich and dream of what it would be like to be aboard one. But by the time I was old enough, they had already become a thing of the past. I've always loved flying in any form of machine. I'm anxious for you to fly the 262. It's a whole different experience in flying."

"Yeah, well, it'll be soon enough. I'm dying to experience it too," I answered.

Hans asked, "What got *you* interested in flying?"

"My dad always had a plane. He taught me to fly when I was a kid and he passed his love of flying on to me."

"Sounds like you have a great father. I envy you for that. Mine died in the First World War. Then my mom killed herself soon after… which left me to be raised by my aunt and uncle. They had no children and didn't want much to do with me, so they sent me to a boarding school here in Munich."

"I'm sorry to hear that. My dad died too, but in this war. They drafted him at 42 years old, and he was killed in the first few weeks of the war."

"That's terrible," Hans said. "Was he flying?"

"No. He was an engineer, stationed in the Aleutian Islands. The Japs strafed the men's barracks while he was sleeping. He died in bed."

Hans replied, "My dad died in the trenches in France."

"Really?" I asked. "My dad fought in France in that war."

The thought crossed my mind that our fathers might have fought each other in those trenches.

Hans said, "Maybe if they'd both survived the war and met afterwards, *they* would have become friends too."

I thought Hans was being a little presumptuous in referring to us as friends. We were 'friendly,' but I wouldn't have said 'friends.'

After landing, we drove into Munich to look for a place to have dinner. The city looked much worse from the ground than it did from the air. Passing over it in my plane only took a couple of minutes, but from the ground, I could see just how large of a city it was. The streets were busy with American military jeeps and trucks, and the sidewalks were crowded with American GIs and the citizens of Munich... mostly women and the elderly. Few buildings were left undamaged in the heart of town. What the bombs hadn't destroyed, fire had. It had the same smell that I noticed in London: the smell of war. It was a mixture of damp burnt wood, sewage, and concrete dust. Munich was a seemingly endless expanse of large buildings made up of townhouses and apartments, most with shops below. The streets were narrow and difficult to navigate, even those that were clear of rubble.

After dinner, we pulled up in front of a large building that was fairly intact.

Hans said, "This is home."

I commented, "It looks like your house was one of the few not damaged by the bombing."

He answered, laughing, "It's the one that most deserved it!"

The front door was open and everything in the house was scattered across the floor. Hans made his way through the mess, picking up a few sentimental mementos. He sighed and commented, "This wasn't a result of the bombings. It was looters."

"I guess people are desperate in these times," I replied.

"People?" Hans asked. "This wasn't from people. It was your American soldiers."

I felt insulted. "Our guys wouldn't be looting."

Hans laughed, "Are you that naïve? Haven't you heard of the spoils of war, Kenny? Soldiers on either side of a war are *encouraged* to take what they can carry from a defeated city."

Maybe I *was* naïve.

Hans stepped onto his balcony to look out over what remained of his city. I stopped and noticed something in the clutter on the floor. I laughed as I picked up a record album and held it up for him to see. Edith Piaf.

He shrugged and said, "I said she sings like a goat. Did I say that I didn't enjoy it?"

He sorrowfully shook his head as he gazed out at the city as dusk began to fall over the silent ruins. "I would stand here nights and listen to laughter and music echoing through the streets. I can't imagine that it will ever be that way again."

There was no power or water. Hans struck a match and lit a lantern. "We might as well sleep here tonight. The couch is comfortable. What do you want to see tomorrow?"

I thought for a minute. "There are a couple of places I'd like to see before I leave. First, I'd like to go back to France, where you shot me down. Hiding behind enemy lines was about the scariest thing I've had to face. I was only there just over a day, but I'd like to go back and walk those streets again, unafraid. Do you understand?"

Hans answered, a little disheartened, "Yes, I understand. And, my friend, I will walk those streets with you as your defeated foe!"

"Hans, Germany may be defeated, but you are personally one of the greatest combat Aces in history. I wouldn't say that *you* were defeated." He was likely fishing for that compliment, but I figured he was entitled to it.

He asked, "You said there were a couple of places you wanted to see. What is the other?"

"Oh. I'm not sure how I feel about my second choice. I'd like to go back to that schoolyard. Do you know where it is?"

"I do," he answered grimly.

"I don't really know why I want to go back or what good it would do. I guess, what I want to know is how many kids died. One or twenty... maybe none! I think I'd sleep better, knowing."

He said, "I would recommend against it, Ken. You can't dwell on it. Do you think it doesn't haunt me? Not only did I lead our fight into that town, but into that schoolyard. These are *my* towns, *my* people."

"If you don't want to go, that's fine. I want to do this, and if I don't do it now, I might not have another chance."

"Okay." Hans sighed. "Okay. So first we fly to Haguenau, then we head north to the schoolyard near Frankfurt."

The next morning, I had to make a few phone calls. Fortunately I had the influence to get the permission we needed to fly to our destinations.

After breakfast, we headed for the airfield and fired up the plane. I wore my uniform so there wouldn't be any confusion about our identities at Haguenau. Hans stood and looked at me for a moment as I climbed into his plane.

He shook his head and laughed. "It is unsettling to see you in *my* airplane, wearing an enemy uniform."

It was a pleasure to fly over Germany and France without having to keep constant lookout for bandits, flak, or targets of opportunity. Before landing at Haguenau, we flew around the area. We found the field where my plane had crashed, but the wreckage had been removed and I couldn't see any sign of where it impacted.

Once we landed, we had lunch, and then I checked a jeep out of the motor pool. Hans and I headed north until we came across that long driveway that led to the home that we had broken into. I parked the jeep at the road and we walked down the drive. As we approached the house, the owner walked out to greet us. I asked him if he spoke English.

"Yes," he answered with a thick French accent. "How may I help you?"

"I am an American pilot who was shot down here last December. I came to apologize for having broken into your home and taken some of your possessions."

I was surprised when the man smiled and offered his hand. "I know who you are, Captain Davis. It's a pleasure to meet you, and don't worry. A woman, Sandy, already stopped by, told us your story, and compensated us for the items we lost. I expected you would show up someday. And this is?" as he turned his attention to Hans.

Hans extended his hand as I introduced him. "This is Major Hans Kirpes... the pilot who shot me down that day."

The man didn't let his surprise diminish his composure. "Now, that I did *not* expect. The two of you are friends now?"

"Now that the war is over, we will be working *together*," Hans replied.

The man said, "This calls for a toast. Come. Meet my wife, and we'll share the details over a glass of wine. This time, you can enter my home as my guest."

Hans and I both gave an accounting of the air battle from our perspectives. Then I went on to explain how we'd stayed the night in the shed, watched them leave for work, then entered the house.

He responded, "Thank you for this visit. Somehow, having met you brings us a peace. Sandy did assure us, though, that you were a good and honorable man."

"Really?" I asked.

The man seemed to sense my confusion. "You looked surprised."

"Well, I only knew her all of 24 hours. She saved me from bleeding to death... where he shot me," as I pointed to Hans. "When I got to the hospital, she never stopped in to check on me. I thought maybe she shipped out before having the chance. But I guess now, I'm a little confused. She must have remained in the area."

The couple looked at each other. The wife said, "She spoke of you with quite a reverence."

"Well, thank you," I offered. "That does make me feel a little better about that." Then I looked around at the house. "I am glad to be able to compliment you in person on your home. It's amazing! It looks like a Frank Lloyd Wright design from America!"

"You're exactly right, sir. He certainly inspired its design."

"Being here made me feel like I was home for a few hours. That meant a lot to me. If you ever decide to come to the

U.S. for a vacation, please allow me to host your visit in my home." I left them my home address and phone number.

After saying our goodbyes, Hans and I walked back towards the road.

He chuckled and said teasingly, "So… *Sandy*! You swine! You had me convinced that you were an old-fashioned Southern gentleman with old-fashioned values. I'm proud of you! You were with this woman only 24 hours with your leg half blown off and you still managed to bed her! Am I wrong?!"

"It wasn't like that!" I protested.

"Your face says otherwise, Major Davis."

"Look, I love my wife and I have a high regard for the union of marriage. Normally, I'd never consider cheating on my wife, but Sandy had given me a strong dose of morphine and we really didn't know if we would live through the next day."

I went on to explain the whole story and my doubts that it really ever happened.

Hans assured me, "If you hadn't bedded her, then she would have come to see you at the hospital. It's that simple. Since you were both married, her conscience got the best of her, wouldn't you think?"

"You could be right about that."

"So, why don't you find her? It would be easy enough. What if she's still here at Haguenau?"

That thought sent a jolt of anxiety through me. "I've thought about that, but what happened between Sandy and me was a fluke, not something that either of us would have planned. If I made a deliberate effort to find her now, I feel that *would* be a betrayal of my marriage."

Hans smiled then said smartly, "Then give me her last name and I will find her."

I smiled and shook my head, "No."

I started the jeep and headed back to the airfield. I changed out of my uniform before we continued our journey north towards Frankfurt. So many of the cities we flew over had been reduced to rubble. We were flying low enough to see people in the towns passing buckets down human conveyor belts, clearing debris from collapsed buildings.

Once we managed to acquire a car in Frankfurt, we drove northwest towards the little town of Limburg where the school was located. Hans didn't say much on the drive up. I knew he didn't think the trip was a good idea. I'm not sure that I did either.

I was impressed that Hans didn't have to ask for directions. He drove us right to our destination. We stood at the edge of the schoolyard and watched silently. It looked much different from ground level. A man walked towards us from the school.

Hans said, "I'll do the talking."

When he reached us, he and Hans chatted in German. I could see Hans point towards the sky and motion to the schoolyard. The man offered a very enthusiastic response. The conversation then seemed to come to an abrupt end, and the man walked back to the building.

Hans explained, "That was the principal of the school. I told him that we were gathering information about an incident that was reported to have happened at this location a couple of months ago. He told me about it. He said that one child and one teacher were wounded and another child died. They seemed to think that it was two American planes that strafed the school."

"But you were in a 262. Americans don't have jets," I said.

Hans turned back towards the car. "Well. That is the way they remember it. Does that satisfy your curiosity?"

"It does, Hans. Thank you. I can sleep better tonight, knowing that it was only one child... and not ten."

As I turned to get into the car, I noticed that a woman was approaching us from the school. I could tell by her walk that she was angry. She began scolding us in German. I didn't need to understand German to know what her beef was. I could see that one of her hands had been replaced with a metal hook. She was likely the teacher who was wounded. My blank expression no doubt tipped her off that I didn't know her language.

She stopped speaking German and asked, "Are you English?"

"American," I answered.

Then she turned to Hans, "And you?"

"German, but I speak English," he answered.

"You are here asking about the day the Americans strafed our school? I have a few things to say about that!" This woman was filled with a rage that she focused on me.

I humbly argued, "According to our information, an American plane was in pursuit of a German jet... that his gunfire was meant for. The schoolyard *wasn't* the intended target."

"That's nonsense! An American plane was chasing a German jet?! I think you have some bad information!" she scoffed.

Hans piped in, "That is the truth!"

She stepped back and looked at both of us suspiciously, then came to a conclusion that made her even more enraged, "It was *you*! You were the one who killed one of my children. And look what you did to me!" She held up her hooked arm.

I was a little afraid that she was going to claw me with it, but instead, she reared back and slapped the hell out of my face with her good hand.

She shook her head in disbelief. "You were so determined to gun down a German jet that you didn't notice our school in front of you?!"

"Yes. And I've been tormented by it since."

"Well good!" she replied. "You deserve to be tormented. And you don't deserve forgiveness!"

Hans said, "It wasn't entirely his fault. I share the blame. I was the pilot of the ME-262 he was chasing. My plane was damaged, and I was so intent on escaping him that I didn't notice that I led our battle into a town... or to a schoolyard."

At first, she looked confused, but that expression quickly shifted back to rage. She reared back and heaved a mighty slap across Hans' face. I could tell that she hurt her hand on that one.

As he rubbed his smarting face, I said, "You were here. The whole thing happened in less than a second, a second that none of us will forget. I've been over it a hundred times in my mind, wondering how it could have been avoided, but our battle was so furious that we didn't have time to think."

She sighed as her anger subsided. "Things weren't as we thought. We thought that Americans coldheartedly strafed our school for the sport of it. Now, I understand how it happened. It won't bring back that boy, or my hand! I was planning on getting married and having a family of my own. But now that the war's over, there are far more eligible women than men in Germany! Who would marry a woman with this?!" she said, holding up her hook.

She quickly turned to me, "Would you?!"

Before I could think, I sidestepped the question. "I'm afraid I'm already married."

Then she turned to Hans, "What about you? Would you marry a woman with one hand?"

Hans backed away, stammering... not knowing how to respond.

I asserted, "Trust me, ma'am. I really don't think Hans Kirpes would make *any* woman a decent husband!"

She was shocked at hearing Hans' name. "Hans Kirpes? *Major* Hans Kirpes?"

Hans nodded as I answered her, "Maybe now you can understand why our battle was so intense. Not only was I flying a P-51 against a ME-262, but against one of the greatest Aces of all time."

She commented, "It's rather remarkable to see the two of you here together. You sought each other out?"

I answered, "Now that the war is over, it looks like we're going to be working together. Ma'am, we were both tormented by the memory of what happened here that day. We came a long way, hoping that facing this place would bring us some measure of resolution. And it has. I thought that there might have been dozens of casualties. I'm also glad that we were able to let you know the truth about what happened. Maybe you could let the parents of the boy who died know that it wasn't a deliberate act."

The woman looked at my cane. "It looks like you suffered an injury too."

"Yes," I answered. "HE nearly shot my leg off!"

"Well good!" she replied, then looked at Hans. "Why is it that you are the only one who hasn't been injured?"

Hans argued, "Oh believe me. I have my share of battle scars, but I would have to disrobe to show you."

"That's okay," I answered. "We will take your word for it."

She turned to me and asked, "I am curious. Your American bombers bombed our cities every day, not caring where the bombs landed. Tens of thousands of people—men, women, and children—died. Why are *our* casualties unique to you?"

I answered, "It was my job to escort our bombers to their targets. From 30,000 feet up, I could see bursts of smoke and fire as the bombs fell on bridges, railroads, factories, and sometimes residential buildings. At times, I would see soldiers running or shooting at me on my strafing runs. But I this time I actually saw the children ahead of my guns…" I couldn't think of the words to finish what I was saying. "I came back around, hoping to see that I hadn't hit anyone, but I could see that I had."

"I see," she said. "Well then, I guess I can forgive you now, both of you, but to be honest with you, it felt better to hate you. I don't know what I'll do with myself now." She extended her arms to me, "Come here."

How wonderful. She hugged me, then Hans.

We hopped in the car and headed back towards Frankfurt.

Hans said, "Well. That's a situation I would have been happy to avoid. I do hope you feel better, even if she slapped you senseless."

"I do feel better, thank you. And yep, that was quite a slap! I've never been slapped before," I replied.

Hans chuckled, rubbing his cheek. "Well, I have... often. You would think my cheek should be callused by now."

I looked over at Hans and laughed, "Some tough sky warrior you are. I wish you could have seen the look of absolute terror on your face when she asked you if you'd marry her!"

"She's not a bad-looking lady," he commented.

"Yes," I replied. "*Striking...* I would say."

Hans countered, "Striking indeed. If it wasn't for that temper, I probably *would* have married her."

"Oh, I'm sure you would have!"

We stopped for lunch at the Frankfurt airport before leaving.

I said, "We've only got a few days left before we ship out to Ohio. I need to get back to Leiston Field to get my affairs in order. I'd imagine you have a few loose ends to wrap up before we go. Did they say how long they expected you to be at Wright Field?"

"I would imagine, as long as it takes to teach you Americans to fly ME-262s in combat. Considering that you're all idiots... that might be a while."

"Idiots, huh? You're talking about the idiots that handed y'all your asses on a platter?"

"*Lucky* idiots," Hans replied.

When we took off from Frankfurt, Hans took us on a course towards the schoolyard at Limburg. We descended on it from the same direction as we had in the dogfight then passed it by. Neither of us said much on the flight back to Munich.

Every time I thought of being stationed in Dayton, I got this little feeling of excitement and apprehension, considering that Sandy was from Cleveland.

When I got back to Leiston, my orders were waiting. I gathered and shipped my belongings on to Wright Field. I still had a little time before my departure, so I hopped on my motorbike and got lost in England's countryside for a couple of days. I sold the bike to a buddy of mine before leaving.

CHAPTER 8: Back to the US

It was a fairly quiet flight back to the States. Even Hans was uncharacteristically quiet. We all had a lot to consider. The war was over, and in leaving Europe behind, I felt that the door to the war was finally closed—at least to the European war. I looked at the anxious expressions of the Germans on the flight. There was nothing for them to stay in Germany for. Their only chance of making a living at their trades lay ahead in a country that, for all they knew, hated them.

Wright Field was everything I heard it was. Not only did they have about every kind of enemy aircraft that was made, but they also had the captured buzz bombs and V2 rockets that were just shipped over. Karl Baur started my ground schooling on the 262 before they had a chance to uncrate the planes.

I knew that it would be a while before I could go home on leave after arriving at Wright Field, so I asked Helen to fly up and meet me that weekend. Hans went with me to meet her.

Even though I was back in the United States, Ohio wasn't familiar to me and being surrounded by Hans and his German associates, it hardly felt like I was home. It wasn't until I saw Helen's face that I felt like I was home. It was wonderful to be reminded of how it felt to have her in my arms. Eventually she noticed Hans standing behind me, staring at her.

She looked past me and said, "Hello?"

I said, "Oh. Sweetheart, this is Hans."

She seemed a little uneasy over meeting him. "Yes. Kenny's told me about you."

He responded, "I hope it wasn't all bad."

"…Aside from you making it your life's ambition to kill my husband?"

"You should be pleased to know that I'm over that now," Hans said, smiling. He took Helen's hand and kissed it. "It is a pleasure and an honor to actually meet you in person, though I've encountered you several times in the sky."

She looked to me for an explanation. "He's talking about my plane, *Heavenly Helen*."

Hans interjected, "Actually, we in the Luftwaffe referred to his plane as the 'Pink Lady.' We could see that bright pink dress from an enormous distance."

Helen coolly commented, "And you shot down… *two* Pink Ladies, from what I understand."

Hans looked at me, then back to Helen. "You *are* a beautiful woman. Now I understand why your husband was indifferent to the friendly girls that Europe has to offer."

Hans scored some major points from me with that comment and put himself on Helen's good side as well. For someone who took such pleasure in being an ass, I was surprised to see that he had an equal ability to be charming.

Hans asked, "What do you say to the three of us having dinner tonight?"

"I'm afraid I'd have to say 'not tonight, buddy.' Helen and I have a little catching up to do. But maybe tomorrow?"

He pouted, "It's my first weekend in a strange country, alone, but *don't you worry about me.*"

"I don't plan to. And you're not alone! You've got Karl and your Messerschmitt buddies here."

"They think I'm abrasive."

I had to laugh, "How surprising!"

Helen extended her hand, "It is nice to finally meet you, Hans, and no… it hasn't all been bad."

Hans gave her a hug rather than accepting her hand. "I can't imagine what good he'd have to say."

We boarded a bus to the transit barracks to arrange lodging for the night.

I told Helen, "I don't know how long I'm going to be here. They sent me here to learn to fly and evaluate these captured jets, but once I do, I don't know what their plans are for me."

Hans commented, "Your next assignment will probably be a desk job, after you wreck a couple of our planes." Then he whispered to Helen, just loud enough for me to hear, "He thinks he has what it takes to fly the 262."

She replied with a laugh, "You *are* abrasive, aren't you?"

Hans smiled, seemingly distant, then gazed out the window. "So, this is America? I'm anxious to see more of it."

I turned to Helen, "How long did you take off from work?"

"I'm here for a week," she answered.

"Great! When you go home, I'll take a long weekend, fly down with you, and drive the Zephyr back." I turned back to Hans, "If you're not too busy, you might want to make the trip with us and help me drive back. That way, you can see Louisiana and a little more of America."

"Y'all can count on me!" Hans replied, not sounding very Southern with his heavy German accent.

I felt a little guilty about leaving Hans alone that night.

In the morning, we met him for breakfast before starting our day. I learned a little more about what the Air Force had in mind for me at Wright Field. The United States' first jet fighter was nearing production—the Lockheed P-80 Shooting Star.

Their plan was that, once I was comfortable flying the 262, I would cross over to—and train in—the P-80. That way, when it came time to offer my evaluation of the performance of the P-80, I'd have something to compare it to.

Aside from being a facility to evaluate enemy aircraft, Wright Field was also the testing facility for most of the *new* military aircraft developed in the United States. It was a busy place with a large group of test pilots to evaluate all of these planes. Again, my contribution to the evaluation process was that of a pilot/engineer who had actually flown against jet fighters in combat.

Hans worked with Karl Baur to develop a jet combat training program that would pick up where Karl's initial 262 training left off. Only they decided that combat training and live target practice would be better suited for a location far away from populated areas... out in the desert. So it was decided to send Hans and the jet combat training group down to Williams Field, just outside of Phoenix.

The German/English language barrier made my classroom training on the ME-262 under Karl Baur a challenge. Though Baur was fairly fluent in English, his textbooks were all in German.

It didn't take long though. Within the week, Karl scheduled me for my first flight. Unlike the P-51 trainers that seated an instructor and student, the ME-262 was a one-man aircraft. So after being taught the theory involved with operating the aircraft, I was on my own when it came time to fly. The German instruments in the plane were marked over in English.

When the engines of the 262 were started up, the sound was like nothing I'd heard before. When they first fired up, they whistled loudly then sputtered into a roar as they wound up. The smell of the engine's exhaust was entirely different than that of the piston aircraft. It reminded me of the kerosene-filled smudge pots that were used to mark construction sites at night on our engineering projects.

Around that time, the name Operation Overcast—which was formed to evaluate enemy technology—was changed to

Operation Paperclip. It was made up of the same people with the same mission, just with a different name.

The guys from Operation Paperclip, Karl, and Hans were all there to watch me on my first flight in the 262. As I taxied out to the runway, the plane did everything that I was told it would do. As I opened the throttles, the plane settled down smoothly, waiting for me to release the brakes. When I released them and began my acceleration down the runway, it was unsettling that there wasn't more vibration. Before I knew it, the airspeed was adequate for rotation and the 262 lifted smoothly skyward. I could see why Hans couldn't wait for me to experience flying one.

I announced over the radio, "It's performing perfectly. I'll take one!"

My first flight was strictly for orientation, which included a conservative flight plan with no fancy maneuvers. That was enough of a thrill for me! Landing was also an experience, since its landing speed was much higher than a normal plane's. I'm glad that I was warned about it. Because of that, I was expecting it to be a lot more difficult than it was. My anxiety over that flight left me exhausted. Keeping the 262 in the air required so much attention that I couldn't imagine flying it while engaged in combat, but I guess you can get accustomed to anything with time and experience. Flying it certainly made me more sympathetic towards the green pilots that I shot down in the 262s. Not only did they have to worry about avoiding me, but they had quite a challenge on their hands, just keeping their planes under control.

That evening, Helen, Hans, and I went out to dinner to celebrate my maiden 262 flight.

I told Hans, "It isn't easy to fly, but everything you told me about the 262 was right on. I'm glad the Luftwaffe didn't have more of them earlier in the war."

"If we had just had the freedom to use them as fighters when we first got them, it would have made a difference in the outcome of the war. That idiot Hitler refused to let us use them as fighters. Until the very end of the war, he insisted that they be used strictly as light bombers," Hans answered.

Helen added, "Let's be grateful for that... speaking, of course, on behalf of the United States."

Hans agreed, "Yes. We should be grateful for Hitler's bad choices!" and raised his glass.

We toasted to Hitler's bad choices.

Helen asked, "I hope I'm not being rude by being so forward in asking, but, what was it like to be a Nazi?"

"Helen. My job in the war was pretty much the same as Kenny's; we just had different bosses. One big difference was that when a British or American pilot logged so many combat hours, they were sent home. Not so with the Luftwaffe... with us, you fly until you die. With me, I started flying in 1942 and flew combat missions until the war ended. That's why the Luftwaffe has so many pilots with one hundred-plus kills."

"You must have had an opinion of the Nazi party," Helen asked.

"Well." Hans sighed. "Old habits are hard to break. If a person expressed a negative opinion about the party in Germany, he'd wind up in some awfully serious trouble."

"You are free to express your thoughts here," Helen replied.

Hans looked around the restaurant. "Well, maybe so. If you listen, you'll notice that a lot of the conversations here are in German. Operation Paperclip relocated nearly every Nazi scientist that the Russians didn't capture and put them right here in Dayton. I have to say, some of these guys were the scary Nazis. If they'd heard me say anything against the Nazi party a year ago, I would have been charged with treason. With these fellows around, I don't quite have the feeling that I've left Germany."

I assured him, "I'm also curious about your true thoughts on it, but if you don't feel comfortable discussing it now…"

"Actually, it would be nice to speak freely about my thoughts. I do have some unique opinions of the whole Nazi-Jew issue. I look at the Nazis and the Jews like a husband and wife. In a marriage, a husband is just instinctively better at some things than his wife and a wife is just instinctively better at other things than her husband. It's a balance."

Helen asked, "So you're saying that you feel like they balanced each other?"

"Exactly, intellectuals come in two extremes… scholars and innovators. Picture a box with scholars to the left and innovators to the right. Everyone falls somewhere between these two extremes. Then picture a vertical scale from top to bottom that measures the degree of intellect. Each of us falls somewhere in the box between the top and bottom... left and right. Usually it's somewhere in the middle.

"On the extreme left, the *scholars* are good at learning from things that they observe or are taught. That works for them, and whenever they have a question, they call on their store of knowledge or their textbooks for an answer. But ask them a question that can't be found in a book, and they're lost."

"On the extreme right are the *innovators*. Life usually forces people in this category to figure things out for themselves because they are *poor* scholars. They aren't good at learning from experience or from others, so they rely on innovation to get them through life. Innovation is like a muscle. The more you use it, the stronger it becomes. The innovators are the people who come up with the ideas that aren't yet in the scholars' books.

"Funny thing is, each group thinks of the other as idiots. The scholars scoff at the innovators because they are such poor scholars. The innovators scoff at the scholars because they can't improvise to solve a problem. The truth of the matter is, they're both idiots and both brilliant, and together, they make a good balance.

"So in Germany, there were two extremes of people. One group was knowledgeable, disciplined... good in business and finance. The other group lived more by their wits. They created brilliant new things, but squandered their money and couldn't manage businesses well. As it turns out, most—but not all—of the scholars were Jewish and most—but not all—of the innovators weren't. The scholars usually employed the innovators, offering them security in return for the profits they enjoyed from the innovators' creations. And all was well... until the innovators decided they wanted the scholar's wealth and influence. The rest is history."

Helen replied, "So, you're suggesting that the Nazis took control of all of the Jewish commerce and justified throwing them into concentration camps by telling the German population that they were inferior people?"

Hans nodded. "You summed it up in one sentence. Right or wrong, that's my understanding of what started the whole mess. Then the Nazis threw people who were indeed considered to be mentally inferior into the camps as well to further convince its citizens of their quest to purify the nation."

I laughed, "Well, it's nice to know that you don't hate the Jews."

"In my opinion, one of Hitler's biggest contradictions was how he said that the Jews must be removed from society because they were mentally inferior... and then he voiced his disdain for the United States, saying that it's a country run by the

Jews. So Adolf... which is it?! Are the Jews idiots or a people brilliant enough to control of one of the most powerful countries on Earth? And who was it that Hitler forced to build the V2 rockets and ME-262 fighter jets? Jewish slave laborers. I don't think that *most* German citizens could be counted on to perform such complicated work."

Helen asked, "So you believe that, in general, Jewish people are more scholastic and the people who aren't tend to be more innovative because they're poor scholars?"

"Right. I don't think anyone is totally on the left or right side of the chart, just closer to one side than the other. Look at Einstein. He's Jewish, but a perfect example of someone on the extreme right of the chart."

I said, "I have a question. If you're right, then why didn't the Nazis just seize the assets from the wealthy Jews? Why did they put the rest of the Jewish population in concentration camps?"

Hans answered, "If the leaders in the Jewish community had decided to call upon their people to take up arms against the Nazis, they would have certainly defeated them. So the Nazis interned the Jewish citizens in prison camps... *before* their leaders had that chance."

I was amused by this perspective. "I guess that would be an effective way to win a war. Make your enemy prisoners of war *before* they have a chance to go to war with you. I suppose that's the most logical explanation I've heard so far for this insanity."

Hans reflected solemnly, "Mankind, no matter what their nationality, has a latent tendency to become evil. Hitler's orders to rid Europe of Jews drew those tendencies out in many of our soldiers. Towards the end of the war, many of them came to relish their freedom to torture and kill. That's why we feared being captured by the Russians. The Russians saw what monsters the German soldiers had become and are hungry for revenge."

Helen and I sat quietly, digesting what he'd said.

He lightened his mood and changed the subject. "I realized something while I was working today."

"What's that?" I asked.

He smiled and said, "When you complete your pilot training on the 262 with Karl, I'll be teaching you jet dogfighting skills."

"Yes?"

"Some of your instruction will be in a classroom, but some will be in actual simulated combat. We will be flying against each other again. Just like old times, huh?"

"Wow. That will be fun! I can shoot you down again!"

Hans got a good laugh out of that. "I admire your confidence, unwarranted as it may be."

My thoughts drifted back to my current training. "You must have been a little nervous the first time you flew a 262. At least when I did, I had the benefit of experienced instructors."

He answered, "Nervous is an understatement. It wasn't until Adolf Galland flew it and gave it his thumbs-up that I gave it a try."

That week at work, Karl kept my flights in the 262 very basic.

My greatest thrill of the week was getting to sit in one of our new P-80 fighter-jet prototypes. It was beautiful, all shiny polished aluminum. Unlike the 262, it only had one engine to manage rather than two. The gauges were in English too. I couldn't wait to have the chance to fly it.

When Friday rolled around, Helen, Hans, and I boarded a flight bound for Baton Rouge. Our destination was Harding Field, which had recently begun sharing its runways with the commercial airliners.

We flew down on one of the new Lockheed Constellations with its long sleek fuselage and triple tail. It made me proud that Hans got to see some of our superior aircraft engineering. As our plane came in for its approach, we circled over Baton Rouge. I pointed out the sights to Hans.

"My family's engineering firm, where Helen works, was involved in building the State capitol building there and the Mississippi River bridge."

"That's quite a bridge," he commented.

I answered, "A big engineering company from up north did most of it. We just took care of little things like approaches and footings. Same with the capitol building: we just helped with the small stuff that needed to be designed on-site."

Hans leaned forward in his seat, looking out of his window as we descended over the huge expanse of oil refineries between the capitol building and the airfield. "Oh my God!"

I pointed out, "It's the second largest refinery in the world. Would have made one heck of a target if you boys had made it over this far, huh?"

Hans pointed out, "We did come close. Maybe not with our planes, but our U-Boats waited for your oil tankers to come down the river to the Gulf of Mexico. We sank a couple... one was even named the *Baton Rouge*."

I'd heard about that. It was unsettling to realize that the war had come within a couple hundred miles of my home.

We landed in Baton Rouge just after noon. The whole family was waiting as our plane rolled up to the tarmac—my mom and Helen's parents as well. After we finished exchanging hugs with our family, they noticed Hans standing there looking rather awkward.

I introduced him, "I'm sure y'all know who Hans Kirpes is. Yes, he's the one who shot me down, but he's also one of the world's top Aces and he's going to teach me a few things about flying jets."

My mom hesitated in shaking his hand, "I'm sorry, Hans, but I find it a little difficult to be cordial to a man who tried to kill my son."

Hans defended himself, "Well ma'am, in all fairness, your son tried to kill me first!"

"That's true!" I added. "And I tried really hard to kill him, but he managed to get away from me and tried to kill me back."

Hans continued, "I shot him down, but then he shot me down. So I think that makes us about even."

"Well, not quite," I argued. "When my plane was disabled and anyone else would have finished me off, Hans pulled up alongside me, saluted, then flew off... sparing me."

My mom responded, "In that case, Hans, welcome to Baton Rouge."

Mom gave him a hug. Helen's parents also gave him a warm welcome.

Mr. Phillips shook his head, looking at Hans as we walked to the cars. "So you're a Nazi?"

"Was... sir," Hans answered. "It was required to become a Luftwaffe pilot."

I pointed to the other side of the airfield out to Hans. "That's where I took my fighter training and flew my first P-51. If we have time before we leave, we'll have to go visit my old commanding officer. I think he'll be thrilled to meet one of the pilots they trained me to fly against."

Hans replied, "That should be interesting."

Helen was anxious to tell her dad about how amazing Wright Field was with its captured aircraft from around the world.

As we drove towards the house, Hans leaned forward and asked, "Are we going to have any Cajun food while I'm here? I've heard about it."

Mom answered, "We will have gumbo for dinner tonight."

Having grown up in Baton Rouge, I took many of its unique qualities for granted. I imagined that it was as fascinating to Hans as Germany had been to me.

"And you have alligators here too?" he asked.

I chuckled, "We do, but I don't think you'll have a chance to meet one on this trip."

As we pulled up the driveway, I could see that Hans was impressed with our house.

He commented, "This is a beautiful house! I didn't know you were from a wealthy family, Kenny."

"My dad designed it. He built it to be reminiscent of the old Southern plantations."

Hans said, "Yes. I saw the movie 'Gone with the Wind.' It does remind me of those beautiful old homes."

We gave Hans a tour of the house and wound up on the second floor balcony overlooking the lake as the sun set over it. Boaters' sails billowed as the warm magnolia-scented breeze blew through the Spanish moss that was draped from the cypress trees that lined the lakeshore.

Our maid, Mary, prepared an amazing Cajun feast that night. It didn't take Hans long to decide that he was crazy about crawfish.

After dinner, Helen and I sat back and listened as the family grilled Hans for stories about his upbringing and life in Germany. He told them how he'd lost his parents at a young age and of how his aunt and uncle sent him to boarding schools for his upbringing. I could see that he liked being included in our family for the evening.

In the morning I called my old C.O., Colonel Windrum, at Harding Field. It was a Saturday, his day off, but he was happy to hear from me and agreed to meet me at his office. I didn't tip him off that I was bringing a guest.

The last time I had seen Colonel Windrum was when I came home after Hans shot me down.

When we walked in, the Colonel shook my hand, "It's great to see you again, Major Davis. Damn, last time you were here, you turned this place upside down!"

I turned to Hans and explained, "They made a big deal out of my coming home... as a wounded Ace. The mayor was here and all the press. Then they even let me take Helen up in one of the trainers!"

Before Hans could respond, Colonel Windrum went on to say, "I heard you've become a double-Ace since then. And that you shot down Kirpes, that Nazi son-of-a-bitch that shot you down! Good going!"

I laughed and answered, "Yes sir. I shot that Nazi son-of-a-bitch down alright."

The colonel seemed a little confused over why Hans and I found his statement to be so amusing.

I motioned to Hans, "Colonel Windrum, I'd like you to meet a friend of mine. Major Hans Kirpes."

He seemed dazed for a second then quipped, "Nawwww! You just about got me there. Good one!"

Hans replied, "As it turns out, Colonel, your government has hired me to assist in fighter jet combat training. We're teaching Major Davis to fly the ME-262 at Wright Field."

The Colonel's face lost all expression. "Holy crap," he said, as he reached to shake Hans' hand. Once he'd heard Hans' German accent, the he realized that we weren't joking. He was beside himself. "Seriously, you're really Hans Kirpes?!"

I answered, "Yes sir. He's the genuine article, a Luftwaffe Ace with over 221 kills to his credit. I expect we might learn a few things from him."

Colonel Windrum asked us to sit down, and he insisted on hearing all the details of our battles, of how we met, and of our adventures since. He picked up the phone and called the field's reporter for *Stars and Stripes* to come do an interview.

"These stories are just too great not to share," he said.

The colonel asked Hans, "I've heard that piston planes are no match for jets, but then Major Davis shot you down in a 262. How did that happen?"

Hans answered, "I'd like to say that he just got lucky, but honestly, Major Davis out flew me. He banked to the right, then dove against his turn, pulling negative Gs, and turned to the left... and got the drop on me."

"Impressive," the colonel commented.

I mentioned, "As soon as I log enough hours in the 262 to start combat training in it, I'll be flying against Hans again. We can challenge each other without having to kill each other."

Hans said to the colonel, "He's feeling awfully cocky because he got the drop on me... once. We'll see how he does when I know what I'm up against. I'll smack that smugness right out of him."

I laughed, "We'll see about that."

The colonel said, "Oh God. This is priceless, where the *hell* is that reporter?!"

Eventually the reporter did arrive, the same reporter that wrote the first story about me.

I was quick to tell Hans, "This is the reporter that said that you downed me with a lucky shot." Then I turned to the reporter, "Do you know that, after he read that story, he made it a personal vendetta to shoot me down?"

The reporter seemed speechless when he shook Hans' hand.

I asked the reporter, "Would you do me a favor and let him know that I explained how he flew up next to me after disabling my plane, saluted me, then flew off... letting me go?"

"You did," the reporter answered. "But we also explained to you, that it's our job is to boost the morale of our troops... not make the enemy out to be a hero. I've got to admit though, when I wrote that story, I had no idea that the major would be reading it, much less that I'd be meeting him face to face. Now that the war in Europe is over, we can be a little more candid about the facts, and to be honest with you, Major Kirpes, I'm anxious to hear about what it was like to fly for the Luftwaffe."

I could tell by the reporter's enthusiasm that he was planning on writing quite a story. This would more than vindicate him for his earlier story. He also asked Hans if he had a photo of himself with his plane. Hans produced one that he just happened to keep in his wallet to impress the ladies. In it, he was wearing his smart Luftwaffe uniform, standing in front of his ME-262.

On the way back from the airfield, I stopped to show Hans the State capitol building with its observation deck twenty-seven floors up. He was in awe of the spectacular view it offered of the city and river.

Hans commented, "This is quite an impressive building. I haven't seen a view like this since the Eiffel Tower."

That Saturday evening, I called up a few friends for a party. Again, Hans was the center of attention. He was his usual obnoxious self. The guests found him to be amusing. They might not have if I hadn't warned them that he'd try to ruffle their feathers for the sport of it.

At six o'clock the next morning, I was awakened by our maid Mary, who was pounding on my door and shouting, "Mr. Kenny. You gotta see the paper!"

By then, the whole house was awake. As it turned out, the reporter for the *Stars and Stripes* for Harding Field was sidelining from his job as a reporter for the Baton Rouge newspaper. Hans and I were plastered all over the front page. The headline read, "Formidable Enemies in the Skies over Europe, Now Friends." It went on to say: "U.S. double-Ace Major Kenny Davis and Luftwaffe Ace Major Hans Kirpes, who are now working together at Wright Field in Dayton, Ohio, make brief visit to Baton Rouge." It also mentioned the fact that we each shot the other down in our air battles and told of how Helen's pink dress on my P-51's nose made me a target for Hans.

Hans was becoming as famous in Baton Rouge as he was back in Germany. That day, we were all famous! I wished that we had time to stick around for a while to enjoy our newfound notoriety, but Hans and I had a long drive ahead of us.

I loaded my civilian clothes into the trunk of the Zephyr, grabbed breakfast, and then we hit the road. I made a quick stop on the way out of town to buy out a store's supply of Sunday newspapers.

"This was a short visit," I told Hans. "If you want to come back again, we'll take you down to New Orleans."

"I would like that. Louisiana seems like a wonderful place to live. And I have to say, your friends and family made me feel very welcome. I haven't felt that kind of warmth before."

"Well. They call that *Southern Hospitality*."

He said a bit distantly, "I envy you, Kenny. I see the love in your home, with your mom, Helen, your friends, and even Mary. I imagine you had a wonderful upbringing."

"I did, Hans. And to top it off, I married the girl I was in love with since grade school. I'm sorry you didn't have a childhood like mine."

"I had friends in boarding school, but they came and went. You see, without the proper childhood nurturing and family support, people like me grow up to be Nazis."

I was glad that Hans could joke about it. "It's not too late to change that part of your life. Why haven't you settled down with one lady?"

"I'll stop looking when I've found one like you have."

I was flattered. "I can't believe that, with all the women you've known, you haven't. How many women have you dated, anyway?"

"How many lovers?" he asked. "I've shot down fewer airplanes."

"Most guys would envy you for that, but it seems like it would get kind of lonely. It means a lot to me to have that one special lady in my life that I want to share everything with... whether it's good or bad. Maybe Helen and I can help you find the right one."

He smiled and nodded, "Okay. I'll hold you to that."

I remembered a talk I'd had with my dad when I was a kid. I had wanted every new toy that came out. He explained that, if he gave me every toy I ever wanted, they would sit forgotten as soon as another one came along. I imagined that's how Hans was towards women. Maybe his good looks, confidence, and charm were responsible for his loneliness.

Hans sat quietly as I drove north to Mississippi. I could tell that he was feeling blue, but I decided to wait for him to break the silence.

Eventually he said, "I have nothing to go back to in Germany. I don't have childhood memories like yours. Of the friends I had, most were killed and some are still in prison as war criminals. The towns from my childhood have been reduced to rubble. Here... there is no sign of war. No burnt or broken buildings. Businesses are prospering, people have work. There's none of that back home."

"Are you thinking about staying and becoming a citizen?"

"I am," he answered. "Like you just said, I can always change my life. The prospects for happiness seem much better here."

As we drove north along the Mississippi River, I gave Hans a history lesson about the Civil War and the effect it had had on the South.

The narrow two-lane highways that led to Dayton passed through the heart of every town along the way. The hotels and restaurants were all unique and one-of-a-kind. Our trip led us through Memphis, Nashville, Louisville, and Cincinnati with dozens of unique little towns in-between.

Whenever I had crossed the country before, it was always by plane or train. The trip by car was as fun and interesting to me as it was to Hans.

We arrived at Wright Field late Monday night. I resumed my flight training the following morning, logging more hours in the ME-262.

On Wednesday morning, I was surprised by a visit from my old friend Colonel Clark with Army Public Affairs.

He said, "I'll get right to the point. You and Major Kirpes created quite a stir down at Harding Field this weekend."

Remembering how critical his department had been of every word I uttered to the press, I had a horrible feeling that Hans and I were in trouble over something we said. I responded, "I thought the interview was okay, since Colonel Windrum arranged it."

183

"Oh, it was. And the reporter telegraphed a copy of the story to us for approval before they ran it. It was actually quite a favorable bit of publicity."

I sighed with relief.

Clark continued, "In fact, so favorable, that we decided to have you do it again—only on a bigger scale. The story would be a great morale booster for our troops fighting in the Pacific. It says that not only did we win the war in Europe, but the Nazis that we conquered are here humbly serving us now. It's a victory story."

"That's great. I'm glad it turned out to be a good thing. What more can I do to help?" I asked.

"Since the story came out, both the Baton Rouge newspaper and Harding Field have been flooded with phone calls and mail expressing the public's fascination with it."

"Really?!" I exclaimed.

Clark said, "And I *like* the hometown aspect of the story and the fact that you brought your conquered nemesis home to meet your family. I'd like to do it again, but I want to have the national press there. And to make it all a bit more spectacular, I would like you and Major Kirpes to fly your wartime aircraft down to Harding and do the interviews in your wartime uniforms."

"Wow. That'll get some attention! Have you asked Hans about it yet?" I asked.

He answered, "No. I thought I'd run it past you first. He might see this assignment as degrading. He can refuse it, but if he does decide to do it, I have to be confident that he'll say the right things to the press. What's your feeling on this? Do you think we can trust him?"

I was amazed that the Colonel would even consider my opinion on the matter. "I'm sure you've already evaluated his records. From what I've seen, he enjoys rubbing people the wrong way just to get a reaction out of them. I don't know whether he'd be that way with the press. I *can* tell you that, if he's been honest with me, he's *not* sympathetic to the Nazi party and never has been."

"He did a good job on your interview at Harding. Surprisingly, we didn't have to edit out *any* of his comments from the interview. With the national media, especially radio, we have to trust that we have the same perspective. Let's call him over to see what he thinks about it."

While waiting for Hans, Colonel Clark and I chatted about some of the good times we'd had while traveling the country together on the publicity tour.

When Hans walked in, I introduced him to the colonel. "Hans, this is a friend of mine, Colonel Clark. He's in Army Public Relations. It's his job to see that, when I talk to the press, I don't say anything that might be detrimental to the Army."

Hans stepped up and shook his hand, "Hans Kirpes. Yes, we had similar liaisons in the Nazi party. Is this about our interview at Harding? I was paying attention to what I was saying… with the understanding that your department would be reviewing it."

Clark replied, "And you did a wonderful job of it, Major. I would imagine that the Nazi Propaganda Ministry was quite strict about what you had to say back in Germany."

Hans answered, "Indeed."

I said, "Colonel Clark told me that the newspaper story on our visit created a fantastic response in the Baton Rouge area. People were thrilled to see you, a Nazi Luftwaffe pilot, helping us now that the war is over. The colonel feels that the Allied world would have the same response if the story were in the national news."

The colonel commented, "Major Davis here tells me that you're not a Nazi sympathizer. I'd like you to give me your attitude towards it."

"Hans explained his opinions regarding the Nazi-Jewish relationship and the Nazi's motives for persecuting them… and his lack of sympathy for their cause."

"Wow," Colonel Clark exclaimed. "I've never heard that perspective before. Is it a popular one?"

"I wouldn't know," Hans answered dryly. "This is my own personal opinion, one that I never expressed out loud before coming here to the States. Everyone had opinions about what the Nazis were up to, but we didn't dare express them unless they were favorable. And if I have an opinion that might be detrimental to your country's welfare, I would keep it to myself as well. But then, there is nothing about this wonderful country that I could have a negative opinion on!"

The colonel laughed, "It sounds like we can count you as an anti-Nazi?"

Hans laughed nervously. "The thought of saying it out loud still scares me, but to answer your question, yes."

The colonel said, "Wonderful, Major Kirpes. I trust that you are a good candidate for this assignment. Believe it or not, we have citizens here in the States who sympathize with the Nazi party. We certainly don't want to encourage them."

I told Hans, "What the colonel wants us to do is to fly back down to Baton Rouge for a *national* press conference— only this time in our wartime planes, you in a ME-262 and me in a P-51, with both of us dressed in our native uniforms."

"So, you are looking to show me off as a living war trophy?" Hans quietly chuckled. "Well, don't worry. I'll put on a show for them that won't disappoint you, sir."

Colonel Clark studied Hans for a moment, then nodded and replied, "I trust that you won't, Major."

Hans continued, "Sounds like fun. I wouldn't miss it for the world!"

"Then I'll schedule this event for next Friday.

Hans asked, "What happens if I slip and say the wrong thing? Are you going to ship me back to the Russians?"

"Well now, there's an idea," the colonel quipped.

"That's not funny!"

"This isn't a funny assignment, Major. It carries a lot of responsibility."

"It's a piece of cake. I've been accustomed to watching every word I say for my entire military career. Colonel, I may be contrary, but I'm not reckless."

"Okay," the colonel said. "We'll see about that. In the meantime, you and I are going to be spending a lot of time together this week before we leave."

When it was time to go, Colonel Clark and the ground support crew flew down ahead of us on a cargo plane that was loaded with the 262's ground support equipment. Hans and I left later in the day to give them time to get down there and prepare for our arrival.

What a break it was to be able to see Helen again so soon! I just wish that it hadn't been so hot. It was sweltering in Dayton that week, and I wasn't looking forward to the summer heat combined with Louisiana's humidity.

I hadn't flown a P-51 since before I joined Operation Paperclip in Europe several months before. After logging as many hours as I had in the smooth, fast ME-262, it was a change to find myself back at the controls of the P-51. The vibration from its massive single engine and prop made me feel like I was riding a jackhammer.

CHAPTER 9: Baton Rouge

The people of Dayton had grown accustomed to seeing the enemy aircraft that we were testing and evaluating in their skies. They would have been amazed to know that on that day, the ME-262 they saw flying overhead was actually piloted by a real Luftwaffe pilot. The spectacle of a P-51 flying alongside a 262 was quite moving, even if the 262 bore U.S. markings. We were instructed to climb to a maximum cruising altitude so we wouldn't startle any ground observers we passed who weren't aware of our mission.

Even though the heat down below was stifling, the air at that altitude was crisp and below zero. All that could be seen of us from the ground were our white contrails. My throttle was set at maximum cruising speed while Hans' was barely halfway there. Even so, the eight hundred mile trip from Dayton to Baton Rouge only took two hours—quite a contrast to the two long days it had taken make that trip by car the week before.

From that altitude, I could only see threads of highways and the clusters of buildings in the towns we passed over. At times like that, I imagined how each of those little specks were houses... homes that contained families whose lives, dreams, and struggles were confined within their walls. I studied my map to try and identify the towns we were flying over as the towns we'd driven through the week before.

When I looked up from my map, I was shocked to see that Hans was gone! I quickly looked around ... but there was no sign of him.

How could he have vanished so quickly?!

In the next instant, whoosh! Hans swooped up to a position right on my tail from below me. I could see him in my rear view mirrors, pointing and challenging me the same way he had in our last dogfight.

I laughed and said over the radio, "Not this time, Hans. Remember, the last time we played this scenario, it didn't turn out so good for you, did it?"

He replied, "That's only because you scored a *lucky shot!*"

"*Ah!* So it's okay for *you* to say that?"

"That's only because you said it first, my friend. I'm entitled." Hans eased his throttle up and pulled back alongside me.

I replied, "I suppose that's fair enough."

After flying in silence for a while, a question popped into my head. "Hans. I've never asked you before. To be a pilot, you had to have a college education. What was your major... Major?"

"Psychology," he answered.

"Psychology!" I was shocked. "How did you do at that?"

"Not so good. The Nazi party decided they would rather throw people with psychological problems into a concentration camp than try to fix them. My career choice became obsolete before I graduated, so I joined the Luftwaffe and started flying."

I laughed, "That was an interesting career choice, since you seem to deliberately alienate people in the first five minutes of meeting them."

"Yes?"

"Is that some kind of test?"

The tone of Han's laugh indicated that I was right. "It's not complicated. When you meet a dog, he'll bark at you and immediately size you up for a reaction. In that instant, based on your reaction, he'll decide if you're someone who should be barked at or someone who should be a friend. The idiots that take my barking seriously aren't people I'd likely want for friends."

I was glad that I took the time to think before responding to Hans' initial rudeness when we were first acquainted. "So, I passed your bark test?"

"Oh... when we first met, I didn't just bark at you. I shot your butt out of the sky! Shooting *me* down in return earned you my respect."

I said, "That's an interesting explanation of your character... or could it be that you're just an ass?!"

He laughed. "That's entirely possible."

"Do you think you'll get your degree and practice psychology when you stop flying?"

"Major Davis... I'm hoping I'll be *dead* when I stop flying."

"I know how you feel. I'd much rather be up here than sitting behind a desk, engineering."

Hans said, "Besides, I do practice psychology in my flying. I can usually size up an opponent in battle in a few seconds to anticipate his moves... whether he's educated or clever, confident or scared. Most are painfully predictable. On our first encounter, I could tell in an instant that you were inexperienced, but I could also see a raw, spontaneous intelligence in your piloting that made you a worthy opponent. In our next encounter, I'm afraid that I underestimated just *how* clever of a pilot you were, when you shot *me* down."

"So you're a psychologist. I'm surprised you never mentioned that."

"Would you do me a favor and keep this between us? I don't tell people about it."

"I suppose you've analyzed me and came up with a prognosis?"

Hans replied, "That is *exactly* why I want you to keep this to yourself. Everyone I meet who knows asks that same question."

"Well?"

"Major Davis. You were raised in a beautiful home on a lake by two loving parents. You had a live-in maid to clean up after you. You married the only girl you ever wanted. You became a pilot and, in no time, became a double Ace; then this Colonel Clark turned you into a national hero... twice! Now, *you* tell *me* what adversities in your life might have caused you psychological damage?"

"Well," I thought. "Having to work with you is a pretty serious adversity!"

Hans laughed. "I suppose that *would* drive most people crazy."

"You said it. Oh, and I cleaned up after *myself*!"

It was time to begin our descent into Baton Rouge. Because of its speed, this process took a little more time for the 262 than it did for my P-51, so now it was my turn to be patient with Hans.

Colonel Clark told me that the newspaper and radio stations would announce our arrival the day before. We had instructions to make a couple of long, slow circles over the town before landing for the benefit of the spectators. I wondered how many of my friends would be among them. We put on a show to where it looked as if I were escorting a captured 262 down.

We made a pass over the field before landing. Flashbulbs sparkled from the crowd on the tarmac as we passed. Once again, Colonel Clark had performed his job masterfully. When we touched down, the ground crew guided us to our parking spots, where they assisted us in deplaning. We were both wearing flight suits from our respective countries. Hans and I approached the crowd, which included Colonel Windrum, Colonel Clark, and other VIPs. We both saluted them. The crowd was eating it up!

The whole publicity event wasn't so much to show people that Hans and I were friends. It was meant to boast of our victory over Germany and to show the country that a Nazi Luftwaffe pilot that they once saw as dangerous and scary was now subservient to us.

The crowd was definitely more interested in our unlikely friendship than the political statement we were making.

I recognized Helen's smile in the crowd right away. She always made me so terribly proud. She refrained from rushing to me like I hoped she would, no doubt because Colonel Clark had already briefed her on this visit's protocol. The press would have to have their turn with us first.

All of the initial questions were directed at Hans. I was impressed that his answers were so eloquent and humble. He made sure to assert his disdain for the Nazi party and for their actions during the war.

They asked about his 221 kills and about his shooting me down. He explained that the Luftwaffe Aces had more kills for two reasons: first, because they could fly three missions a day since they were flying over their homes; and secondly, because they were never allowed to quit flying once they began. Hans assured the reporters that, if he and I had flown the same number of missions, we would have likely had the same number of kills.

When the reporters were done with Hans, they turned to me, wanting to know what it was like to befriend a former enemy.

"This isn't the first time it's happened," I answered. "After the First World War, a number of enemy pilots became friends. Since Major Kirpes and I couldn't manage to kill each other up there, I guess we were *destined* to be friends."

Hans piped up, "Even so. We may kill each other yet!"

After ten more minutes of answering questions, Colonel Clark dismissed the press and I was finally able to hug my wife.

The colonel said, "Don't make any plans for tomorrow night. We've been invited to have dinner with Governor Jimmy Davis. I'll expect to see you both in full dress uniforms. Oh, and the governor made a point of asking me to invite your mother."

"Wonderful," I answered. "I'm sure she'd like to see him and his wife again. He was a congressman when Dad was working on the capitol building, and they became friends."

I invited Colonel Clark to come home to dinner with us. When we got there, Mary had a wonderful dinner waiting for us on the front porch overlooking the lake. Helen's parents were there. Mom was happy to hear about the governor's dinner invitation. It was still quite warm, and the cool breeze blowing off the lake under the canopy of oak trees was refreshing.

As Mary poured Hans a glass of iced tea, he leaned back and sighed.

"This… is the life. What an amazing home and what an amazing family. What do I have to do to get adopted?"

Mom raised her glass to him and replied, "You're hereby adopted by the Davis family, Hans. You might live to regret it, darling."

I could see that he was trying not to show how moved he was by the gesture as we all raised our glasses to concur.

Helen commented, "It's going to be a wonderful dinner tomorrow night, Hans. I'm sure there will be some eligible ladies there. Maybe we can find you a nice Southern Belle."

Hans held up *his* glass. "Here's to my finding a Pink Lady of my own."

In the morning, Hans and I drove to Harding Field. Colonel Windrum invited us to share our stories and wisdom regarding our dog fighting experiences with the instructors there. Most of them hadn't actually seen a fighter jet before, much less one from the Luftwaffe.

When we got home, we relaxed before having to dress for dinner.

Hans asked, "We're having dinner with the governor, at his home?"

"It'll be at the governor's mansion, downtown," I answered. "It looks a lot like the White House. And this will be more than just a dinner if Colonel Clark is responsible for the event." I looked at my watch. "It's about time we got dressed."

When I got up to our room, Helen was already getting ready. She'd laid my uniform out neatly on the bed. As she sat at her vanity, applying her makeup, I kissed her neck.

"The best part of this little trip is having this unexpected time with you."

Helen squeezed my hand that rested on her shoulder.

I told her, "Since I've been back to the States, I haven't had any time alone with you… outside of the bedroom."

"Well," she said. "Your new best buddy has been with you every minute. I really think we need to find him a girl."

"He doesn't have any trouble finding them, but for whatever reason, he doesn't end up keeping them. I don't know if that's his choice or theirs."

After dressing, I stood in front of the bathroom mirror to adjust my tie. I remembered the night I stood in front of that same mirror, getting ready for the dance where Helen and I first got together. I looked back at her in the bedroom and smiled with contentment. Life was good.

Helen and I went downstairs to find that my mom and Hans weren't down yet. I poured us a glass of sherry to help calm our nerves. We embraced those few moments we had alone together and walked out onto the porch to watch the sun set over the lake.

Hans walked up behind us, seeing our sherry, "*That,* looks like a good idea!"

We turned to see him in his full dress uniform. I heard Helen gasp. Wow! He looked absolutely incredible. I was envious.

I complained, "It's just not fair! You damned Germans could have won the war simply based on how impressive your uniforms are!"

Hans' uniform was proudly adorned with all of his medals, topped with an Iron Cross. Helen grabbed the camera to get a picture. When Mom came down, I had her take a picture of the three of us—the two opposing pilots with the Pink Lady between us.

Mom said, "You three don't have to say a word! Seeing you just standing there together, takes my breath away."

Hans looked down at his uniform and said sadly, "This will probably be the last time that I'll wear this uniform in public."

The four of us piled into the car and headed to the mansion.

Hans asked me, "Is this your first dinner with the governor?"

"It is for Helen and me, but Mom and Dad got invited to the governor's mansion quite a bit back when Huey Long was governor. He was the governor responsible for the new state capitol building. Everybody loved that man!"

Hans asked, "But wasn't he the governor that was assassinated?"

"Okay," I answered. "So, there was at least one guy that didn't love him!"

Mom said, "That was tragic. We were certainly fond of him. This will be the first dinner with *this* governor for me. Last time your dad and I saw Jimmy Davis, he was a congressman."

When we pulled up in front, white-gloved servants opened our doors and a parking attendant took the car. Music from a live orchestra spilled out into the warm night through the open doors. Colonel Clark was there to greet us. Helen took my arm and Mom took the colonel's arm as he led us into the main hall where the governor was waiting with his wife. We were met with an enthusiastic response, being the guests of honor. The mayor and Colonel Windrum were also standing with them.

When we approached them, the governor took Mom by the hands and said, "Mrs. Davis. We were so terribly sorry to hear about your husband. Devastating news!"

Mom thanked him for his concern, and then the governor turned his attention to Hans and me. "And you boys made quite an entrance yesterday! We're used to seeing P-51s and P-47s fly over town from Harding Field, but never one escorting a Luftwaffe jet... and by a pilot that was raised and trained as a fighter pilot right here in Baton Rouge. You made the town proud, son."

Next, the governor turned his attention to Hans. He chuckled nervously. "My gosh, you strike an imposing figure in your Nazi uniform, Major."

Hans politely corrected him, "It's a Luftwaffe uniform, sir."

"But, you *are* a Nazi?" he asked.

"Was… sir. It's with great relief that I can say that I am no longer a Nazi."

He replied, "Well, it might come as a surprise you, Major, but you're not the first Nazi that Louisiana has played host to. There are hundreds more of you here."

Both Hans and I were confused by that statement.

The governor went on to explain. "We have quite a number of German prisoner of war camps in the State. One of them is right across the river in Port Allen. With so many of *our* young men over in Europe fighting, we're terribly shorthanded in our businesses and farms. They don't have to, but if they want to, the prisoners can go into town and work with local merchants or on the nearby farms. They earn script that they can spend at the commissary. A lot of them join sports teams with their fellow prisoners. And they enjoy hot meals and sleep in warm beds. That's a damned better life than they'd be living if they were still overseas fighting! Hell, I wish our guys fighting overseas had such a comfortable life!"

One of the reporters asked, "Major Kirpes. We learned from your last visit that you'll be training our pilots, jet aircraft dog fighting techniques. How long are you here and when are you planning on returning to Germany?"

"It's funny you should ask, because after my recent visit to Baton Rouge, I informed Major Davis that I've decided to apply for citizenship here, if you'll have me. I think Louisiana would be a wonderful place to live."

The governor chuckled and patted Han's shoulder, "I like hearing that."

Colonel Clark asked, "Major Kirpes. Over in Germany, did you listen to any American music?"

Hans replied, "Of course. You Yanks produce some *wonderful* music."

The colonel asked, "Have you heard the song, 'You Are My Sunshine'?"

"Yes..." Hans answered. "Yes, that's one of my favorite American tunes. When I'd fly a prolonged mission... as Major Davis can confirm, it gets pretty boring up there. I'd pass the time by belting out my favorite tunes over the roar of my engine. That was one I often sang!"

Colonel Clark placed his hand on the governor's shoulder, "Well, that tune originated from our very own singing Governor... Jimmy Davis."

Thinking they were joking, Hans looked to me for confirmation. I nodded.

Governor Davis looked distressed over the prospect. "So, Major. When you were on a mission to shoot down *our* young bomber pilots… you were singing *my* song?!"

Hans was a bit lost for words. "Yes, I suppose I was." Then he smiled and said, "I can't believe it. It's an honor enough to meet Louisiana's governor, but then to find out that you're one of my favorite American musicians as well! Louisiana is becoming a more fascinating place by the moment!"

After the reporters finished with us, we all posed for photographs before settling down for dinner. At dinner, Helen was so poised and confident; you'd think that she was born an aristocrat.

After dinner, we all drifted into separate groups. Helen was chatting with the other women while Hans and I talked with the mayor, the governor, and the colonels.

After a while, Colonel Clark looked around and noticed that Hans hadn't returned from a trip to the restroom. "Major Davis. Do you know where Major Kirpes disappeared to? He's supposed to stay within earshot of me. Would you be a pal and go find him for me?"

I stole a quick kiss from Helen as I passed the ladies in search of Hans. I saw him chatting in the next room with a group of men… my least favorite guests of the gathering.

I patted Han's shoulder and explained, "Your presence is requested in the other room."

One of the men he was talking with protested loudly, "What's the hurry there, Major? We're having a conversation here."

"Sorry," I apologized. "The colonel has us on a short leash."

The man said, "Oh well. Okay. It was good to meet you, Major," handing him a card. "Give me a call. We'd love to have you speak at one of our functions."

I led Hans away from the group as quickly as I could and warned him sharply, "You can't be seen talking to those guys!"

He was a little annoyed by my lack of diplomacy, "Why?! They were telling me about the nigger problem."

"Hans! You can't say that!"

"What?"

"You can't say the word 'nigger'! It's a hurtful and degrading word for Negro."

"I thought that's what Negroes were called here."

"Yeah, well… that's a word *they* use. I don't suppose you know anything about the Ku Klux Klan?"

Hans examined the business card as he answered, "They were explaining it to me."

"They hate anybody that isn't white and Christian— Jews and blacks alike. They think the Nazis had the right idea in killing the Jews, so to them… you're a hero."

Hans seemed a little embarrassed that he hadn't realized. He asked, "What are they doing here, in the governor's house?"

"You'll find members of the KKK in government office, police departments, and throughout our society. They're a pretty well-organized and scary group. They do enjoy freedom of speech and the right of assembly in this country." I sighed before continuing, "I just hope the press didn't see you talking to them. You've come to this country hoping to shed the stigma of being a Jew-hating Nazi. One picture of you chatting with these guys in the press would be all that's needed to convince the country that that's exactly what you are: an enemy of Jews *and* blacks."

Hans asked, "Why do they hate blacks?"

"I don't know. Some people can only feel good about themselves if they're belittling somebody else. You're the psychologist; you tell me why."

Hans said, "They did say that they thought that Negroes aren't smart enough to be free."

I laughed. "Isn't that *exactly* what you said about the French?!"

"Yes," Hans answered. "Only these guys aren't kidding."

I shook my head, "If you turn on the radio, half of the music you hear is performed by black musicians. That takes a great deal of creativity! Do you think any of those guys you were talking to could create anything original? The only thing they can create is hatred and anger. Trust me, Hans. You need to stay away from those guys. They're nothing but trouble."

"My only experience with American Negroes was with those Red Tail P-51 pilots. I flew against those fellows a few times, and I'll admit, there were some damned impressive pilots."

"Right, the Tuskegee Airmen! They never lost a bomber under their protection."

When we returned the governor's group, Hans announced, "I just had the experience of meeting your Louisiana Nazis; interesting fellows."

The governor was amused, "So you met the Klan boys. I bet they liked you!"

"Oh, they did," Hans answered. "I just wish I'd had a little warning about them."

The mayor said, "I bet you thought you left that behind you in Germany. They're mostly talk, but we still keep a pretty close eye on them."

Hans said, "I must admit that I'm surprised to see a group like that flourishing here. They were invited?"

The governor shook his head and answered, "One of our most influential senators is one of the Klan's leaders."

The mayor changed the subject by asking me, "Are you coming back to Baton Rouge when the war's over?"

"I wish I knew how long that would be. Right now I'm training in the 262, but when the P-80 is ready for action, I'll likely ship out to the South Pacific to see how it fares against the

Japanese Zeroes. I hear the Japs are developing jets of their own."

A congressman in the group said quietly, as if he were telling me something confidential, "I don't think I'd worry too much about that happening, son. Let's just say that uh, there's something in the works that will likely bring this war with the Japanese to a speedy end."

Colonel Windrum asked, "The B-29s?"

"They'll be involved, but that's all I'm going to say about it other than the fact that we expect the war to end before the year is done."

"Wow." That was some good news. "I guess I should start making plans for what to do with myself when the war ends."

Hans asked, "I hope they'll still need *my* services when the war ends."

Colonel Clark said, "I'm sure they will. The Russians ended up in possession of 80 percent of Germany's aircraft manufacturing facilities. So they also have captured ME-262s. The Russians may have the aircraft, but fortunately we have the elite ME-262 pilots of the JV44 squadron who know how to most effectively operate them in combat. '*It ain't the tools that make the carpenter.*' So to answer your question, Major Kirpes, your being a ME-262 JV44 Ace combined with your fluent English means you aren't going to have to worry about your job."

I asked, "I don't suppose I can share the good news about the war ending soon with my wife? We're both a little worried about my being shipped to the South Pacific."

Colonel Clark answered, "No... you can't repeat what you heard here, but what you can do is tell her you found out you won't be going to the South Pacific. Just don't say why." Then he looked to Hans, "I don't think I need to say that the same applies to you."

Hans lifted his glass. "You can count on my discretion."

I glanced over to Helen, anxious to share the good news with her. She was already looking my way, trying to get my attention. Subtly, she pointed to Hans and me and motioned for us to join her group.

I told my hosts, "I want to go over and see how my wife is holding up."

"By all means," the senator said, gesturing in her direction.

I grabbed Hans' arm, "Don't worry, Colonel. I'll be sure that Hans doesn't give away any national secrets to the ladies."

Governor Davis assured us, "You boys can relax about the Klansmen. I'll send somebody over to explain to them that their talking with you is... counterproductive to your mission here."

"Thank you, sir." That was a relief. We left the group and approached the ladies.

My mom proudly introduced us to them. I noticed an attractive young lady that I hadn't met before standing next to Helen.

Mom continued the introduction as she moved to one of the older women that I recognized. "You remember Mrs. McAdams from the garden club?"

The garden club, yes. That was a group of ladies that met at our house throughout my childhood to supposedly discuss gardening. What they really did was drink sherry and gossip. They always smelled heavily of perfume and brought cakes, cookies, and lots of hugs. It was part of the warm memories of my childhood.

She gave me a big hug and said with her overwhelming Southern drawl, "My goodness, Kenny, look at you. All grown up and a war hero! Baby, I see you're walking with a cane. Your mama said this man shot you?" She turned to Hans.

"Yes ma'am," I answered. "But that's only because I missed him! I'm sure my mom also told you that he chose to spare my life that day. He's a good man."

"Well, sweetheart. For you to say that about a man that shot you, I'll take your word for it. And yes, your mama told me that he's a good man too."

Hans politely bowed to my mom, "Thank you. That was kind of you."

"Well," Mrs. McAdams said, "that being the case, it should be safe to introduce you to my granddaughter, Theresa.

She's come to stay with us from Atlanta while she's going to LSU. She's studying to be a psychologist!"

I don't know about Hans, but I couldn't hide my surprise at her career choice. "You're kidding!" I said. I glanced at Hans, whose expression forbade me from sharing his secret.

She was instantly offended. "Oh? You think it's outrageous to think that a woman can be a psychologist?!"

I couldn't give away Hans' secret, so I had to think fast for a diplomatic response, "No, not at all. I think it's wonderful that you made that choice. I'm impressed! A lot of women place limits on their career choices because of their gender. My wife, Helen, is the office manager of the family engineering firm. I'd never be fool enough to think that she couldn't do something because she's a woman."

She eyed me suspiciously and replied, "I'll accept that." But the tone of her voice made it clear that, although she accepted my answer, she sensed that it wasn't entirely honest.

Theresa appeared to be a contradiction. Though she was very pretty and dressed like a Southern debutante, she was confident and well-spoken with hardly a trace of a Southern drawl. Hans seemed intrigued.

He offered her the formal German gesture of clicking his heels before bowing to take her hand. "It is truly my pleasure."

"It's refreshing to see that not *all* gentlemen are from the South, Major Kirpes. I'm pleased to meet you as well."

"Hans will do. I'm a civilian now."

"They called my great-grandfather 'Colonel' until the day he died. The Civil War's been over for 80 years."

"Then you can call me whatever you are comfortable with. I am fascinated with your career choice. I'd love to discuss it further, Theresa."

"It would be my pleasure," she answered.

They walked over to the fireplace and sat together. Mrs. McAdams seemed to approve. I led Helen away from the earshot of others.

"You know why I was so surprised to hear that Theresa was studying psychology?"

"You did seem overly surprised by it. Why?"

I answered, "Hans told me something that he asked me to keep in the strictest of confidence. Hopefully, you're better at keeping a secret than I am. Hans majored in psychology in Germany."

"Oh my God," Helen shouted as she grasped her face. We both looked over to see if Hans had seen her reaction. He was too engaged in conversation with Theresa to have noticed.

"Why on Earth doesn't he want people to know that?" Helen asked.

"He says it's because... first, before he could earn his degree, the Nazis decided that crazy people should be gassed rather than fixed, so he gave it up to become a pilot. Secondly, he says it bothers him that everybody that hears about his education wants him to analyze them. Nobody wants to hear the truth, so he has to lie to them. He says *I'm* okay though."

"Yeah… right, of course he does," Helen laughed. "Do you think he'll tell Theresa about it?"

"That's his choice. Besides, if I know Hans, when she asks him where he came by his knowledge of psychology, he'll probably tell her that they teach that stuff in elementary school in Germany."

We wandered back to the group of women that Mom was talking with.

Mom commented, "It looks like you've lost Major Kirpes."

I pointed towards the fireplace, "We found him a sitter."

Mrs. McAdams said, "Oh. Maybe I should have warned him. Theresa is a very opinionated and outspoken girl. Young ladies weren't like that in my day."

"I'm not too worried about Hans, ma'am. I can tell you from experience… he'll be fine," I replied.

The band played "Moonlight Serenade," the song that Helen and I had first danced to.

I led Helen over to Hans and Theresa and said, "Hey buddy. The colonel gave me strict instructions not to let you out of my sight… and I want to dance with my wife. Think you two would want to join us on the dance floor?"

"Thank you," Theresa said. "I don't think Hans would have asked me otherwise."

For a few minutes, I was able to forget about everyone else's business to enjoy dancing with my wife in the governor's ballroom.

We spent the rest of the night chatting and rubbing elbows with the other guests, except for the Klansman. Colonel Clark seemed to be happy with the way Hans handled the press and politicians that night. When the night came to an end, Hans escorted Theresa and her grandmother to their waiting car. He kissed her hand and wished her goodnight.

As they drove off, Hans sighed and turned to us, "That has got to be the most disagreeable, stubborn woman I've ever met."

I asked, "Did you two talk about psychology?"

"We did. Every opinion I expressed, unless I was quoting Freud, was ridiculous and utter nonsense."

"Maybe German psychology is different than ours?" Helen asked.

"Sigmund Freud was German... or Austrian, anyway!" Hans replied. Then he gave me a suspicious look. "I take it you've shared my little secret with Helen?"

"Sorry. I don't keep secrets from Helen. So, are you going to see Theresa again?"

"Oh, most definitely," he answered.

"But you said she was stubborn and disagreeable?" Helen asked.

He answered, "I don't know what to think about her. It seems that she's just challenging me… and I can't resist a good challenge."

I joked, "Maybe you can't figure her out because she's crazy. I think most people that grow up seeing a psychologist want to be one when they grow up, don't they?"

Damn. I meant it as a joke, but there was a painfully long and awkward silence after my comment, leaving me to suspect that maybe that had been the case with Hans. After all, in his youth, he'd had to deal with some pretty difficult issues. I was afraid that I might have really put my foot in my mouth!

Helen asked, "So Hans, I'm curious as to how Theresa rated on your learner/thinker scale?"

He didn't hesitate in answering, "She's scholarly… most definitely! I don't think she respects anyone's opinion if it differs from what she's learned in her textbooks. The problem with that is that no two students interpret a lesson the same way."

"And I take it that you two have different concepts about psychology?" I asked.

"Drastically, and she's so confident that her perspective is right that it makes me doubt mine. I'm looking forward to figuring that out," Hans commented.

I suggested, "I guess we'll have to plan another visit soon then, huh?"

"Or…" Helen said, "I can see if she'd want to make a weekend trip to Dayton with me."

"That's a great idea." I gave Helen a hug. "Let's go find Mom so we can get out of here."

That was the first time I'd seen Hans humble. I always had the impression that he was bigger than life and never doubted that he was entitled to his overwhelming self-confidence. He seemed to have always had his choice of women, so what made Theresa different? Then I remembered how I was around Helen before we got together. Could Hans have finally met a lady that had that effect on him? That was an encouraging thought.

We rounded up Mom and said our goodbyes to our hosts, then waited for the parking attendant to bring the car around. As soon as we had our privacy in the car, I was able to share my good news of the night.

"I heard something tonight that made me awfully happy."

"What's that?" Helen asked.

"I was pretty much guaranteed that I won't be shipping out to the South Pacific."

Mom said, "That's wonderful, honey. So, have you decided if you're going to stay in the service or come home?"

"I'm still awfully excited about being one of the first pilots to fly the P-80. The United States will maintain a military presence in both Germany and Japan after the war ends. I'd love to fly our jet fighters in peacetime. Maybe not for a career, but at least until my enlistment is up."

I glanced back at Hans for his opinion on the issue. He was staring out the window, most likely thinking about Theresa.

Helen commented, "I'd imagine that the war will be ending soon with Japan since we're bombing Tokyo. The end came pretty quick with Germany after we started bombing Berlin."

The mention of Berlin drew Hans back into the conversation. "You know, Kenny, I kind of got the feeling that the senator was bragging in a way, to let us know that he knew something that we didn't."

"I think you're right... now that you mention it. I guess we'll find out what his secret is soon enough. At any rate, it looks like I'm not going to get the chance to take my revenge on the Japanese for Dad."

"Thank God for that," Mom said. "No more fighting. Sweetheart, do you think there's a chance that we could buy back the family's interest in the firm?"

"That's a thought. After being owners though, I don't know if the crew would want to go back to being employees, even if they haven't done a good job of managing the firm."

Helen replied, "They're still lost without your dad. All that business that was generated with our last publicity was just temporary. The new accounts stayed with us just long enough to realize that those guys can only manage simple projects. Now they are complaining that they can't afford to keep Mom and me on the payroll."

I didn't like hearing that, even if it didn't come as a surprise. "That's not good. You keep the books, Helen. *Can* they afford to keep the family on the payroll?"

"It's tight, and I don't think they can for much longer," she answered. "I've given some thought to giving up my position at the firm. Maybe I could train one of their wives to manage the books, but if I did that, I wouldn't be there to cut your mom's check every month. If it gets any tighter for them, I don't think we could count on them to do that."

We continued the conversation as we arrived home. I said, "We can't force them to pay out money they're not capable of making. I'll have to give this some thought."

Hans piped up. "I have a thought. The hell with them! Open a storage facility here like mine back in Munich. Mine pays my bills and then some, and continues to do so while I'm on the other side of the world."

"Storage facility?" Mom asked.

I answered, "Hans has a couple of buildings in Munich that are divided into little storage units, each about half the size of a garage. They're always rented out. I don't know, Hans. Your storage units are in a country where hundreds of thousands of people's homes were destroyed... people who need to store their stuff. I can't imagine they'd do well here."

Hans argued, "It will work, and when it does, it will take care of you for the rest of your lives. Trust me! In fact… I'll guarantee their success. If they don't show a profit in the first six months, I'll buy them from you for what you invested into them."

Mom replied, "That's an awfully generous offer, Hans."

"I'm serious. I'm that confident in it," Hans proclaimed.

"Hans may be right about this, Mom. Maybe it would be better to give it a try *before* we have to rely on it."

"Well, son. If you think it's wise, we can start looking for a location for it. Do you think it would do better in town or out of town a ways?" she asked.

Hans answered, "I would suggest closer to town, where it's convenient for people to access it when they need to."

Helen commented, "It's not that easy to find vacant land close to town. Maybe we could find an existing warehouse that we can divide into smaller units."

I was impressed with that thought. "That might be a lot quicker and maybe even be cheaper than *building* a facility… and easier to get permits for."

It was decided. The Davis family would speculate on personal storage units.

I wanted to turn in early that night to have a little time alone with Helen since we had to leave the next morning.

It was hot and humid in Baton Rouge that last week of June in 1945. Heat and humidity make it tough for any aircraft to take off. Since the Me-262 required more runway than our planes, we took off at dawn while the morning air was still cool. Soon we were at altitude where the air was clear and cold again.

Hans' voice crackled over the radio, "Kenny. Does your mom like me?"

I didn't hesitate in answering, "Well, of course she does. She adopted you, didn't she?"

"No, I mean, does she…. *like* me?"

I was both shocked and amused at the sincerity of his question, "You mean, as in romantically?"

"She's always hugging me, squeezing my hand and calling me sweetheart and darling. I'm not sure what to think about it."

I had a good laugh before keying up my microphone to answer, "Hans, that's just the South. Once you're family, that's just the way it is!"

Hans was quiet for a moment before his reply, "I'm not too experienced at what it's like to *have* family. It means a lot to me that you've included me in yours."

CHAPTER 10: Dayton

Once I was back at Wright Field, I continued to log hours in the 262. I loved everything about that aircraft except for how long it took to lose speed, both in flight and upon landing. I was told that the Lockheed P-80 solved that problem with the addition of air brakes. That would have given the F-80 an important advantage if it had flown against the ME-262.

Those of us that were lucky enough to be chosen to train in the ME-262s would be the first to train in the P-80s. We would be the *only* pilots trained for the P-80s at Wright Field though. Future P-80 students would be trained down at Williams Field near Phoenix. Once Hans and his colleagues mapped out the combat training program, they would also be shipped to Williams Field. So when I completed my training at Wright Field, I'd be transferred down there for combat training.

The prospect of flying the P-80 was a little scary. A number of test pilots had died while trying to master them, but then around 200 young pilots had died while learning to fly the ME-262 when it was introduced in Germany. I could only hope that they worked most of the bugs out of the P-80s before we got them.

By the end of July in 1945, the first P-80s showed up at Wright Field. Before I could fly one, I had to go through ground school training first, like I did with the 262. The most amazing thing I learned in my schooling on jet engines was how much simpler they were than the piston engines. The basic engine in my P-51 had twelve cylinders. Each had a piston, connecting rod, two valves, two push rods, and two rocker arms. That's eight moving parts per cylinder. That times twelve cylinders equals 96 moving parts. Add the crankshaft and camshaft, and that brings the total moving parts in the P-51's basic engine to 98. The radial flow jet engine in the P-80 had one moving part: a shaft with a compressor blade on one end and a turbine blade on the other.

Like with the 262, there were no P-80 two-passenger trainers at that time. So it was important to be prepared for that first flight alone.

The information passed on to us from the P-80 test pilots was priceless. The transition from the 262 was an easy one since the P-80 only had one engine to manage rather than two.

Time passed quickly over the next couple of weeks as we logged hours in the new jets. Helen and Theresa were scheduled to arrive in Dayton on August 3rd for the weekend.

Hans was a little nervous about Theresa's arrival. It was a ten-mile drive to Dayton Municipal Airport from Wright Field.

The passengers de-planed, and as I expected, it was easy to spot Helen by her smile. Theresa was dolled up, looking mighty impressive. She wasn't smiling though. I'd say that she looked apprehensive.

I grabbed a hold of Helen. Hans took Theresa's hand and politely said, "It's nice to see you again."

They both seemed a little uncomfortable, but I could tell that Hans was glad she made it. We gathered the bags and headed for a restaurant in Dayton.

We hadn't gotten very far when Theresa asked, "I'd like to know where I'll be sleeping tonight."

Hans replied without missing a beat, "In a bed, I would suppose."

Annoyed, she quipped, "In whose bed?"

"Well," Hans answered, "since I arranged for a room for you at the Field's transit quarters, I would imagine that the bed belongs to the United States government."

She wasted no time in coming to the point. "And were you planning to sleep in that bed as well?" she asked.

"Is that in invitation?" Hans asked. "We hardly know each other."

I could see that he was getting into trouble, fast. I guess he couldn't stop himself from antagonizing her.

She got angry and defensive and loudly protested, "I was simply asking what you expect of me."

Hans chuckled and answered, "Theresa. I can say that I honestly have *no idea* of what to expect from you. That's the very thing that intrigues me about you. As far as your virtue is concerned, I can assure you that it's as safe as you'd like it to be."

I interjected, "I'll vouch for him on that, Theresa. But as to whether he's going to aggravate you, I make no guarantees."

Hans said, "I'm hoping that we'll be able to enjoy a little mutual aggravation on this visit."

Theresa seemed to be at least slightly amused by his sense of humor and relaxed a bit.

"You can't blame me for being apprehensive about your intentions. A good-looking, world-famous Ace invites a lady for a weekend away from home..."

Hans replied, "You think I'm good-looking?"

She continued, "Yeah... well. Somehow I don't think you doubt yourself in that regard."

There was an awkward, rather uncomfortable silence.

Helen broke it. "Have you boys decided where we're eating? How about German cuisine?"

Hans answered, "I just happen to know of the perfect place."

It hadn't taken Hans long to find the popular hangout for the Germans who were imported to Wright Field. When we were seated, I ordered drinks for the group, thinking that a stiff drink might ease the tension between Hans and Theresa. Helen settled for an iced tea.

I asked Helen, "Any luck in finding a place for a storage facility?"

"Yes," she answered. "I found a ten thousand square foot building really close to LSU. We thought that, with the students and faculty coming and going, it might be a good location."

I nodded in agreement and looked at Hans for his thoughts on it.

He answered, "That sounds good to me."

Helen went on to say, "I'm putting the figures together now on what it would cost to convert it into two hundred square foot units. I just happen to know a few engineers that are helping me with the layout."

I smiled proudly, "What a smart gal I married. You know, if this new business works, and we're not relying on the firm anymore, we can hire somebody to run it so you can quit and come up here!"

She happily agreed, "I've been thinking the same thing! That way, all *three* of us can be together."

I was a little confused that she would include Hans. "You, me, and Hans?" I asked.

"No," she answered. "If I included Hans… that would make *four* of us."

I was still confused, "Are you saying that Mom wants to come up too?"

"No," she replied teasingly.

I could see that both Hans and Theresa were realizing something that I wasn't.

"Oh… my God!" I realized what she was saying. "You're saying you're…"

Helen nodded excitedly and took my hand to place on her belly.

I was so overwhelmed that I couldn't think of what to say. I took her hand and said, "Thank you, sweetheart!"

I don't think she expected to be thanked. She replied, "Anytime!"

"A baby," I said in disbelief. "Yes, honey. We have to get you up here as soon as possible, or I have to relocate to Baton Rouge somehow."

Hans asked, "You're thinking about requesting a transfer to Harding Field?"

I said, "Hans. I don't care if I get transferred down there to sweep floors. I need to be with my family."

I was too focused on Helen to notice Hans brooding. I realized later that his feelings were likely hurt over my not being concerned over whether he and I were separated. After all, we *had* adopted him.

I said, "I feel like such an idiot that I was the only one at the table that didn't know what you were saying. Of course, if *I* were a psychologist, I'd probably have picked up on it sooner."

Though I hadn't directly said that Hans was a psychologist, I implied it. The instant it was said, Helen and I both looked over to Hans and Theresa. She probably wouldn't have picked up on it if it weren't for our reaction.

Theresa looked around at the three of us, trying to figure out what we were concerned about.

"What?" she asked. "I don't understand."

Hans sighed, "I uh... I don't share this with many people, but my major at the university in Munich was... psychology."

Theresa's reaction to the news wasn't good. She looked angry and confused. I was really hoping that Hans would manage to smooth things over with a little of his diplomacy.

He continued, "I didn't graduate. I was a year shy of earning my degree and I became a pilot instead. I'd rather not tell people that I was *almost* a psychologist."

"You all knew this and didn't tell me. You let me go on, professing my knowledge about psychology, knowing that Hans was... I'm so humiliated!"

I have to admit that I took a little pleasure in seeing her humbled after belittling Hans' opinions about psychology at their first meeting.

Theresa pulled away slightly when Hans placed his hand on her shoulder, "Please don't blame them. I didn't earn my degree, so I don't really like to talk about it. I asked Kenny to keep it private before you and I met." He glanced up at me as he continued, "But it seems that Kenny hasn't been doing a very good job, keeping it a secret."

"You should have told me," she said meekly.

"And I would have, but we're still strangers, Theresa. You're here so we can overcome that. And I have to say that I really enjoyed your perspectives on psychology. The fact that we understand what we've learned differently will make for some interesting debates, don't you think?"

Theresa conceded, "I suppose." Then she sat up straight and said with a cheerier disposition, "We're here tonight, celebrating Kenny and Helen's baby!" She turned to Hans and shook her finger, "So, Mister... I'll talk to you about this another time!"

A baby! What fantastic news. I didn't quite know what I was in for, but I knew that my life would be changing forever. I was just grateful that I was done flying combat missions in the war.

Hans and Theresa seemed to be hitting it off. Maybe that little bump in their getting acquainted helped them to move past their inhibitions. I was glad that they were keeping each other occupied so Helen and I could turn our attention more towards each other.

At the end of the evening, Hans dropped us off at the transit quarters. When Hans bid Theresa goodnight, they shared a parting kiss that appeared to be at least a bit more than just a friendly kiss.

It was a relief to get back to our room. At last I had Helen to myself... for the first time as the mother of my forthcoming child. I was a little nervous over how to touch her, but she assured me that I wasn't going to break anything. Realizing that Helen was creating a new life from the two of us made her seem much more of a woman... so much more desirable.

The sun was already out and warming up the day when we awoke. Helen and I hurried to get ready, knowing that Hans would be there soon to pick us up.

After knocking, we had to wait a while for Theresa to answer her door in the adjoining room. When she came to the door wearing nothing but a blanket, I figured that she forgot we were supposed to meet Hans.

I said, "You'd better hurry and get ready. We don't want to keep Hans waiting."

We heard Hans' voice from beyond the door, "Don't worry, my friend. You're not keeping me waiting."

Theresa grinned and sheepishly opened the door to reveal Hans sitting up in bed, enjoying a cigarette.

"I thought you went back to the barracks!" I said.

"I did," Hans answered. "But it was lonesome there."

"It's good to see you two getting along better. We'll be back in our room when you're ready. And, uh... don't hurry."

I shook my head as we headed back for the room. "I really didn't see that coming. I figured they could only tolerate each other at best."

Helen and I made the most of our little extra time alone together.

It was nearly noon before we took the ladies out to the flight line to see our planes. I took a picture of Helen posed by the nose of my jet in the same sexy position of her image painted on the nose of my P-51. All that was missing was a pink dress.

Since everyone's attention was more inclined towards romance that weekend, I suggested that we drive north 140 miles to Toledo where we stayed overnight in a hotel on the shore of Lake Erie. It was nice to share that little vacation with Hans and Theresa.

We had to wake pretty early Monday morning in order to get the girls to the airport in order to be at work on time. We had a lot to talk about, so we weren't listening to the car's radio.

After we dropped the ladies off and were on our way back to Wright Field, I flipped the car's radio on and heard the news. We had dropped an atomic bomb on Hiroshima. The reports were saying that it completely destroyed most of the city. I'd heard talk of the atomic bomb, but it was mostly top secret. What horrible news. An entire city of people wiped out with no warning. I guess that was the ultimate payback for their surprise attacks, but somehow the news brought me no satisfaction or comfort.

Hans commented, "That must have been what that senator was talking about, the one who told you the war with Japan would end soon."

The reports also said that after dropping the bomb, we gave the Japanese an ultimatum to surrender, or face more of their cities being annihilated. I couldn't imagine their refusing to submit to that ultimatum.

Hans and I were scheduled to fly that day, so we did, but it was difficult to focus on it. Things were bound to change in our lives. The next couple of days passed slowly as we waited to hear Japan's response to the ultimatum... but none came.

On Wednesday, August 9th, the news was announced that we followed through with our promise and dropped a second atomic bomb on the city of Nagasaki, which met with the same destruction as Hiroshima before it.

I was relieved to hear that the second bomb brought forth an informal concession from the Japanese Empire. On the 15th, Emperor Hirohito formally announced over the radio in Japan their surrender. It was over. The Second World War had come to an end.

Not long after that, Hans was transferred to Williams Field while I remained behind to finish my P-80 training at Wright Field. I missed him when he left.

The good news was that it looked like the P-80 program would continue as planned, regardless of the war's end. I'd be able to enjoy flying our new jet fighter without having to fly it into battle.

CHAPTER 11: War's End

Once I completed my basic P-80 training at Wright, my orders came to relocate to Williams Field, which was located in Mesa, Arizona—just outside of Phoenix.

That was my first experience with the desert. What a contrast it was from Baton Rouge, or anywhere else I'd been for that matter.

Hans gave me a grand welcome when I arrived at the airfield. In the short time he'd been there, he'd already managed to establish himself as a celebrity. After getting settled in, I began my combat training with Hans as my instructor. That was a little strange. I was rather confident that he couldn't teach me anything I didn't already know, since I'd downed him in combat. He surprised me though. Not only did he teach me a few new things, but I also came to realize that he was a damned good instructor. With his resounding air of confidence, you couldn't help but have faith in his instruction.

His instruction included actual dog fighting practice. Flying against Hans in simulated combat was something that we'd both been looking forward to, but flying against him in an in an aircraft that I wasn't familiar with put me at a disadvantage.

When I wasn't training with Hans, other instructors were training me in more advanced aspects of flying the F-80.

One thing I'll always remember was how horribly lonely my solo night flights were. In practicing night navigation, I couldn't have any help, and no companionship. I was completely alone in the vastness of the night sky above the desert. There was nothing below but darkness. All there was to see was the moonlight glistening on the plane's polished aluminum wings and the dull red glow of the gauges in front of me. Once in a while, a cluster of lights from a small town would pass under me in the darkness. My feeling of solitude on those flights was no doubt amplified by how much I missed Helen. It was a tease, being back in the States but still being separated from her.

Whenever I hear the lonely howl of a single jet somewhere up in the night sky, I remember those days and still feel a pang of loneliness.

Williams Field was almost exactly twice as far from Baton Rouge as Baton Rouge was from Dayton. Hans and I still made it home almost every weekend to see Helen and Theresa. I loved being home in the fall. There was a chill in the air. I missed how people burned the oak leaves that they raked from their yards. Nothing else smells like that. That wonderful aroma signified that the holidays were nearing.

It was looking like the storage facility would be ready by the end of the year. Unlike Hans, who paid a law firm to oversee his units, we chose to hire a full-time on-site manager.

As much as I missed being home, I loved flying the new jet aircraft. By my standards, it was about the most fantastic job anybody could have.

When the time came for the grand opening of Davis Storage, I played on my celebrity status. I met with the reporter from the newspaper who'd written the story about Hans and me. He liked the aspect of the two of us working together to open a new business in Baton Rouge, so he wrote a great story about it. It was better than any advertising. When the story came out, the phone rang off the hook and the units filled almost overnight.

Hans had been right about there being a need for storage in the United States too. He was also right about it providing an income for the family that would relieve us of our dependence on the firm. That really took a load off of my shoulders. It also meant that, soon, Helen to quit the firm and join me.

Once my training at Williams Field was completed, I would be transferring to a permanent assignment at Muroc Army Air Field in California where a flight of forty-five new P-80s had just been delivered. Muroc was in the Mojave Desert, not too far from Los Angeles. It was still in the desert, though, and I wasn't too crazy about the desert. The thing I was excited about in my transfer to Muroc was that Helen could join me there.

When the workday was over at Williams Field, there wasn't a lot to do. Hans and I would pass the time with the other pilots, playing cards. They loved it when Hans would spin yarns about flying for the Luftwaffe.

He surprised me one night when he said, "I've been thinking about when you proposed to Helen on Christmas... that was a pretty good idea."

"What brings that to mind? Are you thinking about popping the question to Theresa?!"

He nodded.

I exclaimed, "That's a surprise! Well, Christmas worked out great for me. Everybody will be there."

He answered, "I'm not sure about it yet, but I see how happy you and Helen are. You don't even look at other women. You're wholly content with your wife and you're so thrilled about the baby that's coming. I want that."

"Yeah, but Hans, you've only known Theresa for a few months. I knew Helen since I was seven."

"Really?!" Hans laughed at me. "You didn't even *talk* to her until a year before you married her. Did you forget you told me that?"

I laughed. "Okay, you have a point. But from the time we *started* dating, we spent a *lot* of time together. She came to work at our firm. Our families became friends. It was after six months of working and playing together that I asked her to marry me. You've only known Theresa a few months, and in that time, you've only spent a dozen weekends together. You haven't even met her parents."

"Maybe I *am* getting ahead of myself. It's just that something's changed in me. Before, nothing was ever good enough. I always wanted or needed more than I had in life, whether it was air victories, women, my home, or my car... I was never satisfied. I see, from watching your family, that you are all happy in life. You're happy because you cherish what you have instead of wasting time longing for something better, something you might never find. I know that if I'm going to be happy in life, I have to appreciate what I have. And Theresa is a great lady. Considering that she's the first woman I've even considered marriage with, you can't blame me for being a little impatient."

"My dad tried to convince me that I was rushing things with Helen. My argument to him was that if I waited, I might lose the gal I was meant to be with. So, I suppose you just need to do what your heart tells you to do. I hope it works out."

He smiled and said, "Imagine, if things go well, our kids can grow up together."

It seemed really out of character for Hans, but it was kind of nice hearing him entertain not only the notion of having a wife, but a family.

Once again, Hans and I headed to Baton Rouge for the Christmas holidays of 1945.

That Christmas was extraordinary. Because the war was over, it seemed that everyone was in the spirit. It was apparent in the crowds of holiday shoppers that filled the stores downtown.

The smells coming from our kitchen were magnificent with the women cooking our favorite holiday dishes. Christmas music filled the house, the fireplace crackled, and the eggnog was spiked and spiced to perfection.

Mom went to the trouble to have Mary prepare separate rooms for Hans and Theresa, having a pretty good idea that one would be vacant.

Hans was a lot more generous than we thought he should have been that year. He bought me a Rolex watch and mink stoles for my mom, Helen, and Theresa. I figured that if spoiling us made him happy and he could afford to do it, then who were we to refuse it? We certainly had a houseful with my mom, Helen's parents, Helen and me, Hans, Theresa, and her grandmother.

As we finished dinner, Hans stood and announced, "I'd like to say something to all of you tonight."

We all quieted down to listen.

"This has been the *best* Christmas of my life... for a number of reasons. First, I'd like offer Kenny a heartfelt thanks for going to bat for me in the Army Air Force's jet combat instruction division. If he hadn't, I would be with my Luftwaffe colleagues this Christmas... as a prisoner of war."

A short round of applause followed his statement before he continued, "And secondly, I don't know if you all know of my childhood. My parents died when I was young. I was raised in boarding schools and my Christmases consisted of a card sent from my aunt and uncle that contained money to buy myself a gift.

"You folks..." He choked a bit before going on, "You folks have shown me what I was missing. And it's priceless." Mom reached up and squeezed his arm. "My only regret is that I wasn't able to meet Mr. Davis. Judging by his family, he must have been a truly wonderful man.

"I've never known love. Perhaps the truly good women I've encountered in my life sensed that, and had the good sense to avoid me... except for one. I think she sees me as somebody she can fix. I think she can!"

I glanced over at Theresa. Her expression made obvious her concern over where Hans was going with the conversation.

He looked at Theresa, "So, the third thing I'd like to say tonight is... it might be too soon to consider a permanent relationship for Theresa and me, but I'd like to let her know that I'm ready to stop looking for anyone else. I'm ready to focus on the *prospect* of a permanent relationship for *us* in the future."

Theresa's eyes got wide as he reached into his pocket to produce a ring case. Hans turned his full attention to Theresa before continuing, "Let's call this a *promise* ring. I still have a home and a business in Germany, and Theresa, you have three years left of school here and your home is in Atlanta. On top of that, I'm working in Arizona now. I appreciate that we have a lot of challenges to overcome, but I hope you are as willing as I am to work towards a future together."

Theresa stood and hugged him, then extended her ring finger to him. She gazed at the ring admiringly after he slid it onto her finger then proudly held it up for the room to see. Damn! The diamond in Helen's wedding ring was dwarfed by the stone in that promise ring. It left little doubt that Hans was serious about his promise!

Theresa hugged him and said, "This is perfect, Hans. I thought you were going to propose, and I didn't know what I would have said. Thank you for not rushing things. You're a pretty smart guy!"

He replied smugly, "Oh... you would've said yes if I'd proposed!"

She smiled and replied, "In your dreams!"

We celebrated the arrival of 1946, confident that it was going to be a year that would bring us all a bounty of blessings. The last year hadn't ended badly. The war was over, Helen and I were having a new baby, we had established a new business to provide for the family, and Hans and Theresa's future together looked promising.

When we returned to Williams Field, my orders to ship out to the fighter group at Muroc in California were waiting. I had a week to report for duty there, so I hurried to be ready for the move. As I was packing, there was a knock at my door. I opened the door to see a familiar face, a face that I hadn't seen since I was in Dayton: Colonel Sanderson of Operation Paperclip.

I welcomed him in, "Wow. What a pleasant surprise. What brings you to Williams?"

"You," he answered.

"Me?" I asked. "What did I do now?"

"I'd like to borrow you. I heard you're being transferred to Muroc to fly P-80s. I'm working in White Sands, New Mexico now. You might have heard that we're working with Von Braun on the research and development of V-1s and V-2s there. We're also working with the German scientists in furthering the development of our own missiles."

He certainly had my attention, "That sounds fascinating!"

"It is, Major. I'll confide in you: our goal is to modify the V-2 rockets to carry atomic bombs to other countries, so we'll no longer need to deliver them by aircraft."

"I've heard of that. What's this got to do with me?" I asked.

"You're the probably the person who least appreciates your own deductive abilities. When we were examining captured aircraft in Germany, we at Operation Paperclip valued your observations. You'd rattle off little insights about a project that we were discussing, figuring you were just making conversation. A number of those insights turned out to be pretty valuable."

"Thank you. No, I didn't realize that I had much value to the project. I certainly wasn't the most experienced or educated engineer observing those projects."

"Well, Major Davis. There are... educated people, and there are insightful people. You're one of those people that can figure things out on the fly."

I laughed, "Hans Kirpes has quite a philosophy about innovative people making the best pilots. Maybe that's where the expression, *on the fly*, came from"

"My situation in White Sands is: in our agreement with the German scientists, they are required to teach representatives from our universities, industries, and military what they know and what they're learning in their research. From what they tell me, Walter Thiel, the V-2 rocket engine designer, was killed in a bombing raid at Peenemünde, and now, they're trying to get back to where they were with the project before they lost him. We have engineers from the universities and industries working with Von Braun, but like when we called on you in Germany, we don't have a qualified representative from the military in the mix. I'd like you to be our representative."

"I'm overwhelmed and flattered... but my wife and I are having a baby soon. I'm looking forward to getting settled into a home and a long-term assignment at Muroc Field."

Colonel Sanderson replied, "Your permanent duty assignment will still be at Muroc flying P-80s, but you'll be on loan to Fort Bliss. You'll be living and working there for the remainder of your enlistment, or longer if you decide to reenlist. It's near El Paso, just south of White Sands. You won't be living at Muroc. The only reason you'll need to go there is to log the hours required to keep your rating current in the P-80."

"You're asking me if I want to work with Von Braun and his team? How could I say no to that?!"

Colonel Sanderson said, "I figured you'd probably jump at the opportunity! Besides, you'd be in Texas, right next to Louisiana."

"Thank you for considering me for this assignment. It'll be an honor to work with those guys. When do I meet them?"

"We can go down tomorrow, and I'll introduce you to Major Hamill who runs the operation. Then you can find housing for you, your wife, and that new baby. Congratulations, by the way."

"Thank you, sir."

"Why don't you round up that troublemaker, Hans Kirpes, and we'll have dinner tonight? It'll be good to see him again."

I laughed, "He'll be envious over my new assignment!"

Over dinner that night, Hans expressed his appreciation to Colonel Sanderson, "Sir. When I asked you to consider releasing me to help with your combat training program, I thought I'd be avoiding a few months of captivity in prison… a year at most. But the men in my unit, JA-44, are still in prison. Nobody can say *when* they'll be released! So this assignment has turned out to be a lot more of a blessing than I had hoped for. I want to thank you again."

"You've proven worthy of the opportunity," the colonel said. "You have not only been a valuable asset in our training program, but from what I hear from Colonel Clark, you've done a nice job in our Public Relations program."

Sanderson thought for a minute before continuing. "Hans. Can you change your schedule for tomorrow and come with us to Fort Bliss?"

The suggestion floored the both of us. Hans answered, "I'd love to!"

The colonel said, "I know that Von Braun and his team are going to resent us planting one of our Army Engineers in their group. I'm sure they've seen the stories about you two becoming friends. Your showing up together might encourage them to be a little more accepting of Major Davis."

Hans quickly answered, "You don't have to ask twice. If I was given the choice of meeting one man on Earth, it would be Von Braun."

I woke early the next morning, brimming with excitement over what the day would bring. It was a typical Arizona morning. The air was crisp, refreshed by the cool desert night. The inviting smell of breakfast drifted over from the mess hall. After breakfast, we boarded a DC-3 and lifted skyward towards Fort Bliss.

As soon as we arrived, Colonel Sanderson took us to meet Major Hamill.

He was one of the few people I've met in my life that I just didn't like the instant we met. He appeared to be younger than me and didn't exude an air of confidence at all. He struck me as timid, the kind of guy who would turn mean if he wasn't getting the respect he felt he was entitled to. This was the man that they chose to oversee Von Braun and his projects?

We saluted and he motioned for us to be seated. He said dryly, on the border of being disrespectful, "Colonel Sanderson feels that I need help in overseeing Operation Paperclip's management of the V-2 rocket program. I've seen your qualifications, Major Davis. You have an impressive flying record, but as far as engineering goes, you have a B.S. degree in engineering with no practical experience?"

Oh, did he rub me the wrong way! It wasn't so much what he said, but how he said it. I was so tempted to turn to the colonel and ask him if I had to work with that jerk. The colonel had briefed me on Hamill's background. Hamill was an undergraduate in engineering himself, with less engineering experience than I had from working at the firm. I would have enjoyed pointing that out, but I knew that it would only challenge Hamill to be harder to get along with.

Colonel Sanderson came to my defense. "Major Davis' *record* isn't the reason he's here. His education and experience aren't his *greatest* assets."

Hamill flipped through my file, looking for an asset that he might have missed.

"He is unusually innovative and has a unique ability to figure things out," Colonel Sanderson said.

It was obvious, by his silent dismissal of the colonel's comment, that Hamill didn't appreciate the value of common sense. Hans shook his head and chuckled, making it apparent that he thought the man was an idiot. Hans' reaction was apparent to me anyway, but Hamill didn't seem to notice.

Next, Hamill made it obvious that he noticed my cane. He didn't comment on it, but his condescending expression implied that he saw me as being physically inferior as well. I have to admit that the thought of smacking him over the head with it brought me a small measure of satisfaction.

Hamill went on to say, "I need to warn you, Major Davis, before you start working with these guys. They're a bunch of whiny babies. They were spoiled rotten in Peenemünde, given anything they asked for. That's because the Nazis counted on this bunch to win the war for them... which they obviously failed at. Here, we have a sensible budget to work with, and it's my job to tell them what's realistic. So, I am telling you upfront that they'll be pressuring you to persuade me to raise their budget and if you're not successful, you're not going to be very popular with them."

I looked at Colonel Sanderson for his response to Hamill's statement.

He nodded somberly and said, "It's true. We aren't placing the same priority on their rocket development program as the Nazis did. It's not wartime, so this research doesn't have the same urgency. We do have a more limited budget to work with."

I nodded, appreciating Colonel Sanderson's insight. "I'll keep that in mind, sir."

Next we walked to a building where the team designed their projects. As we walked in, Hans and I were both thrilled to see Wernher Von Braun at a chalkboard, chatting with his associates. He paused, annoyed that we had interrupted them. He wasn't at all what I had expected to see. He was a young man who looked more like a movie star than a scientist. I noticed that his arm was in a cast.

Colonel Sanderson introduced us.

Wernher quipped, "Yes, we know who you are. You're our new supervisor—a pilot with a degree in engineering." He stepped back and motioned toward the blackboard, "Do you have any idea what we're discussing here?"

The pressure of being put on the spot by such an extraordinary man made my mind go blank. It was obvious that I was struggling for words. I looked at the board and shook my head. "To be honest, I would need time to study this to tell you what it means, but at a glance, my impression is that you're calculating thrust and trajectory."

Von Braun smiled, impressed. "Not bad!" He turned to Hamill, "That is more than our gracious host, Major Hamill, could have surmised."

It couldn't have been more apparent that the animosity between Hamill and Von Braun went both ways.

Actually, I hadn't come up with my conclusion because I understood what was written on the chalk board. I just figured that thrust and trajectory were the things they'd most likely be talking about.

Von Braun turned to Hans and extended his hand, "Major Kirpes. I've heard a lot about you, both in Germany and here. Over 200 kills and a ME-262 Ace! Impressive!"

Hans bowed and said something to Von Braun in German, to which Von Braun responded in kind. Hamill angrily demanded, "English! Werhner, I've told you to speak in English when we are present!"

Holy cow! Damn, did I want to smack this guy! I couldn't imagine why Colonel Sanderson would allow this pimple-faced kid to show so much disrespect to such a great man. But then I calmed down and thought for a second. Maybe it was military protocol to treat prisoners with disrespect to make them more manageable? If that's what was going on there, then someone needed to clue me in, because I was inclined to make it known that I admired the hell out of these people and that Hamill needed his butt kicked for his attitude.

I shook his hand and said, "Sir. To meet you is a tremendous honor, and the opportunity to work with you and your team is a blessing beyond compare."

I could tell that the compliment touched him, especially after tolerating Hamill's disrespect.

He bowed in formal German fashion and replied, "Thank you, Major. I expect that working with you will be my pleasure as well."

Colonel Sanderson told Von Braun, "Starting Monday, Major Davis will report to you—not so much as a supervisor, but as a student and observer... but don't be surprised if this young man comes up with a useful insight now and then."

Von Braun smiled and said, "Yes. I would assume that anyone who can shoot down three ME-262s in a Mustang—one of which was flown by Major Kirpes—*must* be, at least, *somewhat* resourceful."

I was flattered that he knew so much about me.

Von Braun looked towards Hamill, "With Major Hamill's permission, I'd like to show our guests around the facility."

Sanderson said, "You guys go ahead. Major Hamill and I have some business to discuss."

As they walked away, I felt an instant relief. I could see that Von Braun felt it as well. Considering that Hamill's treatment of Von Braun and his crew might have been intentional, I resisted the inclination to apologize for his behavior.

Instead, I asked Von Braun, "So, how do you like living in Texas?"

He answered, "I find it rather difficult to form a positive emotional attachment to the area. Part of that may be because we're living in rundown housing that resembles a POW camp, and partly because we can't leave Fort Bliss without an escort. We refer to ourselves as 'Prisoners of Peace!' "

He went on to say, "I asked to have vinyl flooring to cover our splintered wooden floors in my housing. The answer was no. On top of that, we have to endure this 26-year-old kid who seems to gloat over having control over people that are smarter than he is. When I was his age at Peenemünde, I had *thousands* of engineers under my direction! Hamill doesn't even understand the basics of what we're doing here... yet he's in charge."

The situation was mind-boggling, but again, I considered that there may have been reasons for Hamill's command that I wasn't aware of.

Von Braun then asked Hans, "How do *you* like working for your captors? It appears that they grant *you* unrestricted freedom to travel?"

Hans answered, "I am indeed fortunate. I would imagine that I have more freedom than you because I'm not nearly as valuable."

Von Braun replied, "As I said. We aren't being *treated* as if we were very valuable. But then, there was a time when Germany didn't treat us very well either. I was arrested once because they felt that my work on the V-2 was progressing too slowly, and they believed it to be an act of sabotage. They also denied me the right to fly my private plane because they thought I might defect. I suppose we can endure the disrespect we're given here. We just keep working, whatever the circumstances. What else can we do?"

I asked Von Braun, "You must be making some progress here?"

"Oh yes," he answered. "The bright side to our situation *here* is that we have plenty of time to think and rethink our designs before implementing them. We're not under the incredible pressure to perform that we were before."

I said, "I will do what I can to help."

Hans added, "And I can assure you that Major Davis is someone you want on your side. Without his influence, I would still be in prison with the rest of my unit. And consider that I am the one who is responsible for his cane!"

He smiled, "Yes. I've heard the stories of how you two have become such unlikely friends." Then he turned to me with a melancholy look in his eyes. "Thank you, Major Davis. And welcome to our team."

Before heading back to Williams Field, Hans and I went over to view Fort Bliss' officer's housing. Its beautiful streets were lined with new white stucco two-story homes with fireplaces and red tile roofs, complete with lush green landscaping. Normally, I would have been thrilled at the thought of living in such luxury, but after hearing of the horrible living conditions that Von Braun was subjected to, it didn't seem fair.

Then I remembered the many people in London who had died and whose beautiful homes were reduced to rubble as a result of Von Braun's work. Considering that and how he had profited from using slave labor back in Germany to manufacture those weapons, I supposed that he should be grateful that he *wasn't* in prison.

I didn't waste any time relocating from Williams Field to Fort Bliss. Meanwhile, Helen resigned her position at the firm, and then organized the shipment of our household furnishings to our new home. Within the week, she flew out to join me. I was relieved that Helen was happy with our housing accommodations... but then I think we'd have been happy living just about anywhere as long as we could be together before the baby arrived.

I'd been driving Dad's 1939 Coupe since I had returned to the States, but it only accommodated two people. It was no longer practical with the baby coming. New car production had resumed for the first time since the war, so Helen and I went to the Lincoln dealership in El Paso to select a new 1946 Lincoln Zephyr 4-door sedan. It was beautiful... tan with whitewall tires. Dad would've been proud!

It seemed like a lifetime had passed since Helen and I had actually lived alone together. Being alone together wouldn't last long though with the baby coming soon. The prospect of being a father began to seem more real to me once I could feel the baby moving inside of Helen. We decorated the nursery together. It really would have been terrible if I'd been overseas and had missed out on that special time together.

It was great, going to work for eight hours and then returning home at the end of the day like a normal person. The only thing I resented was not being able to discuss my day with Helen, since it was rated top secret. Just as in my experience with Operation Paperclip in Germany, I couldn't talk to anyone about my work outside of the group.

We worked out of portable buildings that had been trucked in to White Sands for our field testing, but most of our time was spent back at Fort Bliss. White Sands certainly fit its name. I had to wear dark glasses for protection from the sand's blinding glare. I especially remember how beautiful the new tan Lincoln looked against the stark white sands there.

Von Braun's team was pretty expansive. In all, 177 German scientists were brought to White Sands; but even with all that help, the program experienced a lot of failures. Often, wayward rockets would explode right over Fort Bliss, El Paso, or other nearby towns. One even strayed over the Mexican border, nearly causing an international incident. Crashing V-2 rockets became so common that civilians took to gathering the wreckage that wasn't recovered by the Army to sell as souvenirs.

I began to realize that most of these so-called German "scientists" were nothing more than subordinates who had worked under Von Braun's direction in Germany. They seemed to lack any kind of creative ability. Hans would have labeled them as being scholars instead of innovators.

At first, the team said that the problems they were having with failed launches were a result of having lost their engine designer in the war, but I was starting to think that the guidance systems were more of a problem. There was a lot of finger-pointing going on as to who was at fault. They were also like a bunch of piranhas, each desperate to claim credit for any bit of success that was made with the project. I didn't need to be involved in their war of pride and egos and was content to simply carry out my assignment as a student and observer. Von Braun was the one who kept them focused and on the right track.

As 1946 progressed, Helen and I settled into the new house and eagerly awaited the baby's arrival.

One night, Helen woke me to tell me that it was time. After such a long wait, it all happened so quickly. I was grateful that it happened at night. If I'd been in White Sands, I never would have made it home in time. Because it was late at night, there was no traffic between our house and the hospital.

Once they processed her in, I was left to wait alone in the lobby. Some time later, a nurse came out to the waiting room to let me know that Helen was fine and that I was the father of a baby boy. I was elated. The nurse asked me if we'd chosen a name for him. My mind was in such a whirl that I couldn't remember the name we had chosen if our baby were a boy.

I said to her, "We agreed to name him after my father-in-law if it were a boy, but for the life of me I can't remember what his first name is. I always called him Mr. Phillips. It's a common name, like John or Bill. Can we ask Helen?"

The nurse replied, "She's sleeping now, but if you want, we can wait."

"No... that's okay. I'm pretty sure it's John... or, Bill. To be safe, I'll say John; but make Bill, or William, his middle name."

She smiled, "Okay. So, John William Davis it is."

"How soon can I see him?"

"Now, if you'd like."

The nurse had me don a gown before entering the nursery. There were several babies in there, but somehow I knew which one was mine.

She wrote up a card bearing his new name, slid it onto his basket, and then picked him up. She wrapped him tight and handed him to me with instructions on how to hold a baby.

I kissed his forehead and said, "Hey, Johnny. It's your Dad."

Almost as if he could understand me, he wrapped his tiny hand around my finger.

What an amazing transition I felt at that moment. I'd known that I was going to be a dad, and I'd had nine months to prepare for it. My friends told me about how wonderful it would be, but I couldn't have known until I experienced it. Holding Johnny for the first time, it's like a switch flipped on inside of me. I was a father.

Once again, I felt a profound sorrow that my dad couldn't be there to share the experience. I knew that my mom would be thrilled to see the little guy. I wanted to call both her and Hans… but it was the middle of the night. I supposed that the news could wait until morning.

They finally let me see Helen. She looked exhausted and weak, but that beautiful smile of hers still brightened the room.

"Uh, sweetheart…" I approached her apprehensively. "What's your dad's name?"

"Ed." When she saw the look on my face, she asked, "Why?"

I knelt beside her and took her hand, "Damn! You're going to hate me. I couldn't remember your dad's name when they asked me the baby's name. I always called your dad Mr. Phillips, and I was pretty sure we didn't want to name the baby that!"

She laughed. "So what is our son's name?"

"I knew your dad had a popular name. I guessed John or Bill, but wasn't sure, so his name is John William Davis."

She squeezed my hand and said, "That's nice. It sounds like a president's name."

So, Johnny it was.

Hans showed up later that day with a teddy bear for Johnny and flowers for Helen.

Helen agreed to let Hans hold Johnny under the supervision of a nurse. Straight from boarding school into the military, Hans hadn't known anyone who'd had a baby before. He was exceedingly careful as the nurse placed the baby in his arms. He looked surprisingly natural holding Johnny.

After a while, Hans looked up at me and said in amazement, "I can't believe you did this, Kenny!"

Helen said, "I helped a little."

Hans and I laughed.

Eventually, the nurse gathered the baby up to return him to his bassinette. As she walked by, I said to Helen, "You know, if I hadn't barged into your life, *you'd* be a nurse now."

She smiled and replied, "I'm exactly where I want to be right now."

CHAPTER 12: Peace

During the war, when every day was a do-or-die proposition that brought with it new challenges, it had seemed like each day lasted an eternity. But at Fort Bliss, life became truly blissful. When my life settled into such a happy routine, time began to pass at a surprising rate.

Life was wonderful—that is, except for the occasional rocket explosion. We launched a total of 32 rockets in 1946. Being a part of a successful rocket launch was intensely rewarding, but watching one explode into a raging inferno was fun too.

The relationship between Hans and Theresa was explosive as well, but that wasn't so much fun to watch. Theirs was a relationship of extremes. Their horrible fights were countered with reconciliations of equal intensity. I couldn't imagine staying in a relationship like that, but neither of them wanted to give up on it.

Hans was under the impression that their friction stemmed from their living so far apart. Theresa finally gave in to Hans' encouragement to move to Phoenix to continue her education. Unfortunately, her old-fashioned Southern family refused to continue funding her education if she left Baton Rouge to live in sin. Hans offered to take care of it from then on. Theresa's moving in with Hans worked out nicely, so he wouldn't be alone after was transferred to Fort Bliss.

That year, Hans and I decided to go in as partners on a light plane to make commuting back and forth between Williams Field and Fort Bliss and Baton Rouge more practical. My mom loved coming out to babysit, which gave Helen and me the chance to take weekend vacations with Hans and Theresa to destinations like Los Angeles. Between Theresa, Hans, and my mom, little Johnny was never in danger of lacking for affection.

That summer, a song—"La Vie en Rose"—dominated the radio across the country. It was by Edith Piaf... the French singer that Hans said sounded like a goat. Even though it was in French, the song sold over a million copies in the U.S. Every time I heard it, I felt a sweet sorrow as it reminded me of France, of Sandy, and of what an ass Hans had been when we met.

The only break in my routine at Fort Bliss was a temporary assignment to Williams Field to build up my hours in the P-80 to keep my rating current. I also had to brush up on my gunnery and dog fighting skills, which meant flying against Hans. I remember one of those training sessions in the summer of '46. I was excited about flying the P-80 again. I'd missed it, and I especially enjoyed the prospect of flying against Hans.

As we headed to the planes on the flight line on our first flight, I took a deep, nervous breath and told him, "You know, I haven't flown a P-80 in months, much less in simulated combat. Since you do this every day, I don't expect things to be very balanced up there today."

"Don't be too sure of that," he answered. "The kids I teach mostly fly by the book. They're no challenge to fly against. Only once in a great while do I come up against one that's even a bit of a challenge. I'm really looking forward to some competition."

I smiled. "Well. Win or lose, it should be fun!"

We taxied out, roared down the runway towards the sky, and flew in a tight formation until we were out over the unpopulated desert. Without having to say a word, we peeled away from each other when the time was right to fight. We turned and headed towards each other at a combined speed of nearly 1,200 miles per hour. At first, neither of us could gain a position, because we were thinking too much alike. What followed was a truly spectacular battle of cunning and grace that, put to music, could have rivaled a ballet. God, did it make me feel alive!

Hans and I decided to call a truce once we scored an equal number of simulated kills. I was convinced that he was being charitable in allowing me the kills that I did score. Soon after, we touched back down in the scorching desert heat and taxied to the flight line.

I let out a loud hoot as I climbed from the cockpit. As I approached Hans, I asked, "Well, teacher. How'd I do?"

Hans grabbed my shoulder and said, "Not bad for a Louisiana Yank!"

Most of Hans' jet combat instruction took place in the classroom. I sat in on a few of the classes to answer questions about the times that Hans and I had flown against each other in combat.

Rather than staying in the transit quarters while I was at Williams Field, I stayed with Hans and Theresa. Over dinner one evening, I got to see firsthand how one of their heated arguments began. On that night, *I* actually started one of them. I complimented Theresa on her hair, because it looked nice.

She said proudly, "I got my mom's hair... and my dad's eyes."

Hans couldn't resist offering the joke she had left herself open to. He said, "That's wonderful, honey... for you, but too bad for your parents."

Her smile quickly faded as she asked, "Why?"

Hans knew he was in trouble when he realized that he had to explain the joke.

"Well," he said slowly and clearly, "if you have your mom's hair and you have your dad's eyes... then that would mean that your mom was bald and your dad was blind."

Her expression shifted to outrage. "That's rude! Why would you say such a horrible thing?!"

Hans turned to me with a look of frustration, but there was nothing I could do to help him.

He uttered, "It was... a joke."

She asserted, "Well, it's NOT funny!"

Oh, but it was. It was funnier yet that she didn't get it. I didn't dare laugh though. What a tragedy that Hans was in love with a woman who not only didn't appreciate his wit, but was instead enraged by it.

It's said that opposites attract. Maybe that's true to someone who enjoys a challenge. I enjoy a challenge as much as the next guy but when I come home, I prefer that it's to someone that I share a similar perspective with, a peaceful and romantic perspective.

I'm sure that back in Hans' days as a playboy, he must have cast aside a dozen women of Helen's caliber only to become infatuated with a girl who wasn't so impressed by *him*. And Theresa, a beautiful Southern Belle, was likely bored by the young men who treated her like a queen. Maybe they *were* a perfect match. And *they* were the psychologists! I wonder if they saw Helen and I as a boring couple.

I was certainly glad to get back home to my peaceful marriage.

Before the year was done, Helen announced that we had yet another member to the Davis family on its way.

Things began to change at White Sands that year too. The government found more American engineers with the background and aptitude for rocket research to join our team. That was a good change for me. I was no longer so outnumbered by Nazi scientists. One thing that *didn't* change was the scarcity of funding.

It was a shame to see Von Braun's dreams stifled. When he first became involved with rocketry, he dreamed of space travel, but the Nazis were only interested in using his talents for the war. Upon coming to work with the United States, he was disheartened to find that they too were only interested in using his rocketry as a weapon.

On the weekends that Hans and I didn't fly to Baton Rouge, we hung out at Fort Bliss with Wernher and his German pals.

During the holidays at home that year, Hans and Theresa announced to the family that they had set a date in June to marry. Theresa's family was still upset because of her living with Hans in Phoenix, so Mom and I agreed that we would host their wedding there at our house. That way, her family could come if they wanted. Either way, Hans and Theresa would have a fantastic wedding.

We enjoyed another wonderful holiday season in Baton Rouge. Johnny was too young to enjoy it, but I could tell that he enjoyed all the fuss and attention the family made over him. It was nice to have him home in the town where all of my own cherished childhood memories had been made.

1947 arrived and began to pass at the same peaceful pace as 1946. That that year brought a few interesting events with it.

The first exciting thing to come along in 1947 was Hans and Theresa's wedding, which was sensational. We were relieved that Theresa's family had forgiven them for their premarital relationship and attended the wedding. Some of our military friends attended from Operation Paperclip, both German and American. Von Braun came with his new bride, Maria. Colonel Sanderson also attended with his wife.

The guest list was quite impressive. A number of local politicians attended as well. The menu catered to the broad variety of guests, from German to Cajun.

Colonel Sanderson pointed out, "Now that Hans is married to a U.S. citizen, his application for citizenship should go a lot easier."

I answered, "Great. Hans also mentioned that, once he's a citizen, he'd like to make his relationship with the Army Air Force official."

The Colonel answered, "That would be ideal, since he's already teaching our pilots. I'll see what I can do to rush it."

Hans took Theresa to Munich for their honeymoon. The last time I had seen Munich, it was mostly in ruins. I imagined that they'd had time to do some rebuilding since then. There were a lot of beautiful sights to see in Munich, even when *I* was there. The country was scattered with castles and ancient villages that were left untouched by the war. Hans still had his car and his airplane there, so I'm sure that he was able to give her an impressive tour of his homeland.

Hans learned that the pilots he had flown with in JA-44 were being released from prison just before his arrival. He was especially glad to see his old boss, Adolf Galland, again. After two years in prison though, it seemed that none of the guys were who they once were. Their new challenge was that of finding employment in the devastated post-war Germany.

When Hans and Theresa returned to the States, he told me about the tension in Europe between the Allies and the Russians over the division of Germany. From the start, Russia had wanted to force the U.S., Britain, and France out of post-war Germany, but we stood our ground in Germany as well as in West Berlin. We were all concerned that this tension might prompt another war.

The second wonderful event of 1947 was the arrival of our second son. Helen chose to give him the name "Billy," which was my second choice when I had been struggling to remember her dad's name.

The third exciting thing to happen that year was the arrival of a new jet fighter, which was to replace the P-80. It was the F-86 Saber. It was primarily designed with German technology by German engineers. Word was that it could break the sound barrier.

The F-86 was certainly worth waiting for. When Hans and I heard that a prototype of the F-86 had arrived at Muroc Field, we flew over to have a look. It was beautiful with its swept-back wings and streamlined form. Being an experimental prototype, the plane had an extensive ground crew and tight security surrounding it. When Hans and I approached the plane, a spokesman for the troops who were guarding it stopped us. He was polite and respectful, but he let me know that the F-86 was off limits to unauthorized personnel.

Then I heard a voice that was somewhat familiar come from the ground crew, "Well I'll be damned if it isn't Captain Davis!"

I instantly recognized not only the voice, but the tall, lanky frame of the Master Sergeant that it originated from. It was Sergeant Lonny Gann, the aircraft mechanic who had helped rescue me when Hans shot me down in France. When he realized that he'd addressed an officer in such a casual manner, he snapped to attention, saluted then followed it up with, "Sir!"

He was a joy to see. I responded with "At ease," then gave him a hug. I turned to Hans and said, "This is the guy that saved my ass in France after you shot me down."

I started to introduce Hans to him, but Lonny interjected, "Oh, I know who you are. I've been following your story. You're the guy that shot him down that day, and you're buddies now! That's amazing."

"War can create some strange relationships, for sure," I answered. The second I said that, my heart sank a little as I remembered the relationship it had created with Sandy. I think Lonny picked up on that, because he quickly looked away and thought of a way to change the subject.

He looked down at my cane, "I see your leg is still bothering you."

I lifted my cane and answered, "Yes. It's not likely that it'll ever be right again, but at least I still have my leg."

Hans added, "And your life." Then he said to Lonny, "And I've heard about you as well. You and the nurse... Sandy."

With the mention of Sandy's name, a wave of anxiety shot across Lonny's face.

I commented, "I'm a little surprised that I never saw either of you again after I was loaded into the ambulance. I thought you might come by the hospital to see that I was alright."

The sergeant averted his eyes again, apparently uncomfortable with the topic. "Well, sir. I can't really talk about that." Then he looked up and excitedly said, "But what I can tell you about is this aircraft. I'm the crew chief. I switched from reciprocating engines to jets early on, and now this is my baby." He pointed to his stripes, which indicated his rank as Master-Sergeant. "And I don't mind saying that our little experience in France helped in expediting my promotions."

I looked at the aircraft and commented, "Hans came over with the ME-262s we captured to help train us in jet combat techniques. They had me fly the P-80 to compare it to the 262. I'm glad to see that they've made some improvements in it over the 262. The air brake is a great feature."

Lonny said, "A lot of the features that were applied to the F-86 *came* from the 262, like the swept-back wing concept.

Boy, we had quite a scare today! The nose-wheel on this bird didn't deploy on the landing 'til the very last minute on a test flight today. I thought we might lose the plane. We're working on fixing it now."

I said, "I can't wait to get behind the stick in one of these. How soon do you think it'll be before these are available to us?"

Lonny answered, "It'll be a while. I can only guess a year, maybe as much as two. We've tested several engines in it, and they still haven't figured out which one they're using yet."

I told Lonny, "You're going to join us for dinner tonight!"

He lowered his head and answered, "No, sir. I don't think I should. As you can see, I've really got my hands full here."

I knew that wasn't the issue, and I should have respected that he either couldn't or didn't want to discuss what had happened in France, but my curiosity got the best of me.

"Sergeant, you're not telling me something. Why?"

"I'm under orders, sir."

"…Under orders not to talk to me about France?"

"Yes sir."

"…Whose orders?"

Still avoiding eye contact, he pleaded with me. "Please, sir, I'm really happy with my career right now. I love my job and everything that goes with it, and I could lose it all in an instant and maybe wind up with a court-martial if I disobeyed my orders."

I grabbed him by the shoulder, "Relax, Sergeant. You saved my life. I wouldn't want to do anything that would mess up yours. As much as I'd like to know what you're keeping from me, I'll let it go."

He seemed relieved, then subtly motioned by nodding his head away from the others that we should follow. With a dead serious expression, he said, "I'm under strict orders not to discuss that incident, but if you give me your word that you won't repeat what I tell you, *understanding that my career depends on it*, I'll clue you in."

"You have my word," I answered.

"Mine too," Hans added. Lonny looked at Hans for a half-second, considering whether he needed to hear what he was going to say; then he decided to go ahead.

"When we were rescued, we were debriefed. One of the things that they were curious about was Sandy's uncharacteristic concern over your welfare. It came out that you two had a bit of a tryst when you were alone in that house. You and Sandy were both married. Since they were planning to send you back to the States as a war hero, they decided that a scandal would be, uh…"

I finished, "Undesirable."

"Yes, sir," he answered. "So they swore both the lieutenant and me to secrecy over the incident and gave us orders never to contact you again."

"Oh," Hans exclaimed. "That explains a lot. That should make you feel better, Kenny." Then he turned to Lonny, laughing, "He was so doped up on morphine, he wasn't sure that... the tryst... actually happened."

Lonny smiled, "Oh, it happened, sir. When I was standing guard, I heard a lot of noise coming out of that house. At first, I thought it was just you hollering because the lieutenant was changing your bandages... but then I heard her start hollering, too!"

Hans gently slugged me on the shoulder, "See! I told you... you dog!"

Lonny asked, "Seriously? You didn't know if that really happened?"

I shook my head, no. "I was pretty sure of what happened, but there were parts I didn't remember at all... like how I got dressed in civilian clothes or how we got to the place where we were rescued. I don't remember any of it."

Lonny laughed, "To be honest with you, sir, you seemed to be pretty damned happy! You were spouting out all kinds of romantic stuff to Sandy."

"No!" I was mortified at the thought of what I could have said to her in that condition.

"Yes sir. You don't remember any of it? You might be better off not knowing."

Hans laughed, "Well maybe he'd be better off not knowing... but *I've* got to know!"

I was laughing about it too. "All right, what did I say?"

"You told her that you loved her and that since she saved your life, she owned you. You offered to run away with her and live on a tropical beach... naked."

"Oh my God, it's worse than I could have imagined. How did she take all of this?"

"At first, we both laughed about it and played along with you. I told you that I helped save your life too, and asked you if I was also entitled to a portion of your ownership."

"What did I say?"

"You just kind'a looked at me for a second, then turned back to Sandy and went on about how you loved her freckles. Freckles, freckles, freckles! You kept saying that... freckles, freckles, freckles!"

Hans loved every bit of the story. Lonny added, "So, we had no doubt by that journey's end that Major Davis had a healthy appreciation for freckles!"

"Oh my God," I said with a realization. "That clears something up. Every time I've come across a gal that's got freckles, this little voice in my head says, 'freckles, freckles, freckles!' "

Then it dawned on me to ask, "You said... 'At first,' you two didn't take me seriously. Did that change?"

Lonny looked a little more serious when he answered, "Yeah. I think towards the end, she started taking you a little more seriously. And I don't think she's ever quite gotten over it."

"Why, are you still in touch with her?"

"Yeah. She's back in Cleveland with her husband now. My wife and I had dinner with them a couple of months ago. Her husband's a doctor... a really nice guy."

Hans asked, "So, are you going to look her up?"

"No! Hell no!" I snapped. "It does comfort me to know why you two never came to see me again, but I think we need to leave things as they are. Lonny, I'm glad that you're already sworn to secrecy on this, because it's never to be repeated again. Agreed?"

He answered, "Yes sir!"

"Good. With that out of the way, do you think that you can break free to join us for dinner tonight?"

"Yes sir," he answered, "as long as you're buying!"

Hans said, "Of course he is, Sergeant. After all, you have part ownership of him!"

I laughed and said, "That only applies if you have freckles."

Lonny said, "I got freckles."

Hans said, "Freckles, freckles, freckles!"

Then Hans said to me, "By the way, I spared your life that day, before Lonny rescued you, saving your life on the ground. You're in the company of two men who saved your life that day. I'd say you owe us *both* dinner!"

"Okay, deal!"

Hans turned to Lonny and said, "So I spared this guy's life and as soon as he gets back in a plane, what's he do? He comes back and shoots me down! What kind of thanks is that? I decided right then: I'm not sparing this guy's life *anymore!*"

I laughed and warned him, "Don't you let my mom hear you say that!"

Hans asked, "You won't tell her, will you?"

Towards the later part of 1947 that I had a talk with Helen about my assignment at White Sands.

I asked her, "Are you happy here?"

"Aren't you?" she asked.

"Not really. It's been an incredible assignment. It's just that I'm getting a little tired of the constant arguing between these guys in their struggle for recognition... and their constant struggle for funding. It's really stressful, but most of all, I hate living in the desert. I've heard you say you're not too crazy about it either."

"What do you want to do?" she asked.

"I thought about going back to my unit at Muroc Field in California. It's right by Los Angeles. I'd like to be flying again, but then we'd still be living in the middle of the Mojave Desert."

I went on to say, "There's one other option that might be worth considering, as far as serving out my term. How would you like to see Germany? There's a flight of P-80s stationed at Giebelstadt, close to Frankfurt. It patrols the German border between the Allied and the Russian occupation. It's beautiful there. You'd get to see all the places that I wrote you about during the war."

"We can go with you?" she asked.

"I wouldn't want to go otherwise. I haven't checked into it that far, but I'd imagine that if it's a permanent duty assignment, there will be family housing there."

Helen was excited about the prospect, so I verified that I could bring my family then placed the request for transfer. Major Hamill didn't hesitate to approve my release from Fort Bliss. I don't think he liked me much more than I liked him.

The next weekend, when Hans and Theresa came for a visit, I broke the news to them about our plans to go to Germany.

Hans was instantly elated. "That's wonderful! I bet I can get a transfer there as well. And maybe even get authorization to fly with you."

I could see that Theresa wasn't wild about the idea. She asked, "Hans, don't I have a say in this?"

"You'll love it there," he replied. "Remember how much fun we had there on our honeymoon?"

She stared down at the floor. "I don't remember it being all that much fun."

Hans said, "Well, aside from the part about your being such a bitch over the airplane."

Both Helen and I were mortified to hear Hans refer to his wife as a "bitch." Neither of us would have guessed that he was capable of such disrespect. He saw our reaction and tried to defend himself.

"My plane hadn't been started since you and I took it up, so the fuel had to be purged again. I showed Theresa where the fuel pump switch was… all she had to do was turn it on when I said to. Then she had an episode where she started screaming and crying. Jesus Christ, she couldn't simply flip one switch!"

Theresa angrily defended herself, "Hans! There were a hundred switches! If I flipped the wrong one, it could have started the motor and cut your arm off!"

"There were maybe a *dozen* switches! And I pointed to the one you needed to flip."

"So you called me stupid!" Theresa said, as she began to cry.

Helen sat next to her and held her as she sobbed. I couldn't think of a thing to say that would help the situation, and frankly, Hans didn't deserve to be rescued from the hole he'd dug himself into.

"I said I was sorry," he snapped.

He didn't seem to be the least bit remorseful for having said something so hurtful and degrading to his wife, but instead, he was angry that he'd been exposed for it. My mind raced back over the years that I'd known Hans, and I couldn't recall having seen that side of him.

"I could go for a little fresh air," I said, and I motioned for Hans to join me.

We walked in the chilly night air for a while before talking.

Hans broke the silence. "I'm married to an idiot, and it's driving me nuts! And she's not going to tell *me* that I can't go back to Germany."

I knew he was looking for the sympathy of a friend, but I couldn't support his treatment of Theresa. I was hoping that I could offer some advice that might help their relationship, but I knew that the wrong word would only make him defensive. I thought before speaking, choosing to use Hans' own thoughts for an argument.

I said, "I'm just thinking about what you told me about how people with different perspectives balance each other out. She doesn't know what you know or think the way that you do, but look at Helen and me... same thing with us, but we make a pretty damned good team!"

"No... it's not the same thing, Kenny. Helen ran the engineering firm when you were away and set up the storage business on her own. She's a catch!"

"And Theresa is doing great, working towards her degree in psychology."

Hans scoffed. "Yeah... about that. She remembers what she's taught alright and gets high test scores, but the way she interprets what she's learned is downright scary."

I smiled and said, "If you want a spouse that knows what you know and thinks exactly like you, I'm afraid that you're going to have to marry a man. Theresa trusted you to accept and respect her for who she is when you married her."

"Even if she's an idiot?"

"It bothers me to hear you talk about her that, Hans. Let's say, for the sake of this argument, that you *were* smarter than she is, or even smarter than most people—men and women alike. That doesn't make them stupid. They are normal. That would make *you* the exception... which would hold you to a higher standard. Your wife is a loving, devoted lady and it's your job to protect and nurture her. I have to be honest with you, Hans. It really bothered me to see you treat her with such disrespect tonight. That can scar a person for life, and if you're not careful, you're going to lose her."

He started to argue, but I cut him off. "One final thing about this, Hans. Your perspective towards Theresa isn't just making her miserable, it's making *you* miserable. You said that you envied my family because we were happy with what we had instead of being miserable over what we didn't. You're my friend, Hans. I'd like to see you happy with what you have. Otherwise, you could spend your life looking and never find what makes you happy. I don't need to sell you on this. These are your words!"

After a while, he replied, "I did say that about you being happy with what you had."

"People envy you for having Theresa as your wife. When you walk into a room with her on your arm, people who don't even know who you are admire you. They figure you must have something going for you to have a lady of her caliber. You say she's smart scholastically. You need that for a balance. Enjoy the strengths she has to share with you, and share yours with her. That's it! I don't want to say anything more about this."

Hans said bitterly, "I guess I'm a pretty rotten husband. I made a real ass out of myself tonight."

I sighed and said, "I've made my share of mistakes, so I'm nobody to tell you how to live your life. I just wanted you to know that it bothers Helen and me to see you treat Theresa that way."

When we got back to the house, Hans gave Theresa a heartfelt apology. She accepted it, but the rest of the evening wasn't very comfortable.

When we turned in for the night, Helen commented, "Theresa said she didn't know what you said to Hans, but it worked."

"I don't know," I answered. "I was as appalled as you were to see him call her a bitch. He's always saying that he wants the happiness he sees with *us*. He'll never find it if he treats Theresa like that."

Helen said, "It seems that you convinced him of that."

"I'm not sure that my intervention was the right thing to do though. Some women actually feel more secure in a relationship when they're treated like crap. If her father treated her that way, maybe she'll only respect a man that treats her the same way."

Helen argued, "No, I'm sure that's not the case with Theresa."

"Well, she never took any other man seriously until she met Hans. Maybe he *is* what she needs. If that's so, I should probably keep my nose out of their affairs!"

"He was awfully mean tonight. I've never seen that side of him."

"I've always gotten a kick out of his sense of humor, the way he's always pretending to be horrible. Maybe he wasn't kidding as much as I thought he was."

CHAPTER 13: Back to Germany

Although I had Major Hamill's blessing to leave Fort Bliss, the chain of command above me opposed the idea of someone with my rank, experience, and ability resigning from such an important position to become a mere border patrol pilot. I argued that my assignment at Muroc was supposed to be peaceful and routine, giving me time to focus on my family. Instead, they had given me the stressful and demanding assignment at White Sands.

They reluctantly gave in to my request.

I had our car and furniture shipped to the little German town of Giebelstadt, which had mostly been populated by people supporting the airfield during the war. It had been used as a Luftwaffe base during the war.

We committed to the housing they offered us there, sight unseen. We arrived to find that our quarters were in a large rectangular apartment building with a red tile roof. It looked a lot like all the other buildings in town. An eerie feeling overcame me when I walked into the apartment, for I knew that Luftwaffe officers had lived there during the war. It wasn't the nice, new housing at Fort Bliss, but it was comfortable.

This was Helen's first trip out of the country. I was happy to see that she was excited over the adventure. I'd never have imagined, in the days when I'd escorted bombers to Giebelstadt, that someday I'd be based there with my family.

They assigned me a brand new shiny P-80 and granted me permission to name it *Heavenly Helen III*. I commissioned an artist to adorn the plane's nose with her image. It would be the first time I could fly a plane in Germany, with Helen's bright pink dress glaring from its nose, where I didn't have to worry about Hans hunting me down.

The assignment was everything I'd hoped for. My daily routine was to fly along the border for a given number of hours, then return home in time for dinner.

What also worked out wonderfully was that I left Hans the plane we bought for commuting to Baton Rouge in return for the use of his plane in Munich. I got permission to move it to the flying club at my airfield.

I chatted with Hans a couple of times a week. He was doing everything in his power to get a transfer to Giebelstadt.

In one of our calls, he said, "They made it clear that they want seasoned combat pilots flying your patrol. How can they say no to me?"

I laughed, "Maybe because a few years ago you were flying against us as our enemy?"

"A few years ago, the Russians you're flying against now were your allies! Besides, they're processing my application for citizenship."

"What about Theresa? Has she warmed up to the idea?"

"She's just being contrary. I'm doing my best to be considerate, but the bottom line is, I'm her husband and she needs to support me in my decisions. Besides... she doesn't need to get her degree because she doesn't need to work! I can provide her with everything she could want or need."

I held to my vow of not interfering in their relationship, understanding that what worked for Helen and me might not work for them. I was relieved to hear him say that she was being *contrary* rather than saying that she was being a bitch.

It dawned on me that I'd kind of missed having Hans around since my transfer to Germany. Before that, I hadn't had much of a *chance* to miss his company... not since we'd become friends.

Of all the sights that I was anxious to share with Helen, the one that she was most anxious to see is where I was shot down.

So, one Saturday morning, we arranged for a sitter and hopped into Hans' airplane. I took her to Haguenau Airfield in France, then retraced the route I'd flown the day Hans shot me down. I showed her where we first encountered the flight of FW-190s, and then I showed her how I'd pursued the one that peeled out from the group for a better position. Next, I reenacted, step by step, how the dogfight went with Hans... rocking the plane back and forth to illustrate its intensity. I then showed her where I was hit, where the plane overheated, and the field I bailed out into and where my plane crashed.

Helen had questions about what happened afterwards with Sandy and Lonny. I'd told her the story before, but that was before Lonny confirmed that I'd truly had an affair with Sandy. Before, when I told Helen the story, I didn't feel so bad about omitting parts of the story that I didn't know were factual. Since I wasn't an experienced liar, I was sure that Helen could sense that I wasn't being honest with her. I hurried past the part of the story where I was incoherent to the part where we were rescued. After I finished the story, Helen was quiet and turned to look out of the window. I couldn't tell whether her silence was because she suspected I'd withheld part of the story or if it was simply silence.

If she had any intuition at all, she had to know that I was agonizing over something. Damn. I wished that I could have talked her out of that trip.

She asked, "Have you seen her since then?"

I answered, "No. I mentioned to you that I ran into Lonny recently, but I haven't seen Sandy since they loaded me onto the ambulance."

Helen was quiet for a while, and then she asked, "Was she pretty?"

"Actually, she was kind of boyish-looking... really sweet though, with a great bedside manner." Damn, I thought. I shouldn't have said that.

Silence again. Then Helen said, "Well, maybe we should look her up. It seems a little odd that you haven't, considering that she saved your life."

"We should," I answered, and to my relief, nothing more was said about it.

After that, our other outings were a lot less stressful. There were so many fascinating places to see that the assignment was like a prolonged vacation. The devastation from the war was starting to vanish as cities began to rebuild.

Flying border patrol was uneventful and routine, but once in a while we'd actually fly alongside the East Germans on our respective sides of the border. We couldn't tell if the pilots were German or Russian, but they were flying ME-262s. We would nod and wave at them before we parted ways.

The first snow came before Thanksgiving, which was just another day in Germany. Thanksgiving was alive and well with the American families stationed at the Airfield though. We were like a little island of America at Giebelstadt.

We made the trip home to Baton Rouge for Christmas. Johnny was just old enough to enjoy the lights, sounds, and smells that come with it. Hans and Theresa made plans to be there as well.

It was a long flight home. When we landed at Harding Field, I saw that almost all signs of its having been a military base were gone. The Civil Air Patrol was still active there, but the flight line where our planes had been tied down was occupied by civilian commercial and private aircraft.

When we got to the house, we found that our room was as we had left it the last time we were there. It was noticeably dusty though. Helen tidied it up without complaining, knowing that our maid, Mary, was getting older and having a tough time making it up the stairs. It seemed that Mom was more of Mary's caretaker those days than vice versa. Mary was family. I didn't want to think of what Mom's life would be like when Mary passed on. Next, I helped Helen ready the guest room for Hans and Theresa.

Johnny was a toddler then and seemed to be fascinated by the lake across the street from the house. He was delighted with the ducks that would swim up to the shore for handouts. It was comforting to think that, before another year passed, I would be home for good and that my boys would only remember the lake house as the family's home when they got older. I sat on the bank with Johnny for a while, feeding the ducks and watching the sailboats. As I walked back to the house, I could see that Helen was waiting on the porch with Billy in her arms. I truly felt the peace and security of being home.

Suddenly, an airplane flew over from behind the house, so low we could feel the vibration from the propeller in the air as it passed. I recognized the plane instantly. Hans and Theresa had arrived. Hans made a wide sweep around the lake then passed again, waving his wings.

We waved back, taking that as our cue to go to the airport and pick them up. By the time we made it down Government Street to the airport, they were waiting for us with their bags in front of the terminal building.

I warned Hans, "There *are* altitude restrictions around here, you know."

"There are—500 feet over populated areas, then on the deck over the water. I just happened to pass over the house when I was headed for the water."

"You scared Mom and Mary half to death."

After exchanging hugs, Hans asked, "What's on the agenda for tonight?

"Well, I thought we'd go out for dinner tonight and give Mary a break. I figure we'll go with Mom and Mary in Mom's car and you two can use the Lincoln while you're in town."

"So where are the babies?" Theresa asked.

"They're home with Mom. We have to pry them away from her while we're here!" Helen answered.

I asked Hans, "Have you figured out what they're doing about your transfer?"

"The good news is that we've put about all the P-80 pilots at Williams through combat training, so until the P-86 comes into service, I've got some free time. They're considering sending me to Germany until then. The only slow-down is their issue with my being a civilian contractor that's not a US citizen."

"That's good news," I said. "It'll be great to have you two out there with us."

I asked, "Theresa. How do you feel about spending some time in Germany?"

She hesitated before answering. "I guess it would be okay for a year or so. I'd have to postpone my schooling. I'm not too crazy about that."

Hans interjected, "It'll be like an extended vacation. The renters in my townhouse moved out last month, so we can fly down in the plane to stay in our house in Munich on the weekends!"

"I'm also not too crazy about living somewhere where I don't speak the language," Theresa complained.

Hans took a breath before responding, "I would think that, if my wife spoke a different first language than me, I'd want to learn it... as *I have*."

I changed the topic to a lighter note. "Hey! What about dinner? I say the Piccadilly downtown. They have a little something for everybody... even sauerkraut and bratwurst."

It seemed that those two could always find something to argue about. We listened to them bicker throughout the holiday visit. It almost seemed like they enjoyed it. We sure didn't. We enjoyed Hans' company and Theresa's as well... just a whole lot more when they weren't together. I was starting to wonder how peaceful our stay would be in Germany once they joined us. They spent Christmas Eve and Christmas morning with us, but, thank goodness, they flew to Atlanta in time to make Christmas dinner with Theresa's family. I was right in my suspicion about Theresa's father being like Hans. It was his opinion that women and children were to be obedient to the man of the house. He thought that Hans was a FINE young man and even gave him advice on how to keep Theresa in line.

It was always tough to leave my mom and Baton Rouge, but this time was a little easier since, with my enlistment coming to an end, we'd be coming home for good on our next trip.

It was a long drive back to Giebelstadt from the Frankfurt airport. A lot of snow had fallen since we'd left, and even though Germany had four-lane, divided freeways long before the United States did, the drive home was still dangerous and slow

Giebelstadt was beautiful under snow, but maintaining the airfield and making the planes ready for our patrols was a challenge. It didn't matter what the weather was like below; on patrol, our P-80s climbed up to where the sky was a clear, deep blue.

It was great to be flying again. I'd gotten what I'd asked for, but I was starting to think that my superiors were right in feeling that flying patrols was a waste of my abilities. The patrols consisted of hours upon hours of mindless flying. It got to be where all I had to look forward to for a break the monotony was an occasional radio check.

Germany was split in half between the Allies and the Russians, with Berlin being located deep into the Russian side. The Allies occupied certain sections of Berlin, so the Russians permitted a corridor between West Germany and Berlin through which supplies (air and ground) could travel. Patrolling that corridor was the most interesting part of our patrol. It was there that it was most important that our presence was known. If the Russians ever decided to get nasty and close that corridor off, the British, French, and U.S. sectors of Berlin would be cut off... deep within Russian-occupied Germany.

Hans called to let me know that his orders were issued. He'd managed to persuade the USAAF to loan him to our fighter group for a temporary duty assignment... to give our border patrol pilots a combat skills refresher course.

I commented, "It amazes me how you're able to get your way when you want something."

Hans argued, "It's not just a matter of what I want. If we were to fly into combat with the Russians, who would win? Be thankful that the JA-44 pilots *weren't* turned over to the Russians. The Russians may have Germany's aircraft, but not our piloting skills."

"Okay, but I'm still amazed that things worked out the way you wanted them to."

There was a bit of silence on the phone. Hans sighed and said, "I don't *always* get what I want. Theresa's not coming with me. She went to the trouble of switching from LSU to the University at Phoenix when we got married. She doesn't want to stop and have to continue somewhere else later. I'm only going to be in Germany until the P-86 is available. It makes sense."

He was playing it off as no big deal, but I could hear in his voice that he was hurt and disappointed, to say the least. Within the week, he arrived at Giebelstadt.

Upon his arrival, I introduced him to his crew chief, and we went out to the flight line to the new P-80 that he'd been assigned. Hans was thrilled when he looked down the flight line and saw the nose of my plane, *Heavenly Helen III*.

He walked down to it and ran his hand across the image. "How nostalgic! I will once again be sharing the skies over Germany with the Pink Lady."

"...Except, now, you won't be aiming to shoot her down. Who would have imagined this four years ago?"

Hans said, "Four years ago, I flew out of this field in my 262! I refueled right here on this flight line!"

I laughed. "And I escorted bombers here to bomb it. We left it a horrible mess!"

He looked around, "Well, it looks pretty good now."

"Yeah... we fixed it."

Hans asked, "What's Helen think about being here? She must find it pretty fascinating, seeing where we fought for our lives in such dark times."

"She wanted to see where you shot me down."

"Oh," Hans said with concern.

"Yeah, I'm not a very good liar. I'm pretty sure that she figured there was more to the story than I was telling her. She had questions about Sandy."

He smiled and said, "I wouldn't worry about it, Kenny. Keep a little doubt in her mind and she'll know she's replaceable."

"I don't agree, Hans. She doesn't deserve the misery that comes with that doubt. And, she's *not* replaceable. I don't want her to get that thought in *her* head. She might decide that *I'm* replaceable."

Hans laughed at that thought then focused on matters at hand. "I need to get organized, Kenny. I'm not sure how long I'm going to be here, so I'm going to schedule some ground classes and make up a roster to where I can spend at least five hours with each pilot in the air."

I said, "First things first though. We should probably go get your car in Munich."

"Would you mind driving me down? It's in one of my storage units there."

"Drive?" I asked, motioning to the civilian planes across the field. "Your plane is moored here now."

"Better yet!" he exclaimed.

"You go ready the plane, and I'm going to call Helen to tell her that I'm flying you down. She'll probably want to have you over for dinner later."

He said, "I'll need to get back early enough to secure some lodging."

"Worry about that tomorrow. You're staying with us tonight. We've still got that couch you like."

"I'm excited to see the boys. I brought them presents!"

"I'm sure they'll be glad to see their Uncle Hans."

On the flight down, Hans asked me, "Do you remember Adolf Galland?"

"Yeah, he was your boss with the JA-44, right?"

"I met with him when I was here on our honeymoon, and since then, we've stayed in touch. Once he was released from prison, he went to live with a lady-friend up north then got work as a forestry worker. It was a meager existence. He did some hunting to supplement his income. It broke my heart to see such a great man so humbled. I sent him some money to help get him back on his feet after he told me about that.

"Anyway, last week he wrote me to tell me that Kurt Tank, the man that designed the Focke-Wulf 190, called him and told him that Juan Peron, the president of Argentina, offered to fund his research in building new jet aircraft. Peron said that he'd acquired some British Gloster Meteor jets for his Air Force and needed someone to teach his pilots to fly them, so Tank contacted Galland. It turns out that Galland is as fluent in Spanish as I am in English. So, he's basically doing for them what I'm doing for the United States. He's living it up down there. He said he has a place for me down there if I ever need it. I wouldn't mind going down for a visit. Adolf says the nightlife is incredible. Peron's wife, Ava, is a famous actress down there... so they're quite the socialites!"

I asked, "What's Tank building down there, a fighter jet?"

Hans answered, "He's continuing the development of his Focke-Wulf Ta183 that he was working on here at the end of the war. It's a single-engine jet fighter with swept-back wings, much like the F-86, only it has a 'T' tail."

That *was* exciting news. "I'd love to see that. Maybe we can take the girls down there for a vacation soon."

We landed at the little airport in Munich where Hans had kept his plane during the war. The bomb craters were all filled in and glass was restored to the windows of the little terminal building. The only evidence of the war was several unclaimed airplanes still deteriorating in the woods that skirted the field.

We hired a car to take us to the storage units. I wanted to be sure that Hans' car started before leaving him. The last time it had been driven was when he and Theresa were there for their honeymoon. Aside from a dead battery, it was in good running order.

Hans pulled onto the road heading towards Giebelstadt and I headed back to the airport. By the time I had the plane refueled and was airborne, I figured that Hans had a pretty good start on his trip. I flew along the road he was taking back to the airfield. When I saw his car, I couldn't resist swinging around in front of him and diving on him as if I was making a strafing fun. I passed over him close enough to see him shake his fist at me… at least I *think* it was his fist he was shaking. He made good time in driving back to Giebelstadt. I was barely home an hour before he arrived.

The next morning, Hans and I went to the morning briefing before we went out on patrol. Most of the pilots knew Hans from their combat training at Williams Airfield in Arizona. He announced that, before he started their refresher training, he'd fly a couple of patrol missions with us. The guys were thrilled to have him along.

The main reason for Hans' push for the assignment in Germany was to create an extended vacation for the four of us, as two couples. It was disappointing that Theresa didn't come along, but at least we didn't have to endure their constant bickering. Hans showed us places in Germany that we wouldn't have otherwise thought to explore. We saw the boarding school where he'd spent most of his youth. He was saddened to see that it had been closed and abandoned.

For the most part, Hans seemed to be okay with Theresa staying behind. But his 30th birthday was a different story. Helen and I planned to take him out for a birthday dinner after Theresa called... only Theresa didn't call. She said she'd call around 7AM, her time, before she left for class. That was around 5PM our time. We waited a while longer, but figured that she might have overslept and been late for class. That's what Helen and I figured, anyway. Hans was considering only worst-case scenarios... that something happened to keep her from calling or, worse yet, that she was otherwise occupied.

I was worried about him. It was unsettling to see him vulnerable. After we got to the restaurant, we had a couple of drinks over dinner, which made him more vocal.

"I bet," he said to Helen, "you'd call Kenny on his birthday, no matter what. You're so lucky to have each other. I love you guys."

Helen returned the compliment. "We love you too, Hans."

Hans waved at the waitress, "I'll take another one, a double, for my friends too!"

"No, Hans," I said. "I have to fly in the morning, and we have to get home to the sitter. I think it's about time we went home."

He argued, "I am going to stay here and finish getting drunk. It's my birthday. You're my best friend, Kenny... you're not going to leave me to get drunk alone, are you?"

I turned to Helen, "Sweetheart. I can't leave him alone. Why don't you head home?"

"Should I come back for you later?"

"We're only a five-minute walk from home. We'll be fine. Hans can sleep it off on the couch."

Helen gave me a kiss and a hug, then hugged Hans, "Happy birthday, sweetheart."

Hans hugged her back, a little too long for my comfort. I patted him on the shoulder, "Better let her go home, Hans."

He let her go and slumped back into his chair with a big grin, then picked up his drink and held it up. "Hey! I love you, Helen."

I gave Helen another kiss and said, "Hey... I love you too!"

She joked before turning for the door, "Better keep on your toes, Kenny. You've got some competition."

I asked the waitress to bring me a double too, then went over to the jukebox and played that popular Edith Piaf song, just to antagonize Hans. He laughed and bleated like a goat.

We drank and laughed until they closed the place down. I hadn't been that drunk since I became an Ace back in England. We had fun though and forgot all about Hans' troubles. As we stumbled home, our voices echoed through the little town as we laughed and tried to sing "La Vie en Rose." God, I imagine that it sounded pretty horrible!

We finally made it to my building and quietly made our way to my door, trying not to disturb the neighbors. Hans headed straight for the couch and flopped onto it, face-first. Helen brought him a blanket.

With a little effort, he managed to sit up, "Did Theresa call?"

Helen smiled and answered, "She might have called while we were out, but if she called, she probably called your place."

"Oh. Okay. Well, I think I need to call my wife. I don't think… she loves me anymore."

Helen scolded him, "Hans. You're not in any condition to talk to anybody right now. What you need to do is get some sleep."

He mumbled to himself for a minute, then said, "Okay. Well, Kenny, you go in to bed with your beautiful, loving… smart wife, and I'll be out here, all alone."

Helen laughed affectionately and said, "I'm sorry, Hans. Sometimes life isn't very fair. You deserve to be with your loving wife."

"Loving wife?" he asked, slurring his words while struggling to sit upright. Then he turned to me and said, more to himself than to me, "You don't deserve Helen, Kenny… screwing that nurse… and lying to her about it."

Oh my God! In the split second that he uttered those words, I was stone sober! It felt as if my soul were suddenly swallowed by an earthquake. The pain, the rage, the disbelief I saw in Helen's eyes in that one second ripped my heart wide open.

I heard it in her voice as well as she demanded, "Is that true?! You did cheat on me with Sandy?"

I looked at Hans, who also sobered up once he realized what he'd said. "Oh God, I'm sorry."

Helen snapped at him with an uncharacteristically cold tone in her voice, "Sorry for what, Hans?! Being honest with me?"

She shot me a look at that would have killed most men, then turned and stormed into the bedroom, slamming the door behind her.

Hans pleaded with me, "I'm so sorry, Kenny. Oh God, I'm such an ass."

Damn, I was mad. "What the hell?! Yes, you are, Hans! Now you need to go and let me deal with this!"

"I'm so sorry. I know you can fix this!"

I pointed to the door. "Go, now!"

He sorrowfully made his way to the door, looking back with a most pitiful expression as he left.

I turned my attention back towards Helen and saw that Johnny had been awakened by the commotion and was standing by his door, watching curiously. I picked him up, hugged him, and put him back to bed.

He asked me, "Where's Mommy?"

I tucked him in, "She's not feeling too good right now, cowboy. You go to sleep and I'll see to her."

I was afraid to open our bedroom door. Whatever was on the other side was going to be bad, very bad.

I walked in to find her packing a suitcase on the bed.

I asked, "Aw, come on, honey. Can't we talk about this? Can I explain?"

She kept her back to me, not answering, and continued to pack.

"It was just the one time. I *wanted* to tell you about it."

"Yeah... sure," she replied. "Like all those times I asked you about her?"

"It was *only* the *one time*. I was out of my head on morphine."

She stopped packing and replied without turning to face me. "I just learned that my husband, who I've trusted completely, is a liar and a cheat. All of a sudden, you're a stranger to me. If you're a liar and a cheat and you're caught at it... *of course* you'd say it was the only time. For all I know, she could just be one of many! Don't expect me to believe *anything* you say. So please... just stop talking and let me go. I'll take the boys with me to your mom's."

That was it. Nothing I could do would stop her. Ten minutes earlier, my life was perfect. All of that was devastated by a few drunken words in a matter of seconds. I couldn't have imagined that I could feel such a horrible, empty sorrow. I could only hope and pray that my angel of a wife would forgive me and give me another chance. I knew that she was hurting, probably worse than me, but maybe... just maybe, she'd feel differently in the morning.

She didn't stop packing though. I sat quietly in the darkness of the living room, hoping she'd stop. It was like sitting in a dream. I wasn't familiar with the emotions that filled me. It was also strange to seeing Helen from such an unfamiliar perspective. Helen, who I always felt that I was one with, had become a separate individual. Not only separate, but isolated from me. Next, she moved into the boys' room, turned on the light, and started packing their stuff.

I cleared my throat. My voice broke the silence as I said, "Honey. It's two in the morning. I'll sleep on the couch if you want to leave in the morning," hoping that it would give her time to change her mind about going.

It was a moment before she replied. "I want to be sure to get to Frankfurt in time to catch a morning flight. You can have Hans drive you up to get the car tomorrow."

She seemed so strong, so confident, and so cold. Again, showing me a side I hadn't known before.

At any moment, I prayed that maybe she would break down, rush into my arms, and tell me that all was forgiven. I kept waiting for that. Instead, she asked me to load the bags into the car while she dressed the boys. I knew that I had to be strong. If she was indeed going, I didn't want the boys to see me fall apart. When she loaded them into the car, I kissed Billy and hugged Johnny.

Johnny asked, "You're not coming, Daddy?"

I smiled and said, "No, buddy. I'll see you soon though. You mind your mom for me, okay?"

When I closed the car door, Helen didn't even look back. She just… drove away. The sound of the car echoed through the streets in the still of night, diminishing as it faded into the distance. Eventually, the night returned to silence. I fell to the front steps of the building and began to weep. I paused now and then to listen for the sound of the car returning. After an hour of waiting, I returned to the apartment to sit by the phone, just in case. I sat there waiting until well after dawn.

My heart soared when it finally rang. "Hello?!"

It was my C.O. "You missed the briefing this morning. Are you flying today?"

"Oh damn. I'm sorry. I... I can't fly today. I should have called."

He replied, concerned, "You sound like shit. Are you okay?"

"I'll be okay. I appreciate your concern, sir. And I'll let you know about tomorrow before the day's out."

I hung up the phone, disappointed that it hadn't been Helen. I again settled back to wait. I'd never heard the apartment so quiet.

Every time I heard footsteps in the hall, my heart would soar, only to plummet as they passed.

One set of footsteps stopped at my door. Instead of hearing a key in the lock, I heard a loud knock. I sprung to my feet and swung the door open. It was Hans.

He was acting like what had happened wasn't that serious and asked, "Are things okay now?"

If he'd been humble or seemed even slightly remorseful, I probably wouldn't have reacted the way I did. I burst into a rage. "Okay?!" Before I could think of anything to say, I reared back and with all my might, I punched Hans in the face, knocking him backwards into the wall where he fell to the floor in the hall. He didn't resist me and didn't get up. Hans put his hand to his face and looked up at me... then, with remorse.

I snarled and screamed at him, "They're gone, Hans! Thanks to you, buddy! They're on a plane back to the States. What the HELL is wrong with you?!"

Then, I'll be damned if he didn't start crying, which of course started me doing the same. I helped him up and we both staggered into the apartment. I didn't care if his face was bleeding. My knuckles weren't in much better shape.

Hans asked, "I made a mistake. Can we fix this, Kenny?"

"Well let's see. My best friend, who I thought would always have my back, stuck a knife in it. Your betrayal cost me my wife and kids. "So," I said sarcastically, "just say you're sorry, we'll shake hands and everything will be fine!"

He pleaded, "Kenny. I was drunk."

"Yeah, you were, Hans. So was I, but you know something? I don't care how drunk I got, there's no way I would have betrayed you like that." I raised my voice as I went on, "You were feeling sorry for yourself because Theresa didn't call you on your birthday. You were envious of how happy Helen and I were, so you leveled the field. The booze just helped you do it! You succeeded! Now we're both alone!"

"That's not it at all. I didn't mean for her to hear what I was thinking. I love you guys. You're my family!"

"We *were* your family, Hans! In case you haven't noticed... I don't *have* a family anymore! So, it looks like we're *both* out of luck!"

"Please. Can you forgive me, Kenny?"

"I don't see that happening, Hans. What you did is unforgivable!"

Hans said defensively, pointing his finger at me, "You did the *same thing*, Kenny. You betrayed Helen, the most important person in your life, when you were on morphine. Okay... so my judgment was off because *I* was drunk. How's that different?"

"That's not the same thing!"

"Why?" he asked. Damn it, I couldn't think of why, but it *was* different.

I argued, "All that matters right now is that my wife has left me with my kids because you betrayed me. What I am sure of is, I don't want to be around you, alright?!"

Hans got up to leave, and then turned back to me at the door. He started to say something, but sorrowfully shook his head, looked down, then turned and walked out.

When he closed the door, I sighed and said, "Goddamned Nazi!"

As the day went on, I resigned myself to the fact that Helen wasn't likely to change her mind any time soon, so I pulled myself together. I had to see the doctor about my hand. It wasn't broken, but it was awfully swollen and sore. I was having a hell of a time getting around since I'd hurt the hand that I used with my cane. I had to trade the cane for a crutch.

In the days that followed, I don't think ten minutes passed that I didn't think about Helen and the boys. Every time I did, there was a horrible emptiness in my gut that followed. I'd been alone for long periods of time during the war, but that was different. At least back then, Helen was with me in spirit. I knew that she wanted to be with me. What hurt me the most, was knowing the misery that Helen was suffering and knowing that it was my fault.

I couldn't bring myself to wash the sheets since they still smelled of her. I worked long hours and did a lot of reading to pass the time.

Hans respected my wishes and kept his distance. I'd hear him over the radio now and then when I was flying. I missed the guy, but wasn't about to forgive him.

A week passed and Helen hadn't called. Knowing that she didn't want to hear from me, I decided that rather than try to call her, I'd write a letter to my mom, asking her to call me when Helen wasn't home.

It took about a week, but Mom did call.

The operator announced that it was a long distance call from Louisiana.

"Hi baby, it's your momma."

It was so comforting to hear her voice. "Oh, Mom, I really messed up this time."

"Yes, you did, sweetheart."

"I'm so miserable without Helen. Do you think she'll ever forgive me?"

"She's miserable without you too, son, but I think her coming home is what she needed right now. She's got some healing to do."

I argued in my defense, "You know, Mom, when I was stationed in England and France… all the guys were out chasing girls and going to bordellos. I didn't! I only messed up that *one time* when Sandy gave me that morphine for my leg."

"Honey," Mom said. "Will you take some advice from a woman's perspective?"

"Sure."

"Don't tell her that. Arguing that you could have cheated more than you did… well, that's just not a good argument. What she needs to hear from you is how sorry you are and that it'll never happen again."

"It won't!" I said. "Do you think she'll give me the chance?"

There was a little pause. "I think so, but not right now. When she's ready… I'll let you know. Okay?"

I got excited over the prospect, "Do you think it'll be soon?"

"Don't press it, Kenny. I have no idea how long it'll take. You need to be patient and give her that time."

"Yes ma'am," I replied.

Mom asked, "How's Hans doing through all of this?"

"Well, I haven't, uh... talked to him since Helen left. I'm pretty mad at him right now."

Mom didn't much like hearing that. "Oh, baby. *You* made the mistake. Don't punish Hans for letting it slip. You might need him to forgive you for something someday. If you haven't talked to him lately, you probably don't know that Theresa divorced him. She filed for it as soon as he left for Germany."

I was really sorry to hear that. "Oh no! They haven't been married that long."

"Well, I'm sure you noticed that Hans never made Theresa feel that she was very important to him. Then when he decided he wanted to go to Germany to be with you and Helen, and she didn't want to go, he left her behind."

I felt bad for Hans, but I could understand how Theresa might have felt. "I know that Hans loves her, in his way. He was devastated on his birthday when she didn't call."

"Why don't you give him a call, baby? I'm sure he could really use a friend right now."

"Mom, you've made my day, just knowing that she might give me another chance! I'll be patient and wait for you to let me know when she's ready, and I'll give Hans a call right now."

Hans didn't answer the phone, so I drove over to his barracks. But his car wasn't there. I waited for over an hour, then scribbled out a note and left it on his door.

"Hans,

I'm still not happy about what happened, but I think our friendship can endure this. I just talked to Mom and she thinks that Helen will be ready to talk to me again soon. She also told me about Theresa. Call me or come over when you read this. Kenny."

I went back to the apartment and settled into the couch. For the first time in two weeks, the torment that had kept me from sleeping subsided. I fell into a deep slumber that lasted without interruption until my alarm went off the next morning. When I woke, I was concerned that I hadn't heard from Hans. I wondered if he was mad at *me*. I figured I'd try him again after the morning patrol.

After my flight took off, we'd barely formed up when I received instructions on the radio to switch to another frequency.

My commanding officer was on the other end. "Major Davis. We have a situation."

"Yes sir?"

"It's your buddy Hans. He's defecting."

I couldn't believe the words I was hearing. "Defecting? You can't be serious!"

"He took off on an unscheduled flight a few minutes ago and we monitored a communication from him to Air Control in East Berlin. It was in German. He asked them to allow him to enter their airspace in his P-80 and asked for asylum."

"Sir, that's nuts! *He wouldn't do that.*"

"He's on a heading for East Berlin right now. I want your flight to intercept him *immediately*. If you can't talk some sense into him, you have orders to shoot him down!"

"I can't shoot Hans down," I answered.

"You *have to*, Major! He's better than any of our pilots. You're the only one who stands a chance of shooting him down. So if you can't talk him down, you *must* shoot him down! That's an order"

The C.O. went on to say, "I'll give you the frequency from his last transmission. He's not answering our hails, but maybe he'll answer you."

I tuned to the frequency and keyed my microphone. "Major Kirpes. Hans… do you copy?"

No response. I repeated, "Hans, this is Kenny. Do you copy?"

After a pause, he responded, "I copy."

"What are you doing, Hans?"

"There's nothing left for me back there, Kenny. I ruined everything in my life. I've lost Theresa, you, Helen, and your family. In East Berlin, I'll be a hero if I deliver this plane to them. I can actually be a citizen there and have a commission in their air force."

"Hans. I have orders to shoot you down if you don't land. Don't do this."

He laughed over the radio. "Shoot me down? That's some wishful thinking, Major Davis."

"I have three other planes in my flight, Hans. We can't let you reach the border."

"Then this should be fun."

"Hans. I talked to my mom last night. It looks like I can work things out with Helen."

There was a pause before he replied. "I'm glad to hear that. I knew you would, my friend."

"Hans, didn't you get my note? I told you about Helen and said that you and I can fix our problems. Did you read it?"

There was a pause before Hans answered. "No. I didn't see any note, Kenny. I stayed at my place in Munich last night."

"We *can* fix things, Hans. We can fix *everything*. Please, turn back. We're closing on you fast. I need an answer now!"

"I wish I'd seen that note, Kenny. It's too late for me to turn back now. I'd be facing life in prison or a firing squad if I did. I'm afraid this is a one-way trip."

No sooner had he said that then I saw him on the horizon. Our paths were to intersect within seconds. There was no more time for conversation. My wingman and I dropped in behind Hans while the other two fighters held in formation to the side. Instantly, Hans pressed his plane to its limits in evasive maneuvering. I'd hoped that I could get a chance to line up a shot to where I could disable his plane by hitting his wing, or possibly knock out the engine without destroying the plane. That was an opportunity he wasn't affording me. I couldn't get a clear shot at his plane, period.

I let a burst go from my guns, knowing they'd miss, just to let him know that I was serious. The battle was so furious that I lost the rest of my flight, who couldn't keep up or catch us. As we continued, I began to remember what it was like to fly against Hans and intuitively began to anticipate his maneuvers. For a couple of split seconds, he crossed my gun-sight, but I wasn't quick enough to take the shot. In those few crazed minutes, I reverted back to flying instinctively, with no regard as to who my prey was. This was a battle that I could not lose!

Once again, it looked as if he were going to cross my gun-sight. I squeezed off another blast. I hit him! I could see the rounds hit his wing and actually heard fragments of his plane pelt mine. He kept flying, but he didn't seem to be quite as agile as he was before. Maybe my hit had affected his controls. Good. This meant that I'd have more of a chance to disable rather than destroy his plane. I was close enough to line my sight up on his right wing then squeezed off a one-second blast from my guns. It seemed like time slowed as I watched my tracers depart my guns, as they raced towards his plane. To my horror, his plane veered to the right just as the tracers reached it, ripping right into the fuselage and into the engine. The plane exploded instantly into a huge ball of fire.

Horrified, I flew up alongside the burning mass, hoping to see that Hans survived, that he would bail out. I couldn't even see the cockpit through the blaze. I looked back behind us, hoping to see that maybe he'd already bailed and I just hadn't seen it. No.

"Oh God, no..." I screamed. "You stupid bastard, what have you done?!"

I circled the blazing wreckage as it plummeted into the forest below, hoping that by some miracle I'd see him emerge. I couldn't leave. I just kept circling.

Choking back my sorrow, I cursed him, "You stupid son of a bitch! Goddamn you!"

My flight caught up with me and confirmed to my C.O. that Hans was down. I returned to the field with them. I landed and taxied to the flight line and shut down my engine. When I climbed out of my plane, my C.O. was standing there to meet me.

He said, "You did what you had to, Major. Kirpes was *not* the man you thought he was."

I stepped up to him toe to toe, put my face to his and growled, "Fuck... you!"

It's funny the way the mind works. Regardless of what I'd just witnessed, I still rushed back to his barracks to see if somehow he was there. The note I'd left the night before was still on his door. Oh God, was I lost! I was alone, with no one that I cared about around. I stared off into the sky... and just focused on breathing.

CHAPTER 14: Aftermath

There was an inquiry the next day. General Eisenhower himself was there with all the other top brass, demanding an account of what happened.

When they asked me for my account, I answered, "Y'all heard the conversation I had with Hans over the radio before the fight. His wife had divorced him, we got drunk together, and then he caused a rift between my wife and me. He was depressed."

"We read the transcripts," Eisenhower said. "Lots of people get divorced and depressed, but they don't turn traitor. Because of a little adversity here, it seems that Kirpes considered East Berlin to be an inviting alternative. That creates a problem for us, Major. We trusted Major Kirpes. Even though he was a former Nazi and a German citizen, we allowed him to fly one of our top secret aircraft along enemy lines, only to have to shoot him down while he was trying to defect. Looking back, that was a really stupid move on our part! Do you see how that makes us look?"

I felt the question was rhetorical, but answered anyway, "Not very good?"

"Not very good at all, Major. The East Germans and the Russians know what happened, but as far as the rest of the world is concerned, what happened yesterday was a training accident, an accident in which a civilian contractor was killed... nothing more. There'll be no mention of his name, his prior military history, or his citizenship. Is that understood?"

"Yes sir," I answered.

"Major Davis. We realize that you and Kirpes were friends. You performed with extraordinary valor in executing your duty as a United States Army Air Force officer yesterday. We thank you."

I sadly replied, "Well, sir. Hans Kirpes *was* a close friend, but to be honest with you, I don't think he was a traitor. I don't think he had any intention of reaching his destination. What I do think is that he used us all to orchestrate his own death by doing what he loved most, flying in combat."

"So you think he committed suicide?"

"That was his mother's way of dealing with his father's death. Think about it, General. If he'd really wanted to defect, why did he give us time to stop him by making that radio transmission with his request for asylum? He could have done that in the corridor. He planned it when he *knew* I was flying... and gave me plenty of opportunity to stop him before he reached enemy airspace."

Eisenhower replied, "So, he destroyed one of our top secret aircraft and made us look like fools for trusting him... all over an emotional tizzy? That's not much better!"

I took a deep breath and turned to my C.O. "I... I don't want to fly anymore, and I don't want to be in the Air Force anymore. You can show your gratitude for my actions yesterday by granting me an immediate honorable discharge. I want to go home, sir."

He walked over to me and said, "I know you've been through a lot. I can understand what you're feeling, but I think you'd better give it a little time before making a choice of this magnitude. Take a week off. I'll start the paperwork, and if you feel the same way next week, we'll send you home on terminal leave until the discharge comes through. Fair enough?"

That sounded like a reasonable proposal to me. Yes, I desperately needed some time to myself.

I went home and sat alone in the apartment, mulling over what had happened the day before. How could I have done things differently? What I couldn't stop thinking about, though, was that the last time I saw Hans, I punched him. Looking at my bruised knuckles, I tried to imagine how he'd felt, being attacked by a friend for an offense that he'd had no intention of committing. I never got to tell him that I was sorry. I took some measure of comfort in the fact that I had told him over the radio that we could fix our friendship. At least he died knowing that it was something I wanted.

The next morning, a messenger appeared at my door with a telegram. I tipped him and opened it. It was in German and the only thing I could make out in it was the name, "Hans Kirpes."

My neighbor's wife was German, so I went next door to see if she'd read it for me. It was from an attorney in Munich,

Hans' attorney, requesting that I come see him at his office. I thanked her for reading it and asked her to call the attorney to let him know that I'd be there that afternoon, and that I'd need an interpreter.

I flew Hans' plane down to Munich. As I flew, I pondered death. My world had been devastated when my dad died, and now again with Hans. I thought about the people I'd killed during the war and of how I'd sometimes wondered if they had families, but dismissed the thought when it became uncomfortable. I realized that each of those pilots who died, each of those soldiers who I'd strafed on the ground, left people behind who were feeling what I was suffering at that moment. I was done killing and was ready to go home and devote the rest of my life to the living. If Helen would take me back, I'd be the best husband and father possible.

Once I landed in Munich, I caught a cab to my appointment, curious about what it held in store.

The attorney began, translated by an interpreter. "Hans came into my office last week to finalize his divorce documentation. Since they hadn't been married long, it was actually an annulment rather than a divorce. So, Theresa has no entitlement to Hans' assets. This left him without an heir to his holdings. He had me draft a will in which he named you as his exclusive heir. I received a letter from him this morning that notified me that I was to contact you to initiate his will since he was, as of this morning, either dead, in prison for the remainder of his life, or a citizen of East Berlin."

"He's dead," I answered sorrowfully.

I was surprised to see how this affected the attorney. It took him a moment to recover from the news. They must have been friends as well. "Hans and I worked together for many years. May I ask what happened?"

"Sorry, I'm not at liberty to discuss it. I can just say that it was a training accident."

Since I wasn't explaining how Hans might have foreseen his death, the attorney quietly sat, trying to make sense of it.

"I understand," he replied, then pushed a folder full of documents over to me. "He left you his financial assets, his automobile, aircraft, home, and storage business here in Munich."

Then he slid an envelope to me, which contained all of the keys. It's a good thing that I was sitting down when I saw the balance in his bank accounts.

I commented, "Damn! He was rich! That's a *lot* of money!"

The attorney explained, "It was his inheritance, from his parents. His aunt and uncle were made trustees of it until he came of age. I've been his attorney since then."

I replied, "I guess his aunt and uncle provided him with everything, except what he wanted the most: a family."

The attorney noticed the sorrow in my reply, "You two must have been good friends."

I nodded.

I held up the balance sheet and asked, "I don't understand this. With this kind of money, he didn't *need* to work. He didn't need to be in the military. And why did he need that little storage business?"

The attorney smiled before answering. "When you have that kind of money, it changes the way people look at you. They no longer regard you as a person. They look at you as an opportunity to be taken advantage of. When you have that kind of money, you either lock yourself away from people, or you keep it quiet. The storage units were a great idea. They offered an explanation as to how he had extra money for the luxuries he chose to enjoy in life, and they *do* provide an impressive cash flow."

"I guess I don't need to ask why he wanted to fly."

The attorney replied, "In the First World War, only the wealthy and titled flew our fighter aircraft. There were few exceptions. It was always Hans' dream to join their ranks."

I grinned as I remembered Hans telling me that the Red Baron was his greatest boyhood hero.

I said, "Theresa had no idea of the wealth she was giving up when she went through with the annulment. I imagine that Hans was devastated over her wanting out of the marriage but I don't think he understood that she felt he'd abandoned her in choosing to come back here without her. I know that he loved her, profoundly. I really think he'd want her to be provided for. Before we finalize this, let me talk to her to see if I can convince her to let me sign his bank holdings over to her."

When I left the office, I didn't bother taking a cab to Hans' townhouse. The walk gave me time to reflect and to enjoy the beauty of Munich. I hadn't seen the building were Hans' townhouse was located since just after the war. It looked nice now. The whole neighborhood was nice. The park across the street was crowded and the streets were busy with pedestrians, much the way it must have been before the bombings.

I unlocked the door and walked into the living room, into what looked like a Davis shrine. A large chair with a footstool sat facing out toward the large windows that overlooked the park. Small tables situated on both sides of the chair were loaded with every photograph he must have had of Helen, the boys, Mom, Theresa, and me. On the right table sat a glass and an empty bottle of brandy. Then I noticed a strategically placed letter, addressed to me.

It took me a little while, but eventually I sat in his chair, put my feet up on the footstool, and opened the letter.

"Kenny:

If you're reading this, I'm no doubt gone. I wanted you to know how much of a difference you made in my life and how grateful I am for it.

I've had a lot of time to think since we last spoke, and I've come to some realizations about myself.

As you know, my dad left me through no choice of his own soon after I was born. My mother, on the other hand, did make the choice to abandon me by taking her own life. I was then given to my aunt and uncle, who abandoned me to the boarding schools where I was raised.

You might have wondered why I made such an effort to be an ass to people.

Everyone that I ever cared about abandoned me. As an adult, I never wanted to give anyone else that chance. I'd meet a girl I liked, but when I found myself becoming vulnerable, it would be time for me to move on. I didn't have the heart to abandon them... so I was rude and abrasive enough to make it their choice to leave.

When I became a Luftwaffe fighter pilot, people admired me for it and the better I became at it, the more I was admired. For the first time, I found a way to where I felt loved and admired... but not in a personal way.

I went through life safe, as an arrogant ass... that is, until we met. I insulted you and expected you to distance yourself, but you didn't. Instead, you offered me your friendship. Why? Why would you do that? What did you see in me the others didn't? As mean and ornery as I could be, you only seemed to be entertained by it.

And then I met your wonderful wife... and then your mom. Then I understood how you could enjoy the good in someone who worked so hard to hide it. The love that your family shared brought you a happiness that I hadn't dared to dream of for myself. Yet, you had it and offered to share it with me. I learned what it felt like to be loved and to belong to a family. The only thing I hungered for then was a wife and children like yours.

I had that opportunity with Theresa. As I began to fall in love with her, I panicked. It scared the hell out of me, knowing how devastated I'd be if she left me. She didn't seem to see the good in me the way your family did. My old survival instincts took over and before I knew it, I was looking for ways to push her away... and offered her reasons to push me away. In the back of my mind I knew what I was doing, but I couldn't stop myself.

Friend, I'm asking you to let her know that I've loved her more than I've dared to love any woman. I want her to know that my hurting her was out of my sheer terror of that love. She deserves a man who isn't afraid to love her.

And as far as you and Helen are concerned, I thought about what you said. Maybe it was my jealousy of your happiness that inspired me to betray your trust. Maybe I did want you to be alone, like me. If I am that much of an ass, I don't deserve your friendship or the love your family has shown me. Your marriage to Helen is one of the most beautiful I've seen. To have destroyed that was, in your words, unforgivable. So I won't ask for your forgiveness. I've ruined the only chance I'd been given at happiness in this life. How likely is it that I'll ever have a chance like this again?

I've decided to move on. I know it won't make up for the loss I've caused you, but I'm leaving you my possessions. They didn't bring me the happiness that I sought in life, but perhaps they'll help you to rebuild yours.

I didn't want to go without letting you know that I've loved you and your family. Thank you for letting me experience that.

Your friend;
Hans

I dried my eyes and said again, "You *stupid* bastard."

I took a deep breath. If only he'd seen my letter, I wouldn't be reading his. If only I hadn't been so stubborn. If only I'd mailed that letter to my mom one day sooner; if only…

I noticed a record on his phonograph and smiled when I saw that it was "La Vie en Rose." I switched it on and sat back to listen to it. The song filled me with a sweet sorrow.

As I sat looking at the pictures and remembering, I dozed off into a sound sleep. I was emotionally exhausted.

I was awakened in the morning by the phone. I didn't answer it, but whoever was calling didn't want to give up. It continued to ring until I finally decided to answer.

"Hello?"

A desperate voice shouted, "Hans!"

I knew the voice. It was Theresa.

"No… it's Kenny."

"Is it true? They came and told me yesterday that Hans was killed."

"I'm afraid it's true, sweetheart. I was there."

"Oh God, I've been calling his room since they told me, hoping they were wrong. I thought maybe he was there at the house." I listened to her cry for a while. "I was so mad at him, over wanting to be out there with you instead of home with me, that I'd forgotten all the things that made me want to marry him in the first place. I was hurt and I was mad, but I never stopped loving him. I just wish he'd died knowing that."

"Don't be too hard on yourself, Theresa. Hans told me why he treated you so badly. I just wish he'd explained it to you."

Theresa asked, "Can *you* explain it to me?"

"After losing his parents and being abandoned by his aunt and uncle to be raised in boarding houses, he was just afraid to let anybody get too close to him out of fear that they'd abandon him too. That's why he was such an ass to people. He said that he loved you more than he'd loved any woman, but he couldn't change his ways with you. But he wished he had. He felt he deserved to lose you… that you deserved better than what he could offer."

She cried, "I only asked him for the divorce to hurt him back for hurting me. I was hoping for an argument, that he cared enough to ask me to change my mind. Instead, he granted it to me without hesitating. I figured he was glad to be rid of me. Why couldn't he have told me how he felt? That would have changed everything."

"I don't think he figured it out until a couple of days ago."

Then I remembered Hans' estate. "Theresa. Did you know that Hans came from a wealthy family?"

"I know that when he lost his parents, his aunt and uncle got a trust to provide for him."

"Well, that trust is substantial enough to provide for you, very comfortably, for the rest of your life. He would have wanted you to have it. With the annulment, you released your claim to it, so he changed his will to name me the beneficiary. But if he's watching us right now, I know he'd want me to convince you to accept it. It wouldn't be right of me to keep it."

She sobbed for a minute, then replied, "Okay."

"He's also left me his car, townhouse, plane, and that storage business. If you don't want to bother with these things, I'll deal with it."

"Okay." Then she asked, "Kenny… *what happened?*"

325

"I can only tell you that it was a training accident. What I can say, though, is that he died doing what he loved." Then I told her, "I'll head back over to the attorney's and sign what I need to and give him your number to work out the details."

"How much money are you talking about?" she asked.

"I don't know the exchange rate offhand, but I can say that it's in the millions."

After I hung up the phone, it dawned on me that this was a decision that I should have asked for Helen's input on. I figured that I knew her well enough to know that she too would have wanted Theresa to have Hans' money. I sure hoped I was right about that.

I decided to write Helen a letter. I sat at Hans' desk and began to write.

"Dear Helen;

I would imagine that by now you've heard about Hans. I hadn't seen him since the morning you left. That morning, I punched him and told him I didn't want to be around him. I know it was wrong of me. It wasn't his fault.

I'm having a hard time dealing with this. Anyway, that's not what this letter is about. I've had enough of the military and flying. I want to come home. Of course, I want to come home to my wife and kids. I respect what you're going through. I messed up, and to make matters worse, I kept it from you. I swear to you that if you can find it in your heart to forgive me, I'll never betray your trust again. I'll be honest with you even if it hurts!

Helen. You're my world. I love you and beg you to take me back into your life, and into the boy's lives.

Mom said that she would let me know when you were ready to talk to me. I'm sorry that I couldn't wait any longer. I've asked for a discharge and I'm coming home for good in a few days. I'll let Mom know exactly when. You don't have to answer. When I arrive in Baton Rouge, I'll look for you when I get off of the plane. If you don't want me back, send Mom to get me and I'll have my answer.

Love, Kenny."

It was nearly noon before I headed back to the airport. I fired up Hans' plane then flew northwest to Frankfurt. There, I hired a car and drove to Limburg, the town with the schoolyard that Hans and I had visited back in 1945.

I went into the school to the principal's office to find out if the teacher we talked to was still there. Unfortunately, no one in the office spoke English. I motioned to them as if my hand were missing. I could see recognition in the principal's face. He led me down the hall to her classroom. When we entered the room, I could see that she didn't recognize me right off... not until she noticed my cane. She spoke to me in English.

"How can I help you?" she asked.

"I'd like to talk. Are you available for dinner?"

She looked at me suspiciously for a moment before answering, "I'm off at four."

I killed some time by exploring the little town of Limburg until she was off. As she came out of the building, she asked, "Where's your friend, Major Kirpes?"

I answered, "That's what I'm here to talk to you about. Is there a good restaurant nearby?"

"Yes," she answered. "My favorite one is just down the hill. There's no need to drive."

I took in a deep breath before going on, "About Hans. He died in a… training accident a few days ago."

She stopped and said, "No!" and was noticeably shaken by the news. "That's horrible!"

"Yes," I replied. "We'd become very good friends since I saw you last. I'm feeling pretty lost right now."

"I'm sorry. Why have you come to see *me*?"

I smiled and said, "Let's discuss that over dinner."

I was relieved to see that she wasn't mad at me anymore. She slid her handless arm through mine as we walked. I think she did it, maybe just a little, to tease me.

After we ordered, I explained, "Hans left me a few things in his will: his house, his car, his airplane, and a little storage business in Munich that generates a substantial income."

"Yes?"

"I don't need it. I'm going back to the States now. Hans and I, out of carelessness, cost you your hand and a child his life.

There's no way we can bring those things back, but maybe if I give these things to you, it'll make your life a little better?"

"To me?! Are you serious?" she asked.

"Yes."

Wondering out loud, she asked, "What would I do with a business, and a home in Munich… and an airplane?!"

"I'd imagine you'd want to sell the plane, but the car is very nice—a Mercedes convertible. The business runs itself. If you move to Munich, you'd have a free home and enough income to where you could live very comfortably and never have to work again."

"And… you're serious?! Doesn't he have family to leave it to?"

"Not here. His ex-wife will be *well* provided for back in the States. He's left his assets here, to me to manage. I feel good about this decision, and I'm sure that Hans would too."

I could see that she was overcome with emotion. "Do you know how much I make as a teacher? I live in a one-room flat and ride a bicycle to work… which isn't easy to do with only one hand. I think I would voluntarily give up a hand for what you're offering!"

We laughed, "Well, good! When would you like to go to Munich to see your inheritance?"

"When can I?"

"Now, if you'd like. I flew the plane up here to Frankfurt. We could be there in a couple of hours. What about your work tomorrow?"

She gave me a condescending smile and said, "I think I'll take the day off."

It dawned on me that I'd never asked the lady her name. It was Marie.

It lightened my heavy heart to see how much these gifts meant to her... to see that *something* good had come from Hans' death.

As we drove to the Frankfurt airport, Marie said, "I don't know what I would do with an automobile. I don't drive. I couldn't drive!"

"You can sell it. Better yet, the child that died in the schoolyard that day... could his parents use a car?'

"That's a wonderful idea. I'll ask them."

I assumed that she was comfortable with the idea of flying to Munich. "You *have* flown before?" I asked.

"Yes... but I must admit, my last experience with you flying an aircraft didn't turn out so well," she said as she lifted her hook.

I laughed. She was a character, all right. I commented, "Your English is great!"

"It should be," she replied. "I teach it."

I asked her, "Do remember when you asked Hans if he would marry you?"

She laughed, "I do. He turned white as a sheet."

"Well, you might as well have been his wife. It's a little ironic that you'll be the woman living in his house that he's providing for, even after his death. That is, if you decide that you want to live there."

We made it to Munich just after dusk.

When we arrived at the townhouse, I unlocked the door and motioned for her to enter, "Welcome home!"

To me, it was a nice townhouse; but to Marie, it was a palace.

She turned to me as she walked through in amazement, "And, you said, this is paid for? And it's mine?"

"Yes, if you want it. And don't forget the storage business. If you decide to live here, you'll have enough income to live a comfortable life. You'll never have to work again."

She exclaimed, "I've died and gone to heaven."

I argued with a heavy heart, "Well... I'm afraid that it's *Hans* who has died and gone to heaven, but what he's left you will make your stay on Earth a lot more comfortable."

I gave her a tour of the house. I'd never seen the upper floors before. It was a four-story townhouse.

I said to Marie, "I'll leave you for the night and be back in the morning. We'll go to the attorney's office first thing."

"You're not going to leave me alone? Where will you go? There's plenty of room here."

"You'll be fine. I'm a married man. It wouldn't be appropriate for me to stay here alone with you."

She laughed, "I trust you. You must not trust me? Are you afraid I'll get my *hook* into you?!"

I laughed then reflected a little more seriously. "You know, I think you *would* have made a good wife to Hans. You have a quick wit. Would you believe that he went back to the States and he married a woman who had absolutely *no* sense of humor?"

"Why on *Earth* would he do that?"

"I think he was finally ready to settle down, but he just wasn't particular enough about *who* he married. Theresa is a sweet enough gal, but I never saw the two of them as a good fit." I chuckled as I remembered, "When we left you that day, after you asked him if he'd marry you... he commented to me that you were an attractive woman and that if you hadn't been so mean, he *would* have married you."

"Me?" she asked. "Mean?"

"Well, you did slap the hell out of both of us!"

She laughed, "Well, that wasn't nearly as mean as you two shooting my hand off!"

"I can't argue that," I replied with a sad chuckle.

It felt good to laugh again, but at the same time, my heart was aching. I gave her a hug as I wished her goodnight.

"I'll see you bright and early, about seven?"

I found a hotel less than a block away. As much as I had to think about from the day, I was exhausted and had no trouble falling asleep once I slid beneath the cool linen in my bed.

I called the attorney before leaving the hotel to let him know what I had decided to do with Hans' assets and that we would be at his office soon. It took a while considering their limited English and my limited German.

I went to pick up Marie, who managed to throw breakfast together. Before we left, she asked me if there was anything I wanted from the house.

Deciding what to keep for a memento from Hans was a sad prospect. I wanted his Edith Piaf record album and the pictures he had of us all together. I thought I'd leave at least a few pictures of Hans for Marie to remind her of her benefactor.

As we walked to the door, I turned back for a minute and looked back into Hans' home. Again, a tide of sorrow welled inside me as I was leaving the home that had housed my dear friend and his life.

Marie must have known what I was feeling. "You can come back any time you like."

I offered her a nod of silent gratitude, knowing it wasn't likely that I would ever return.

I was weak with sorrow as we walked to the attorney's office. We must have been a sight. There we were, walking down the street—me with my crutch and Marie with her hand-hook.

The attorney had arranged to have an interpreter there for me. It didn't take long to make the amendments to the documents for Theresa. The interpreter expressed the attorney's concern over how Marie would get Hans' car to Limburg.

I answered, "I'll give her a hand."

Marie gave me a dry look and raised her hook, as if I'd intended the pun. "Why, thank you."

I told Marie, "You'll be collecting rent from the storage units at the first of the month, which should give you the cash you need to make the move and to get settled in." I placed the keys to the airplane on the desk and told Marie, "I'm leaving the plane at the airport here for you to sell. I'll catch a train back to Giebelstadt."

"I can't thank you enough," she said.

I left that day, knowing that I'd probably never see Marie again.

On the trip back, I realized why I felt such relief in finding a good home for the things that Hans had left me. I felt that he'd wanted me to feel guilty over abandoning him, no matter how justified it was. Leaving me his assets was actually an act of spite. By passing those assets on to others who were more entitled to them, I was refusing to accept the guilt I would have felt by profiting from his death. I felt guilty enough as it was.

This way, Hans would be taking care of Theresa for the rest of her life and maybe Marie, once she was living in a city as large as Munich, would meet a man who could see past her missing hand and appreciate her for the colorful lady she was.

The next day, I walked into my commanding officer's office and let him know that I hadn't changed my mind. He reluctantly produced my discharge file.

"We're sorry to lose you, Major," he said. "Again, we appreciate how difficult it was for you to carry out your orders, and we owe you a great debt."

I'm glad they didn't feel compelled to issue me a commendation for my valor. They likely knew that I'd refuse it anyway.

I said, "I've called around, trying to find out where Hans' memorial service will be."

The C.O. lowered his head. "There won't be one, Major. In fact, there won't be any record of Major Kirpes being attached to this unit. Colonel Sanderson will meet with his friends and family back home to brief them on the fact that his work here and the incident that claimed his life are strictly confidential."

I understood.

The C.O. slid the file to me and asked me to take it to processing. After signing what seemed to be a hundred documents, I was a civilian. I didn't know what to think about it. I'd wanted out in the worst way, but being free was a scary feeling.

I went to the airport to book a flight home, and I gave myself a few days to wrap things up in Giebelstadt. I sent Mom a telegram to let her know when my flight would arrive. I chose to send a telegram instead of calling because I was afraid that, if I talked to Mom, she'd let me know what Helen had decided. If I didn't know, I could hold on to the hope that she'd be waiting for me at the airport when I got there. I needed to believe that until then.

I boxed up our belongings and arranged to have them, along with the car, shipped back home.

Before closing the door to the apartment, I tried to remember the good times I'd had there with Helen and the boys, but all I could remember was that one horrible night and the morning after. Those were memories that I wanted to leave behind.

I found Hans' car parked at the airfield. His overnight bag from his trip to Munich was still in the seat. The car still smelled of his cologne. I started it up and headed north towards Limburg.

I arrived at the school and handed the car keys to the principal and said, "Marie."

Once Hans' car was delivered, I caught a train back to Frankfurt and stayed the night in a hotel near the airport, where I spent a sleepless night in anticipation of what my reception would be from Helen when I got home. It wasn't until I boarded my flight and it was underway that I was able to fall asleep.

By the time we touched down in the States, I was wide awake. I was riddled with anxiety on the final leg of the flight to Baton Rouge.

I hadn't really considered what I would do if Helen wasn't there. I supposed I could get an apartment. But then, I told myself again, she *will* be there. She had to be! As the plane descended into Baton Rouge, I took deep breaths to ease my raging anxiety.

When the plane taxied up to the tarmac, my seat was on the wrong side of the plane, facing away from the terminal. I couldn't see if Helen was there. As I made my way down the sky-stairs, I searched the crowd. I didn't see Helen's magic smile, but my heart leapt for joy when I spotted her bright pink dress!

It seemed to take forever to make my way through the crowd and into her arms. We both laughed and cried a bit, heedless of the people around us.

I wiped her tears and said, "Baby. Let's *never* do this again. I *can't* live without you. I'm so sorry I hurt you…"

She put her fingers over my mouth and said, "I'm so sorry about Hans."

"Yeah, I was feeling pretty alone over there, having lost you and then Hans. But now, you are here! Thank God! Where *are* the boys?"

"They're at your mom's. She thought it might be a good idea for us to have a little time alone first."

"Ah. *Smart lady,*" I said.

CHAPTER 15: Home

Nearly seventy years later, the elderly Kenny Davis sat exhausted after telling his story to his grandson.

Norm sat quietly, digesting all he'd been told. All he could think to say was, "Wow."

Kenny said, "That was in 1948. Since then, my life has been… normal."

Norm said, "This story is amazing. More than amazing! And nobody in the family knows anything about it, other than that you were a pilot in World War II."

"Does it surprise you that I didn't tell the family that I cheated on your grandmother and killed my best friend as a result of it? No, when I got back to Baton Rouge in '48, I took a job as an engineer with the State of Louisiana until I retired in 1978. Sadly, the last project I was involved with was the closing down of the downtown airport and converting it into a complex of parks and state buildings." He stared as he reminisced, "That's where I learned to fly… and where I took your grandmother up on our first date.

"Anyway, since I came back home, I raised my two boys the best I could and then welcomed my grandchildren and a few great-grandchildren into the world. It's been wonderful just being a husband, a dad, and a grandfather.

"Life was pretty great until my mom died, and then your grandmother followed her fifteen years ago. Once again, I realized the sorrow of having lost my Helen." He smiled, "Now she truly *is* my *Heavenly Helen*. I keep waiting until it's my turn to go... but I guess God doesn't want me just yet."

"Well, sir," Norm said, "you promised me a unique story, and you certainly delivered one. I have so many questions! You met so many fantastic people. And Wernher Von Braun, the man that built the rockets that put us on the moon, was a guest at your house?"

"He was." Ken paused, "If I were given a chance to change *one* thing in my career, it would have been my choice to leave Von Braun and White Sands. I should have stayed there instead of going to Germany. If I'd stayed, I could have been part of Von Braun's team in the space program. Hans would never have gone to Germany and he'd still be alive. You would have grown up with his grandchildren. Wouldn't life have been different if not for that one choice?"

Norm pondered for a minute, "So many things make sense to me now, like what happened to your leg... and why you keep that old Lincoln in your garage. And you definitely answered the question of how the family came to be in the storage business. And crazy Aunt Theresa from Atlanta... she's not really a blood relative?"

"Nope." Ken smiled. "She was Hans' wife. I never told her *or* your grandmother that Hans' death was a suicide. I didn't want them to feel that they contributed to it. Aunt Theresa, though, always carried the guilt of how she ended her relationship with him. She never remarried. I think she has always been in love with him. I mean... he's a pretty tough act to follow!"

Ken pointed at Norm's computer, "You can get on that computer of yours, Norm, and find all the people and places I told you about, except for Hans Kirpes. Not only did they erase the incident of what happened on that day, but they erased his entire life. There's no mention of him as one of the world's greatest Aces—no mention of him anywhere at all. There isn't even a grave that I can go visit."

Norm asked, "Your watch. Is that the Rolex Hans gave you for Christmas that year?"

"It is. Almost 70 years old now. I've had it repaired a few times, but it's still ticking. It's the only thing I have to remember him by... this and my bum leg."

Kenny studied the watch for a moment then went on to tell Norm, "If you're planning on publishing this story, you need to call it fiction. The government might not want light shed on what happened back then, even now."

"Yes sir," Norm answered.

"There's one more thing I'd like to ask of you, Norm. I had all the excitement and fame I wanted in my earlier life. From the time I came back home, I just wanted to lead a quiet, private life with my family. I'm old. I won't last a whole lot longer. Would you wait until I'm gone to write your story?"

That was a huge request. Norm couldn't wait to share his grandfather's story with the world, and especially with his family, but he agreed to respect his grandfather's privacy and wait.

Kenny sadly went on, "My sons and some of you grandkids have been complaining about my living in that big old house alone. As long as I live there, Norm, I'm *not* alone. When I walk up to the front door, I see my wedding out on the front lawn... the band playing on the porch. I walk into the living room and hear Bing Crosby singing 'White Christmas' with Mom, Dad, Helen, my in-laws, and Mary all chatting around the Christmas tree. I see the joy in Hans' face as he offered Theresa her promise ring. As long as I can come home to that house, I feel like they're all still around me."

Norm looked up at the picture on the wall of his elderly grandparents. "I *can* imagine it now, Grandpa. Thank you. I can see you and Grandma, young and beautiful, soaring through the skies above Baton Rouge. You've brought your memories to life for me."

"Good. As I shared my story, I could see in your face how much it meant to you. That means a lot to me, Norm. Thank *you*."

EPILOGUE;

Two years later, Major Ken Davis slipped away from this life to join his wife and his buddy, Hans.

Since Norm was the only family member who seemed to truly care about the storage business and about his grandfather's life, Kenny left him controlling interest in the storage business, the house, and all of its contents—including the cherished Lincoln Zephyr.

Ken's remaining assets were divided among his quarreling descendants.

Norm gladly became the guardian of his grandparent's memories.

So now, when Norm goes home to the lake house, *he* pictures the wedding on the front lawn, his grandfather surrounded by his family at the Christmas tree and all of the wonderful memories created within its walls.

Once Norm and his family settled into the lake house, he was ready to tell Kenny Davis' story. He sat at his grandfather's desk and opened his laptop. He looked at it for a minute, smiled, then closed it and put it aside.

He stood, then walked over and opened his grandfather's old record player, which still had an Edith Piaf record sitting on its turntable. As he switched it on and lowered the needle onto the record, the scratchy music began to play. He then went to the closet where he found Kenny's old manual typewriter. He set it on the desk, blew off the dust, inserted a new ribbon, loaded a piece of paper into it, and began to type. The title read, "Sky Knights."

The old typewriter hadn't seen much action since it was removed from the offices of Davis Engineering so many years before. It came to life, first with a clicking and then with a clatter... issuing the words of a story that would revive the memories of Kenny, Helen, and Hans. Through the story, Hans was rescued from his banishment from history, and the trio, along with their tragedies and triumphs, would live on forever in the minds and hearts of its readers.

The End

Made in the USA
San Bernardino, CA
22 December 2018